TEASE THE COUGAR
COUGAR CHALLENGE

DESIREE HOLT
MARI CARR
MARI FREEMAN
CIANA STONE

ELLORA'S CAVE
ROMANTICA® PUBLISHING

HOT TO TROT
Desiree Holt

Buying a ranch on eBay was the wildest thing Autumn Kelley had ever done. Past forty, she'd pretty much written excitement out of her life. But then she discovers the ranch comes with a foreman who makes her pulse pound and could give her an orgasm just by looking at her. As if that isn't enough, he has a friend equally as mouthwatering—and the two of them take Autumn on an erotic trip that outdoes any fantasy she could ever have imagined.

If sex with one hot boy toy is fantastic, sex with two at the same time is a whole new level of amazing. But what happens when Autumn inevitably has to come down from the orgasmic high?

ASSUME THE POSITIONS
Mari Carr

Damn Cougar Challenge!

Rachel's thankful for the new friends she met while attending an erotica-book convention. They instantly connected and began sharing the relationship woes unique to older single women on their Tempt the Cougar blog. Then Monica issues that challenge… How is Rachel going to convince a younger man to have sex with her? Hell, even *she* doesn't want to look at herself naked. To control her growing angst, she makes a list of eligible men then… Nothing. It's been too long and her divorce was too painful. She'll never be able to do this.

Ethan, one of Rachel's physical therapy patients, is pissed when he learns of the challenge. Not because he finds it silly—because he's not on Rachel's list! So he does what any self-assured young stud would do. The luscious police officer gives her a copy of the *Kama Sutra* then asks her to make a new list.

And assume the positions…

SIN ON SKIN
Mari Freeman

Wild women do…

That's the theme for the friends Stevie Jones found at an erotic-romance convention. But as the women share their experiences with younger guys on their Tempt the Cougar blog, Stevie discovers she's the least wild of the bunch. Finding a younger man isn't the problem; after a lifetime of unfulfilled desires, Stevie needs a younger *alpha* man. In the meantime, getting a tattoo is an easy, safe way to begin ramping up her wild side.

Tattoo artist Errol knows instantly what Stevie needs, and it's not just a bit of ink. He's hot, young—and he's just invited Stevie to his private BDSM club. Before you can say "green light", Stevie is experiencing things she'd only read in her favorite erotic novels. Sinful toys, spanking benches and voyeurism are just some of the stops on what will become the wildest ride of her life.

CAM'S HOLIDAY
Ciana Stone

Fantasies about being with a younger man? Before her husband left her for a younger model, they wouldn't have crossed Cam's mind, but now she has plenty. After meeting a group of ladies at RomantiCon, Cam and the women form a blog celebrating younger men—Tempt the Cougar. Then they challenge each other to find a younger man to make their fantasies come true. It's not a husband hunt. It isn't about love. It's about a night of hot, steamy sex.

When Lee Holiday enters Cam's life, he seems like the right man for the job. A personal trainer, he makes it clear he'd love to ring Cam's bell. And ring it he does. Repeatedly. Cam's found sexual nirvana. Only Lee's not going to be happy with a short-term, sex-only relationship. He wants the whole nine yards and is out to prove to Cam that he's more than just a holiday from her normal life. He's the man of her dreams.

An Ellora's Cave Romantica Publication

www.ellorascave.com

Tease the Cougar

TEASE THE COUGAR

ഔ

HOT TO TROT

Desiree Holt

&

Dedication

ဆာ

To all the cougars in the Cougar Challenge. Thanks for including me. To Ciana, the wonder woman, who pulled it all together. And to all cougars everywhere. Read it and take that next leap.

Author Note

ဆာ

You'll find the women of *Cougar Challenge* and the Tempt the Cougar blog at www.temptthecougar.blogspot.com.

Trademarks Acknowledgement

ဆာ

The author acknowledges the trademarked status and trademark owners of the following wordmarks mentioned in this work of fiction:

eBay: eBay Inc.

Instant Messenger: AOL LLC LTD LIAB CO

Lone Star Beer: Olympia Brewing Company

Chapter One

∾

Dear blog friends,

Okay, I've done it this time. What we talked about at the erotic romance convention? Totally changing our lives? I know I've always been the safe one. The prim and proper one. The one who held back. But we agreed to make a change and wait until I tell you the change I made.

I bought a ranch on eBay!

That's right. A cattle ranch in South Central Texas. Cashed in everything I had, sold my condo, quit my job and headed for Bypass, Texas. And let me tell you, a more fitting name for a bump in the road could never be found.

But I got to the ranch, finally, and I nearly turned around and left. The pictures on eBay must have been taken someplace else because the ranch is the sorriest broken-down place you've ever seen. I barely was able to find one bedroom to stash my gear.

It does, however, have Mitchell Brand, the former foreman who would make anyone's mouth water. I could barely keep from drooling. Six foot four of hot hunkitude, with dark brown hair, blue eyes, a rugged face and a body that you itch to run your hands over.

So my experience is limited. So what? I'd be more than a willing student to this guy. I took him to dinner in the nearest big town, to discuss business of course—quit laughing—and all I wanted to do was lose myself in those eyes. That and rip his clothes off.

Yeah, that's right. Prim and proper me wants to have hot sex with the man of everyone's dreams.

I know one thing. The ranch might be a mess but with Mitchell Brand there I'm in the right place.
Stay tuned.
Autumn

* * * * *

No one had ever told her South Central Texas was hotter than any place in hell. Even with the air conditioner on—and thank god it was a new one—Autumn Kelley still felt beads of perspiration on her skin. She swiped at her forehead with her arm and brushed back the few strands of honey-blonde hair that had come loose from the ponytail holder. Bypass, Texas had turned out to be just that, a wide place in the road that people passed by, little more than an intersection with a combination gas station-general store-diner.

And the ranch! Oh yes. Sweetgrass Ranch. Where she planned to start her new life, amid the cows and horses and young—but not too young—cowboys. She could hardly believe she'd been the successful bidder on eBay, scrambling to get the cash before the seller changed his mind, or went to the next bidder.

The day she drove down the bumpy gravel road, more than a week ago and saw it in its too, too awful flesh she wanted to cry. Or maybe slit her throat. The buildings and land were in terrible disrepair, the few cattle and horses wandering aimlessly around not much better. It was so far from what she'd bargained for. What she'd spent a huge chunk of money for.

All she could think at that first glimpse was, *What the hell do I do now*? Had she lost her everlovin' mind? A lone pickup, covered with dust, was the only vehicle in the parking area. Any hope it might belong to Henry McClain, the rat who'd swindled her into buying this place, disappeared when she remembered he'd told her he wouldn't be there.

Probably off on some island spending my hard-earned money.

Of course, no one buys a ranch on eBay unless they're nuts, right? But she'd needed a change so very desperately. If she hadn't pushed herself to go to that erotic romance convention, she might never have broken out of her shell. She'd still be dating men who just as often as not, couldn't get it up, and didn't believe sex and imagination belonged together. She'd be hiding from the world in her sterile condo and working at a job she hated. Never have had the courage to take this leap of faith. At forty-one she was stuck in a holding pattern, unable to move back, too chicken to move forward.

Just like, in many ways, the women she'd met at the convention. They were all about the same, gravitating toward each other as if drawn by invisible strings. She'd felt very lucky to hook up with them. They made her want more from life than she had.

The last day, giddy with their new friendships and probably one too many margaritas, together they'd made a pact. Each of them would do something totally out of character to give her life color and excitement, to embrace sexual experiences they'd only read about until now. To test the waters with younger men who would certainly have more staying power than the men they were all used to. To not only push the boundaries but maybe erase them completely.

One of the women who happened to be internet savvy even set up a blog where they could post about what they chose to do and keep in touch with each other. Empowered by the doors unlocked that she'd kept shut for years, she'd come home and plunged ahead. And in the months during which their friendship had strengthened, she'd gathered the courage to take a leap of faith.

But the beginning had almost been the end.

She sighed, stretching her tired muscles, as that first day slammed into her again.

* * * * *

Looking at the ranch when she pulled up next to the house she thought, *Holy shit. What am I getting myself into?* Buildings in a sad state of disrepair. A few scrawny cattle nibbling in the pasture nearest the house. Two horses swishing flies with their tails in the corral. She wanted nothing more than to get her hands on Henry McClain.

She climbed out of the SUV, brushed a few stray hairs away from her face and straightened her shorts and tank top as best she could. Henry had told her the ranch hands were keeping the place running, no worries. She had all the legal papers in a folder in the SUV. All she had to do was find someone, introduce herself and take over.

Yeah, right.

And then she caught sight of a hunk straight out of the wettest wet dream, the most mouthwatering specimen of manhood she'd ever laid eyes on, heading toward her from the barn. She hoped this was the foreman Henry had mentioned. Mitchell Brand. Just looking at him was enough to make her nipples twinge and her crotch dampen.

Ohmigod! I hope he's planning to stay.

Wait. I'll find a way.

She was already composing an email in her head to the ladies.

Well over six feet, with broad shoulders, lean hips and a build she could tell was solid muscle beneath the dark t-shirt and worn jeans that clung to every line of his body. Most of his face was shadowed by the brim of the western hat he wore but she could still see the square line of his jaw.

The first thing she thought was, *I wonder how old he is.*

On legs only slightly unsteady she walked across the gravel to meet the man, holding out her hand. "Hello. I'm Autumn Kelley, the new owner of Sweetgrass Ranch."

The sensuous mouth broke into a grin and a laugh rumbled up from somewhere deep inside him. "Mitchell

Brand. Mitch. Good old Henry didn't tell me that A. Kelley was a woman. And a gorgeous one at that."

Autumn made a face. "Good old Henry and I never met in person and I'm sure he didn't care what I looked like."

"Tell me." If she could have seen his eyes clearly she was sure they would have been looking her up and down. "Is it true you bought this place on eBay?"

She sighed. "Yes. What gave me away, the idiot sign on my forehead?"

Mitch Brand chuckled. "No, darlin', not at all. It's just that…"

"It's just that no one in his or her right mind would buy this place, right?" Autumn swallowed back the bitter taste in her mouth. "But I'm here, for better or worse. And it sure looks like 'worse' is the operative word."

"Well, then. Welcome to…" His grin widened. "What's left of Sweetgrass Ranch."

"Thank you. I think." She looked around. "Where are the others? I don't see anyone else here."

"Others?" She could hear the amusement in his voice. "Darlin', I'm the only one here. Everyone else took their shit and split."

Darlin'? Oh, right. She was in Texas. He probably called every woman darlin'. The feel of his calloused palm against her softer one sent tingles the length of her arm. Still, she snatched her hand back from his and tucked both hands in her shorts pockets. It wouldn't do to jump him five minutes after she met him. Would it?

"I was assured by Mr. McClain that there was a full crew and this was a functioning ranch," she told him. "He guaranteed me of that."

This time Mitch Brand threw back his head and laughed, a full-throated sound. "I'll just bet he did. He said he'd find a sucker on eBay and I guess he did."

15

Heat crept up Autumn's already hot cheeks. "You think that's funny? You don't see me laughing, do you?""

With an effort he collected himself. "Henry's been trying to unload this place for a year. Didn't put a single penny into it. No self-respecting buyer would touch it."

"But the pictures," she protested. "They were gorgeous." She looked around. "Cattle everywhere. Men on horses." The sick feeling in the pit of her stomach was growing worse by the minute.

"Taken three years ago," he explained. "I told Henry that would get him into trouble but would he listen to me? Not one word. And don't think you can find him. He lit out of here the minute your check cleared the bank."

Autumn could feel perspiration gathering on her skin again. She felt hot, clammy and sticky and at a loss how to deal with her situation.

"So why are you still here? Why didn't you leave with the others?"

He cocked his head, a grin of amusement still tugging at his mouth. "Well, darlin', I'm in a little different position from the other guys who worked here. I made a good living as foreman of the ranch and I have a solid savings from my rodeo days. I can afford to take my time about my next move, so I decided to hang around and see who showed up. See if I wanted a part of it."

"A part of it," she repeated slowly. "What exactly does that mean?"

"First of all, let's get out of this sun. It's as hot as hell without burning up at the same time." He took her arm and led her toward the porch, gesturing toward two ratty chairs. "Have a seat."

"You haven't answered my question yet," she pointed out.

"All right, then. I will."

16

He tipped his hat back and she could finally see his face, a heart-stopping sight. Piercing blue eyes looked out at her from beneath enviously thick lashes, as dark as his hair. Deep trenches carved into his cheeks, giving his face an even more rugged look and tiny lines from the sun bracketed his eyes. He was definitely all male and as sexy as sin. For the first time in her life, Autumn wanted to leap at a man, tear off his clothes and hers and shout, "Fuck me!"

What in hell is happening to me?

"Let me ask you a question first." His eyes were like twin beacons on her face.

"What?" What he could possibly want? A job? With everyone else apparently missing she was ready to chain him to the fence, even if he hadn't been the young stud of her dreams. She twisted her hands together and wondered if the beads of perspiration on her face would start trickling down her cheeks. Why the hell hadn't she taken a hankie out of her purse?

"Are you serious about this ranch business, or is this just some kind of game to you? What I mean is, are you taking a break from your high-maintenance lifestyle or are you committed to this? Now that you've seen the place, have you got the guts to make this a productive ranch again?"

Autumn pulled in a deep breath and let it out slowly. *Be honest*, she told herself. *You have nothing to lose.*

"First of all, my lifestyle was anything but high-maintenance." She swiped at the perspiration on her face. "I probably shouldn't tell you this but to answer your question, this is no toy for me. I cashed in everything I had to buy this place. Sold my condo, quit my job." Pointing to the SUV, she added, "Even traded in my car. I've burned all my bridges so I have no place left to go. Except here."

"To a broken-down ranch without much to recommend it."

She sat in silence for a moment. "I guess you think I'm pretty stupid, doing this."

"I don't know." He studied her face. "Are you?"

Autumn heaved a large sigh. "I guess I am. But..." She stopped, not about to blurt out all her secrets to a strange man, even if he was completely mouthwatering.

He watched her, not breaking the silence, either. Finally he said, "Well, how about this. Since I hung around out of curiosity, I'm at a loose end. You got any money left in your pocket to pay a stingy salary, handle some repairs and begin restocking the herd?"

"I-I don't know. How much will all that cost?"

He lifted his hat, ran his fingers through his hair and settled the hat on his head again. "A lot less if you have me doing the bargaining for you. And I won't cost you all that much. Enough to get by on. For now. And a place to sleep."

The hot look in his eyes burned into her. Did he mean in her bed?

She wet her lips with the tip of her tongue. "I can handle that. I...have enough cash if I'm careful.

"Good." He stood up and held out a hand to her. "Then why don't you come on down to my house, I'll get you a cool drink, which you certainly look like you can use."

She frowned. "Your house?"

"Foreman's house, actually. Goes with the job." He grinned. "And it's in better condition than anything else around here. Come on. I don't bite."

Oh but how she wished he did.

When she still hesitated, he said, "We'll talk about how you came to own Sweetgrass Ranch, what needs to be done to it and you can convince me why I should stick around."

* * * * *

18

Her first sight of the inside of the house almost made her want to cry again. Then she remembered the pact, squared her shoulders and dug in. Mitch had been very blunt about what it would take to put the ranch on its feet again but he'd also helped her draw up a budget she could afford. And he'd been right about sniffing out bargains for her. She listened to him on the phone with one supplier and was sure he came from a long line of con artists. While he'd gone about ordering new fencing, checking cattle sales, ordering building supplies and looking to see what men he could rehire, Autumn had attacked the house from top to bottom.

When she finished she realized it was only dirt and grime that had made the place look so dilapidated. Once she had everything cleaned and polished, she could appreciate the wood floor, the furniture gleaming with age and furniture polish, the windows everywhere that gave her magnificent views of the ranch. Two of the men Mitch hired scraped and painted the outside of the house and a trip to the nearest big town brought her linens and dishes to replace the ones she threw out.

As soon as she had satellite service hooked up, she logged onto The Blog.

Hi everyone,

Just want you to know I got here okay, to my beautiful new ranch, which looks like a leftover from The Great Depression. But not to worry. It came with a man who could light anyone's fire. Mitch Brand is the quintessential cowboy, yummy and mouthwatering. And younger. Exactly the kind of man we talked about. And the chemistry between us is not to be believed. Zing!

More later,

Autumn

Each day she made a little more headway. While she cleaned and polished, the men Mitch had found swung hammers, strung fences and wielded paintbrushes. She'd set a budget with Mitch right at the beginning and was determined to stick to it. And Mitch was the original *wunderkind*, true to his word that he could stretch a dollar until it snapped.

But working with him every day was an exercise in her self-control. And sometimes, when she caught him looking at her, she saw heat in his eyes that almost scorched her. How long had it been since any man had looked at her that way? Certainly not the oldies but goodies she'd dated.

Now, more than a week into her new role as a ranch owner, all she could think of was how she could get him into bed. With the lights off, of course. She looked much better in the dark.

She glanced out through the big kitchen window, watching him at work in the hot sun, shirt off, naked back gleaming in the heat. An unfamiliar wave of lust sweep over her, leaving behind a maelstrom of wild sensations. What would it be like, she wondered, to be naked in bed with him? To feel that thick cock his jeans couldn't hide pressing into her body? Sometimes at night she imagined she could feel those work-roughened hands exploring her body, playing with her nipples, sliding his fingers into her very needy cunt. It was all she could think of as the chemistry between them heated up daily.

Sometimes when he handed her something, or took something from her, just the brief contact of their hands nearly sent her up in flames. And his eyes would get that hot, hot look in them again.

This morning she'd actually awakened masturbating, bringing herself to a climax with the image of Mitch fucking her still so vivid her mind.

Ohmigod!

Well, this was her objective, right? To be a cougar on the prowl, find a younger man who pressed all her buttons and indulge in wild monkey sex. She just hoped when the time came she didn't chicken out.

The back screen door slammed and she looked up to see Mitch standing in the utility room. The current sizzling between them was almost palpable. Did he feel it too?

"Don't forget the auction coming up," he told her.

The following week he was taking her to her first cattle auction to buy a small lot to begin restocking the ranch.

"You said we're only going to bid on a small lot. Right?"

"Yes. You don't want to run cattle for beef," he told her. "Too expensive and you're in effect just starting out. You want a breeding ranch. A bull that can sire champions. Cows that can drop quality calves. Much smaller and easier to operate."

She'd been learning a whole new language along with everything else.

And working hard to keep her hormones under control. When she'd visualized a younger man she hadn't expected one quite so...seasoned. Or completely masculine. Every time she looked at him her palms itched to rip off his clothes.

She tried to push the erotic thoughts away and smiled at him. "Gotcha."

He looked at his watch. "Five o'clock, boss lady. Time to knock off for the day."

"But..." She looked around, not half finished with what she was doing. "You go on. I want to keep at this for a little while."

"You have to eat," he pointed out.

"I'll just fix a sandwich. Go on."

"Uh-uh. Not tonight." He moved closer to her. "You've been at this every day since you got here. Tonight I'm taking you out to dinner. You deserve a break."

Dinner? With Mitch? Was she finally going to get her chance with him? God, she hoped he wasn't taking pity on her because of the ranch. Or just taking his boss out to dinner. It had been hard enough working so closely with him for the past week. She'd never been so attracted to a man in her life.

21

She was sure if he asked her to strip down for him in the yard she'd so it without hesitation.

"D-Dinner?"

Why do I have this terrible habit of stammering like an idiot around him?

But she remembered The Pact. The Women. The Blog.

Go for it. What the hell. This is what I wanted, right?

"Is there a decent place to eat around here?" she asked.

"The Armadillo Bar and Grill," he said with a grin. "Not exactly around here but close enough. You can get everything from a steak to a beer to the finest bourbon. It's where everyone kicks up their heels. Or just hangs out. Be ready at seven, okay? We'll have a great night."

Ready? At seven? A great night? Oh, hell.

Her first inclination was to turn tail and run. Just pick up her stuff and go home to die a thousand deaths. But she didn't want to be that woman anymore. Advice from the group over the months filtered through her mind.

Do it, Autumn. That's why you're here, isn't it?

But she needed shoring up.

Mitch had barely headed back to his own house before she raced to the little den, opened up her laptop and went directly to her Instant Messenger list. No time now for the blog or even email.

Please, please, please let someone be online. Ohmigod, you'd think I was a fainting virgin.

Still, the realization that tonight would probably be The Night had her shaking with nerves. There was a big difference between talking and doing. She checked the list, breathing a sigh of relief when she saw Rachel was logged in. What a stroke of luck. Good, solid practical Rachel. She'd tell it like it is.

Flexing her fingers, she typed frantically.

Autumn: Help! Help! Help!

Rachel: Okay, what do you need?

Autumn: The gorgeous hunk I blogged about has asked me out to dinner. Tell me quick what to do.

Rachel: Shower and bathe every crevice in your body and douse yourself with that jasmine scent you love. He'll love it when he peels you out of your clothes. Wear one of your tank tops so he can get an eyeful of your cleavage, and have a hell of a time. Oh and wear your hair loose.

Autumn bit her lip, hesitant to voice the fear she'd pushed back. But if she couldn't ask practical Rachel, who then?

Autumn: What if my age turns him off? I don't think he knows how old I am, really.

Rachel: Oh Autumn, don't be silly. He wouldn't have asked you out if he was turned off. It's clear to me that this guy is really into you. Go out with him. Have fun.

Autumn: Are you sure?

Rachel: This is that whole new life thing you said you wanted when you bought the damn ranch on eBay. I mean it seems to me the old, boring, conservative Autumn would be the type to stay home and watch the house fall in on her but you aren't her anymore. Were you serious about changing or was it all talk? This is your chance to do what you set out to do. Break free! Be wild and crazy. Hell, get laid!

Autumn smiled. She could almost hear Rachel's voice, urging her. Pushing her.

Autumn: Thanks.

Rachel: Any time. Oh and limit yourself to two drinks, cookie. I remember you and the margaritas at the convention.

Autumn laughed at that one. Typing her thank you, she signed off and went to get ready. She didn't ever remember being this nervous about a date — if you could call this a date — before in her life.

Chapter Two

ഇ

The Armadillo was exactly what she expected a Western bar and grill in the boonies to be. The floor was concrete but the walls were aged and polished paneling. A long bar took up part of one wall, tables and chairs and a few booths occupying most of the remaining space. At one end was a postage-stamp-size clearing for a dance floor and a small stage where a band was setting up.

"I hope they don't play too loudly," she commented as she sat down at one of the tables.

Mitch took the chair to her left, his legs touching hers, heat flaming through her from the point of contact. She tried to shift her position but there wasn't much room to move around. He glanced at her, lips twitching, as if he knew what she was doing and Autumn just buried her face in the plastic-coated menu.

Autumn did her best to keep her head on straight where Mitch was concerned but the sensations rocketing through her body made it difficult. She'd taken Rachel's advice and dressed in a brand-new, skintight pair of jeans and an embroidered tank top, one with two buttons at the scoop neck that she casually left open. Every few seconds Mitch's eyes would stray to the swell of her breasts. If he caught her watching him, a slow, hot as sin smile would creep over his face.

She was sure from the heat she felt and the tiny grin lifting one corner of his mouth that she was blushing furiously. She lifted her glass of ice water, draining it completely, hoping it would cool her off. Mitch's knowing smile didn't help much.

Come on, Autumn. Seductresses don't blush and act like shy virgins. You wore the damn top to catch his attention, so don't play coy.

The food was excellent. Trouble was she had difficulty concentrating with Mitch sitting so close to her, his very masculine scent teasing at her nostrils, her eyes glued to the muscles in his jaw and throat as he chewed and swallowed. It had been bad enough riding in the truck with him, very aware of the play of muscles in his arms as he drove and the way the worn denim stretched over his thighs. But sitting here with him her mind, let loose from its usual prison of inhibitions, kept picturing him naked.

Just as it had every day since they'd met.

She took a sip of the ice-cold beer in front of her and it suddenly occurred to her that this was the second Lone Star beer she'd downed without even realizing it. She'd been working long days, as much to get the house in shape as to work off the unfamiliar sexual energy charging through her. She knew she needed to get to a bed and crash but—surprise, surprise—she wanted Mitchell Brand to be in it with her. Now the band was tuning up and they opened up with something slow and sultry, matching her mood exactly.

"Come dance with me, Autumn." Mitch covered one of her hands with his. "A little music will relax you. Come on. Just one dance."

Dance with him? Let his body press close to mine? Am I ready for this?

Before she realized it she was on the dance floor, her body plastered to Mitch's.

Oh, lordy, I am in such big trouble here.

They moved almost in place, Mitch's strong, muscular arms around her, cradling her to his chest, one hand at the nape of her neck. Her breasts were pressed into the hard wall of his chest and it was impossible to miss the hard thickness of his cock pressing against her through the fabric of their clothing. An electric charge seemed to pass straight from his body to hers, making the crotch of her panties even damper and her breasts more sensitive.

Touching him was everything she'd imagined it would be. His muscles rippled against her as he moved with slow, measured steps, his scent teased her nostrils and the heat of his body transferred itself to her. She felt suddenly daring, a brand-new sensation for her.

A scene from an erotic romance she'd read recently flashed through her brain, a scene so similar to this she might have recreated it herself. When she'd read it, she'd wondered if things like this really happened. Did you meet a man and immediately fall in lust with him? A tiny shiver raced down her spine at the thought of what she was doing. People who knew her would be in shock.

Well, the people who knew her saw the old Autumn, a woman afraid life was passing her by. She'd vowed with the others to change her life and open herself up to new experiences.

She sighed, her mind fuzzed around the edges and her body relaxed from the long day and the beer. She'd been fantasizing about this man since he strolled lazily across the ranch yard to her. Now she had the reality and she wasn't about to miss out on whatever happened next. She might have been inhibited but she wasn't any shy wallflower, either. It might be scary but she could step forward and take what she wanted. If it was offered, that is.

She tucked her head beneath Mitch's chin and nestled it against his shoulder. Mitch's hand pressed more firmly against her back and his hips ground against hers. She answered him with movement of her own hips, wishing there was nothing between them but skin.

"I think this would be a good time to make our exit," he murmured in her ear in a soft, low voice. "Don't you?"

"Hmm?" She tilted her head and looked up at him, thinking she could drown in his eyes.

He was breathing heavily, working to keep himself under control. He kissed her ear lightly and just touched it with the tip of his tongue. Delicious shivers raced through her. "Let me get the check and we can get out of here."

"Oh." She shook her head as if to clear it. "No, wait. My treat, remember?"

"Save your money, darlin'. This one's on me."

* * * * *

They were mostly silent on the drive home. Mitch found a country music station and turned it on low volume.

"You need to learn Texas-style music," he told her, letting the deep baritone of a familiar voice fill the silence in the truck cab.

By the time they reached the ranch, between the beer, the dancing and the music, Autumn was feeling as mellow as she ever had in her life. She dug into her purse for the keys to the house but Mitch shook his head.

"Uh-uh. I've got a better place for you to spend the night."

Butterflies did the two-step in her stomach and her palms were suddenly damp. She knew what he had in mind. The same thing she did. Could she actually go through with it?

When he helped her out of the truck, it seemed the most natural thing in the world for her to take his hand and let him lead her around the barn to his house. On the porch he looked hard at her, eyes boring into hers.

"We both know what's going to happen, Autumn. We've been building toward this since you got here. If you want to change your mind, this is the time."

She stared back at him.

Suck it up, Autumn. This is what you came west for. This is what you've been panting after all this time. A younger man who could fuck your brains out. So what's holding you back?

But her own fears and insecurities surfaced. She had to ask The Question. All the way home she'd debated with herself the wisdom of this. What if he tossed her out when he found out how old she was? Or worse yet, humiliated her in some way? Or — worst of all — pitied her? She suddenly felt like an idiot old woman who'd saved her virginity too long — certainly far from the truth. But still, she had to *know*. She just had to *know*.

"I have to ask you something first," she finally got out.

Autumn, the women would smack you silly.

I don't care. I have to ask first.

Shit, shit, shit.

He cocked his head, a quizzical expression on his face. "I give blood every month so I'm always tested and I'm disease free. And I'm careful with the women I...spend time with."

She shook her head, fisting her hands. "That's not it."

"Okay. Fire away."

"How...how old are you?"

His eyes narrowed, the shadows from the porch light making his face look harder, rougher. "What the hell kind of question is that?"

Autumn wet her lips with the tip of her tongue, digging her nails into her palms. She had to do it, that was all. "I just want to know how old you are. Is there something wrong with that?"

"Yeah, there is." He glared. "Why don't you tell me how old *you* are?"

She closed her eyes and breathed in and out. This was it. Push to shove. "How old do you think I am?"

Mitch frowned. "I don't know and frankly, I don't care. But if you want my age, well, tit for tat." He scratched his neck. "That's the first time any woman's ever asked me that."

Just tell him.

"I'm...forty-one."

When he didn't say anything she opened her eyes to find him staring at her.

"So?"

"Didn't you hear what I said" I am forty-one years old. Forty. One. Years. Old."

"And *that's* what this is about? Your age? Darlin', I'm thirty-two but sometimes I feel like fifty. Now can we please go inside?"

"And that makes me nine years older than you. Don't you get it?"

"What I get is that you are a beautiful, desirable woman and age is just a number." He pulled her to him and slammed his mouth to hers, a predatory kiss that stole her breath. When he lifted his head, he said, "Does that answer your question? All right, then. Let's go inside." He got out his keys and opened the lock.

They were barely inside before he had her backed against the door, his body pressed against her.

"I wanted this the minute I saw you." His voice was thick with need. "You made me so hard I was barely able to walk. Damn it, woman. Just looking at you makes me crazy. Does this feel like I give a good goddamn how old you are?"

"No," she breathed, unable to believe he really meant what he was saying.

This is going to work. Yes, yes, yes!

But then she couldn't think anymore as his lips came down on hers.

His mouth burned against hers as he ate at it, licking it with his tongue before pressing inside the warm cavern. Every place it touched tiny flames leaped to life. At the same time his hands, big and warm, slid beneath her tank top and cupped her breasts, thumbs chafing the nipples through the thin fabric of her bra.

In the dark every sensation was magnified, every touch more erotic. Autumn was liquid in his arms, the kiss melting her. Pulses began to throb low in her body, her cunt quivering with the need to be filled. She wrapped her arms around Mitch's neck, taking a brief moment to ask herself once again what the hell she was doing before giving herself completely to the feelings sweeping over her.

"Too many clothes," he mumbled, breaking contact long enough to pull her tank top over her head and get rid of her bra.

His head bent to take a nipple into his mouth, sucking it, grazing at it with his teeth and wrapping his tongue around it. Autumn moaned with pleasure, pulling his head tighter to her body. Her breasts felt full, as if the skin was too tight, her nipple ready to burst with sensations.

As he moved his mouth to the other breast his hands were busy unfastening her jeans and pushing them, along with her panties, down her body. She stepped out of them, kicked them away and gave a sigh of bliss as his hand slid between her thighs, his fingers probing her slit.

"Oh, Jesus." He lifted his mouth from her nipple. "Darlin', you are so wet I could slide my cock inside you right now without any trouble. We need to get someplace more comfortable than this. The first time I fuck you isn't going to be standing against a door."

He lifted her up and carried her into another room. Autumn had her eyes closed, her head against his shoulder, unaware of where she was until she felt Mitch dip and use one arm to move something. Then she was lying on crisp cotton and she opened her eyes to find herself in his bedroom. A click and the bedside lamp came on, throwing soft light and shadows.

Mitch stood beside the bed, looking down at her, a hunger in his eyes she'd never seen before from any man she'd been with. All her insecurities came charging back and she had to resist the urge to cover herself.

"Please turn off the light, okay?" She tried to smile. "I like the dark."

He sighed even as his gaze continued to travel over her. "Autumn. Darlin'. You have a very sexy body. I want to see every bit of it. You have nothing to hide, trust me. I have no reason to lie to you."

She tried to pull her thoughts together and not make herself sound like an idiot. "I know all the women you've been with are much younger than me. My body isn't..."She searched for the right words. "It isn't what theirs is."

A quick spurt of anger flashed in his eyes, then was gone. "First of all, you have no idea what kind or how many women I've been with. In the second place, none of that means a damn thing. It's you I want. And let me tell you, I am so hard looking at you it's a wonder I haven't split my jeans. Forget about age, Autumn. This is just us, you and me. Wanting each other. So let me see you. All of you."

He bent her legs at the knees and placed them wide apart, exposing her completely. She automatically reached her hands to shield herself from his gaze.

"Don't," he said, as if reading her mind. "Your pussy is so beautiful to look at."

She let her arms fall to her sides, clutching at the sheet, as he spread her legs even wider and looked at every inch of her cunt. She could only hope he meant what he said.

One lean finger reached out and traced the length of her slit, coming away glistening with her juices. Autumn could barely hold herself still, tremors racing through her as she quivered with need.

Mitch lifted the finger to his mouth and licked it with deliberate slowness, then ran his tongue over his lips.

"Delicious." His Texas drawl in that deep voice was like warm maple syrup. "But I knew it would be."

His eyes never left her as he stripped off his shirt and toed off his boots. She lowered her eyes to his waist when his hands went to his belt buckle, unfastening it and lowering his zipper. When he pushed down his jeans and boxers together, his cock sprang free, thick and hard and swollen, a drop of liquid already beading on the dark, plum-colored head. The dark hair on his chest arrowed down across flat abs to the thick dark curls that surrounded the root of his shaft. Below it the sac with his testicles hung against his thighs.

Autumn's mouth dried up like the desert at the sight. God, he was the most magnificent specimen of man she'd ever seen. At that moment she didn't give a damn how old either of them was. She just wanted *him*. Any way she could get him. She squeezed her legs together as little pulses of pleasure vibrated in the walls of her vagina. None of the few men she'd had sex with even came close to the sight Mitch presented.

He grinned, heat flashing in his eyes. "Like what you see? You'll like it even more when I'm inside you." He knelt on the bed between her legs. "But I have other things to do first. Hang on for the ride, darlin'. We're cranking into high gear."

If she thought the other kisses were scorching, this one was off the charts. Her entire body was suffused with heat and her skin felt much too tight. There wasn't an inch of her mouth his tongue didn't explore. His hands cupped her head, holding it in place to give him better access. When he broke the kiss, she felt a sudden loss of warmth.

But in the next instant his mouth trailed down the column of her neck, stopping to kiss the sensitive spot behind her ear and the place where her neck and shoulder joined. Who knew that was such an erotic spot on her body?

His lips brushed over the hollow of her throat, pressing lightly against the pulse beating there before moving to the slope of her breasts. His tongue outlined the shape of each mound, licking closer and closer to first one nipple, then the other. When his teeth closed over one of them and bit gently she jerked, a soft cry rushing from her throat. She gripped his shoulders, arching into his mouth, bracing her feet on the bed to push against him.

When he'd spent enough time on her nipples that they were rigid and swollen to bursting he shifted and licked his way down past her navel to the curls covering her mound. The tip of his tongue trailed a line back and forth just above the curls, making her blood heat and the pulses in her body increase in their intensity.

"Mitch," she breathed, trying to push his head lower.

He chuckled, the sound vibrating through her. "Does that sweet little cunt want my attention?" he asked his face buried in her curls. "All right, then."

He pushed her thighs apart, spread her labia with his thumbs and pressed an open-mouth kiss right at the core of her pussy.

"Oooh," she gasped, hitching her hips.

Sensations unlike anything she'd ever felt before raced over her like jagged bolts of lightning. Shock waves pulsed through her as Mitch's tongue traced the opening of her vagina, then lapped at her slit. When he used the tip to flick her swollen, aching clit, she cried out in need, begging him for more.

"Like that?" He lifted his head, his face slick with her juices, a lustful grin on his face. "Tell me how you like this." He bent his head and without warning plunged his tongue into her cunt, his thumbs pinching and rubbing her clit.

She bucked beneath the erotic assault, her senses going haywire, her body on fire. The harder he tongue-fucked her, the more he tormented her clit, the harder she bucked beneath him, her hands ripping his hair, feet pressing into the mattress. She exploded without warning, the orgasm rumbling up and bursting with incredible speed. She shook in the grasp of it, spasm after spasm rocketing through her, hips moving, pussy contracting around his tongue.

The last flutter had barely died away before Mitch lifted himself, grabbed a condom from the bedside table, sheathed himself and plunged into her with one swift stroke. His hands wrapped around her breasts and his mouth pressed against hers, her juices still on his lips. He rolled and thrust, pulling back then pushing all the way into her, again and again, faster and faster, stealing her breath.

They came together, falling over the edge, wrapped in an erotic storm that shook them, their bodies shuddering, his cock pulsing inside the latex sheath as spurt after spurt of semen surged into the reservoir and the walls of her pussy contracted and milked him, harder and harder.

Autumn was tumbling through space, through a black void, Mitch her only anchor as her body gave itself over completely to the storm.

And then they were still, Mitch collapsing on her as they struggled to draw breath into their oxygen-deprived lungs. Autumn wound her arms around his neck, holding him close, unable to tell if the thudding heartbeats knocking against her ribs were his or hers.

When he lifted himself from her and slid from her body, she made a small sound of protest.

"I'll be right back, darlin'." He kissed her lightly then headed to the bathroom to dispose of the condom. When he crawled back onto the bed he pulled the covers over both of them and snapped off the bedside lamp. Pulling her toward him, he spooned his body around hers and kissed the top of her head.

"Mitch?" she muttered sleepily.

"Yeah, darlin'?"

"I don't... I mean, I'm not usually... That is..."

God, I sound like an idiot. Why can't I keep my mouth shut?

He kissed her again, this time on her shoulder. "It's all right, Autumn. We'll talk tomorrow. But everything's just fine." He licked a slow circle with his tongue. "Whoever said women reach their sexual peak later than men must have been thinking of you. Because darlin', you are the hottest thing I've ever laid my hands on. And we're just getting started."

As she tumbled into a black void of sleep, her last thought was that the reality was much better than any dream.

Chapter Three

ℒ

At first Autumn thought the pounding she heard was in her head but forcing her eyes open she realized someone was at the door.

The door? What door? Where the hell was she?

She looked around at strange surroundings, bewildered. Lifting the covers, she realized she was completely naked. And sore in strange places.

Then it all fell into place in her brain with a loud *thunk*!

She was in Mitchell Brand's little house. Thirty-two-year-old Mitchell Brand. Her very own boy toy. She hoped. Exactly what she and her blog ladies had talked about. Jesus! She'd actually gone and done it and the sex had been beyond anything she could have imagined. And if she remembered the bits and pieces of what he'd said, he planned for them to do this again.

But now someone was knocking on the door in a manner that said whoever it was, wasn't going away.

Mitch rolled off the bed and yanked on his jeans. "I'll take care of it," he said in a low voice. "Don't worry about a thing."

He disappeared into the living room, yelling, "Okay, okay. Hold your water. I'm coming."

Autumn pulled the covers up over her, hiding beneath them, the faint murmur of male voices drifting into the bedroom. She prayed Mitch could get rid of whoever it was without giving away any information. The sound of the door closing was followed by that of bare feet padding on the wooden floor into the room.

"You can come out of hiding," Mitch said, amusement in his tone. "It's safe."

She peeked cautiously over the edge of the blanket and sheet. Mitch had stripped off his jeans again and slid under the covers beside her.

"Who was that?" she asked.

"Randy Churchill. I'll tell you about him later." He reached for her, his hands skimming over her body, sparking her nerves to life.

Autumn pushed away from him, hard as it was to do it, especially with his steel-like cock pressing against her body.

"I need a shower worse than anything," she told him. "Please?"

Heat flashed in his eyes. "I think a shower would be just the thing." He pulled her out of bed with him. "Come on. We'll see if this shower really holds two people."

She caught only a quick glimpse of the bedroom in the daylight as he led her to a doorway in one wall. Aged oak paneled the walls and the floor, all polished to a fine sheen. The furniture was a darker oak and a couple of western-themed prints hung on the walls. That was all that registered on the edge of her consciousness before she found herself in the bathroom. She looked warily at the small and efficient stall shower.

"Don't you worry, darlin'," Mitch told her as he turned on the water. "This will be just right for us."

She closed her eyes in bliss as the hot water sprayed over her body. But they popped open when she felt a hard male body plastering itself against her.

"I told you we'd fit," Mitch grinned down at her. "Just a little close quarters, that's all. His hand moved across her shoulders, smoothing something on her skin. "If anyone had told me I'd be bathing a gorgeous woman this morning I'd have had them committed. And you are gorgeous, darlin'." He bent his head a little and nipped her earlobe. "You just stand here and let my fingers work their magic.

Autumn closed her eyes again and sighed as his hands coasted over her skin, rubbing the lather in with gentle strokes. First her shoulders and her back, then he turned her around and rubbed the rich lather across the upper slope of her breasts. When he took her nipples between his fingers and twisted them pleasure streaked directly to her pussy, intensifying the low beating of the pulse in her womb that had set up its cadence the moment Mitch's hands touched her.

"Such beautiful nipples," he murmured. "Like raspberries just begging to be plucked. I can't wait to get them in my mouth again."

She arched into his touch, grabbing his forearms for support. She remembered the hot wet heat of that mouth on her last night and her legs trembled, her knees almost buckling.

"Easy, easy," he said, that maple syrup voice wrapping itself around her. "We haven't even gotten to the good part yet."

"Oh?" She was breathless. "What's that?"

"Well, this for starters."

His lather-coated fingers brushed over her pubic curls and slipped between the folds of her labia, rasping her clit as he stroked past it. Autumn clutched at him for support, shaking with need, moaning with pleasure as his fingers thrust inside her and massaged the walls of her pussy.

"Oh, god, Mitch," she whispered, her voice catching in her throat. "More. More, more, more."

"I'll give you more, darlin'. Just hang on for the ride."

He added a third finger, stretching her tight walls, his mouth pressed to her ear, tongue tracing the outline of it over and over. She was falling into an erotic fog that thickened with each thrust of his fingers in and out of her clasping sheath. The tendrils of an orgasm began to steal over her, unwinding through her body but just as she was about to give herself over to it, to ride his fingers to ecstasy he pulled them from her cunt and turned her around again.

"Put your palms against the wall and lean forward," he ordered, applying lather to her back again in wide swaths.

She was hanging on the ragged edge of need, ready to beg for release, when he slid his slick fingers through the cleft of her buttocks, resting the tips against the puckered ring of her anus. She jumped slightly at the contact. She had never been fucked in the ass before, never been taken there by anyone. Oh, she'd read about it in her erotic romances. A lot, as a matter of fact. And been utterly curious about how it would feel. Now the thrill of something dark and forbidden made its way through her bloodstream, exciting her and arousing her even more.

"Don't fight it," Mitch's breath was warm against her ear as his fingertips pressed against that dark spot. "I can make you feel so good, Autumn. Take deep breaths."

Slowly, in tiny increments, his fingers pushed past that tight muscle. When they were fully inside her dark channel flashes of hot and cold washed over her. She trembled even more, pushing back against his finger as much as the tiny shower permitted, moaning as his finger moved in and out.

Water washed over her thighs and she realized he'd lifted the handheld head from its place on the shower wall and was pressing it against her clit. Muscles quivered, nerves fired and she was lost in such a wave of sensation she could hardly catch her breath.

"One of these nights I'm going to fuck you here," he told her in his incredibly deep voice. "Consider yourself warned."

His finger moved faster, the showerhead pressed harder, moving up and down and she crashed into an orgasm that shook her from head to toe. Mitch dropped the showerhead and reached around to hold her, his fingers rubbing hard on her throbbing clit as he took her through the spasms, then the aftershocks.

She was limp when the last shudder died away, leaning back against Mitch, held up by the strength of his arms banded around her.

"I didn't get to return the favor," she finally managed to say.

"There'll be plenty of time for that. Don't worry." He shifted her so she faced him, taking one of her hands and wrapping the fingers around his thick cock. "I'll have trouble bending over today but I'll let you make it up to me tonight." He brushed his mouth against hers. "Okay?"

She nodded, then cleared her throat, looking at him with the water spraying around them, a sudden attack of nerves gripping her. She hadn't realized when she set out to do this how important his opinion of her would be. Why should she even care? But she did. Unexpectedly.

"Mitch, I don't usually... That is... Oh, hell. Never mind."

Here I go again. Idiot of the year.

She pulled herself from his arms, opened the shower door and managed to step outside. She was drying herself with one of the big towels on the counter when Mitch stepped out next to her.

"Look at me, Autumn," he commanded. "Right now."

Reluctantly she lifted her eyes to his. "I need to tell you..." Her voice trailed off at the look in his eyes.

"That you don't usually jump into bed with a man five minutes after you meet him? You think I couldn't tell that? Darlin', I've been around the block more times than you can count." He placed a finger under her chin and tipped her face up, placing a soft kiss on her mouth. "You're changing everything in your life, though, aren't you? New place, new lifestyle." His eyes flashed with fire. "New sex. Right?"

She nodded, unable to say anything.

41

"Okay, then. Consider me your guide. For the ranch...and everything else." He smiled at her. "I like you, Autumn. You've got guts. And if you're up for an adventure, I'm just the man who can give you one."

"Despite the age difference?" she teased.

After last night she couldn't even imagine going to bed with anyone older than she was anymore. Mitch was older than his years with a toned body and incredible stamina. She felt as if she should growl like a cougar, the nickname for older women who paired with younger men. Now she knew why they loved it so much. And she hoped now that he could see her in the light of day Mitch would not feel differently.

"I thought we put that to rest last night. Like I said when you brought it up, age is nothing but a number. I'm interested in you, the woman, no matter what." He pushed her wet hair back from her face. "You know, it works the other way too. I could be worried that I don't measure up to older men."

She'd never thought of it that way. "That's ridiculous," she blurted.

"My point exactly. So are we okay?"

She sighed. "Yes. Okay."

"All right, then. Let's get dressed, I'll make us some breakfast and tell you about Randy Churchill."

Having put last night's clothes back on, Autumn sat at the kitchen table, watching Mitch deftly slip bacon and eggs onto plates and carry them to the table.

"I should hire you to cook," she teased, savoring the taste of the scrambled eggs. "Meanwhile, I want to know about this Randy who practically knocked the door down and then explain what our plan is for today."

Mitch took a sip of hot coffee, watching her over the rim, his eyes thoughtful. "Randy and I have been friends for a long time," he began. "I wanted to hire him to work at Sweetgrass when Henry made me foreman but Randy said Henry had no real interest in the ranch. He didn't want to get stuck with a loser and he was right."

Autumn raised an eyebrow. "I'm still surprised you didn't feel the same way."

He put his mug down carefully. "I was tired of the rodeo circuit and tired of having no place to call my own. I had plenty of experience and I wanted a place to live. I figured if Henry didn't make it here, there was a good chance the next owner would."

"Only you didn't think the next owner would be a flaky female who bought the place on eBay," she finished for him.

"I don't think you're flaky, Autumn. Not for a minute. The way you did this might be strange but it's obvious you're committed to it. I want to help you so you don't fall on your face."

She lowered her eyes, focusing on her eggs as she carefully scooped some onto her fork. "And what's in it for you?"

He shrugged. "A place to live and a chance to put this ranch back on its feet." He grinned. "And the unexpected pleasure of some really hot sex."

Heat bloomed on her cheeks. "About last night..."

"It was great," he cut her off. "I think we said all we need to on that subject." He paused and looked at her. "Unless you don't want a repeat."

Now she knew she really *was* blushing. "I do," she said in a soft voice.

"All right, then. Now. Back to Randy."

"Yes. What did your friend want this morning? Why isn't he at wherever he works now?"

"Gossip flies around here," Mitch chuckled. "He has a few days off and he wanted to know about the woman I had at The Armadillo last night."

"And he came all the way over here to find out? What's the big deal?"

Now it was Mitch's turn to drop his gaze. "Randy and I...share a lot of things."

Autumn swallowed a bite of bacon to hide her surprise. "You mean you tell each other about your dates? Like high school boys?"

"Not exactly," he mumbled.

"Then what, exactly?" Then her jaw dropped as a stunning thought hit her. "You mean you share your *women*?"

"Hey, don't make it sound like we're committing murder," he said defensively and rose to refill his coffee mug. "Don't tell me you've never heard of ménage."

Of course she'd heard of it. Hadn't she read about it in her erotic romances? Hadn't it been one of the things she and the blog ladies had discussed and fantasized and giggled about at the convention.

But holy shit!

When she set out on this erotic odyssey with a plan to change her life, she hadn't expected the possibility she might be dropped into the middle of one.

"So, let me guess." She buttered a piece of toast to give herself something to do while she organized her thoughts. "He wanted to know what I looked like, if the sex was great and if I was interested in...expanding the participation. Have I got that right?"

Mitch's face colored but when he looked at her his gaze was solid. "That's about it."

"About it? What else could he want?" Autumn snapped her fingers. "Oh, wait. He wanted to know if he could jump right in and join us this morning. Right?"

He dipped his head once. "But don't worry. I set him straight."

"That right?" She bit off a piece of toast and chewed it slowly. "Exactly how did you do that?"

Mitch stared at her for a long time before answering, as if trying to get a clear read on her. "I said he was not welcome in our bed unless I invited him. And anything that happened there was strictly up to you. And it is." He lifted her free hand and kissed the knuckle. "Nothing will ever happen unless you want it to, Autumn. You don't have to worry about that."

She was grateful for his reply. "Thank you."

They ate in silence for a moment.

Autumn stared into her coffee cup. "But if I hire him, even for a short while, that's going to signal to him that I agree to being...shared."

"In a manner of speaking. Yes. But it's your choice, darlin'. All the way. No one's feelings will be hurt if you say no."

When she and her friends had started out on their odyssey, she'd thought it would be courageous enough just to get a younger man in her bed. Now she was on the verge of jumping into a ménage. How wild was that?

"Can I wait until I meet him to give you an answer?" She hoped she didn't sound as timid as she felt.

Mitch laughed, a warm sound. "I wouldn't expect anything else. Anyway, Randy wants to meet you. I can send him packing if you want." A slow grin spread over his face. "And by the way, he and I are the same age."

Two of them? Would that make her a double cougar? She swallowed the hysterical urge to laugh.

"You mean he's still here? Waiting?" She lifted her eyes and stared at him. "For you to talk to me about this?""

"Uh-huh. He's watching the guys sweat in the sun and drinking coffee."

"And speaking of that, what will the guys you hired think when they see me walk out of your house? Never mind the

45

situation with Randy." Something she hadn't considered in her mad rush to fall into Mitchell Brand's bed. But then she'd never been a ranch owner before, either, trying to exert authority over a bunch of sweaty testosterone-laden males.

He grinned. "They'll think I know how to take care of my boss." Then his face sobered. "Seriously, Autumn. It won't be a problem. Trust me on that."

"If you say so." She swallowed her doubts.

Together they cleaned up after breakfast. When the last dish had been put away, Autumn drew in a deep breath, let it out slowly and told Mitch, "Okay. I'm ready to face the world."

The first thing she saw when she walked out onto the porch was the man leaning against the corral and watching the house, as if he'd been waiting specifically for this moment. He was as tall and lean as Mitch, his t-shirt and jeans clinging to every muscle of his body. His tan western hat was tipped low over his face, blocking any view of anything but his chin. Much as Mitch's had been that first day. Her legs began to wobble and little jolts of sexual energy fired throughout her body.

Holy shit! Did they grow them this way in Texas?

Mitch cupped her elbow and urged her forward. Without his supporting hand she was sure she would have fallen as weak as she suddenly felt.

"Randy Churchill, meet Autumn Kelley, new owner of Sweetgrass Ranch."

Randy tipped his head back and Autumn had to swallow at the sensuously masculine appeal of his face. Vivid green eyes traveled over her slowly from head to foot and back again, sending shivers racing over her spine. Sensuous lips quirked in a grin above a rough-hewn jaw. The chemistry that arced between them was almost visible.

"Pleased to meet you," Randy drawled.

He held out his hand and when Autumn took it a wave of electricity shot up her arm and through her body.

It must be the Texas air. In thirty-four years no man has made erotic thoughts dance in my head. Now, in three days, I've met two of them. I'm either in luck or in trouble!

"Same here," she said, quickly dropping his hand.

Randy looked at Mitch with a broad grin. "That's a fine lady you've got here, my friend. Mighty fine." And his eyes swept over her again.

"She's not anyone's to 'get'," Mitch corrected, resting his hands on her shoulders. "Autumn's a woman with a mind of her own."

"I guess so, buying a ranch on eBay sight unseen." He looked around at the activity. "But y'all look like you're pulling things together here." He shifted his gaze back to Autumn, then to Mitch. "Think you can hire on one more hand?"

As close to her as he was, Autumn could sense the sudden tension in Mitch's body. Was he waiting for *her* to answer? Was *she* supposed to take the lead? This was more than just another worker on the place. Just as they'd discussed at breakfast, if she hired Randy, she'd be telling Mitch she was agreeable to whatever sexual arrangement he had in mind.

Her nipples tingled with anticipated pleasure and a pulse began to beat low in her cunt, her liquid soaking the crotch of her panties at the idea of both men naked in bed with her. Pleasuring her. Taking her places she'd never been before. Erotic images were running through her mind, dark and forbidding and so thrilling she almost trembled with the force of them.

Well, they'd all made a pact, hadn't they? Wait until she posted *this* on the blog.

She swallowed, hard, looked up at Mitch and nodded.

His hand slid from her elbow up her arm in a slow, caressing gesture, coming to rest on her shoulder. His thumb gently stoked the sensitive spot where shoulder and neck were joined.

"Okay, then," he agreed. "I can use help getting the barn back in shape, especially the stalls for the horses. And they all need checking over and grooming." He chuckled. "Think you can handle that?"

Randy gave an answering laugh. "I've been shoveling shit since Day One. I think I can do it with my eyes closed."

"Then go on into the barn. I'll meet you there in five."

Randy held out his hand to Autumn again. "Pleasure to be working at Sweetgrass Ranch." He winked. "I just know I'm going to enjoy the hell out of it."

Autumn felt the same tingles shoot up her arm to her body. This man was as much sex on the hoof as Mitch was. She could barely handle him. What would she do with two of them? Shivers of anticipation tickled at her.

"Why don't you go on up to the house," Mitch said. "I'll check on how the men are doing, then get Randy started." He bent and put his mouth to her ear. "I might sneak away for a cup of coffee."

Her heat factor rose a notch. "Okay. See you later. Bye, Randy."

Chapter Four

While the coffee was dripping, Autumn quickly stripped off yesterday's clothes, put on fresh undies, jeans and a clean shirt and brushed her hair back into a ponytail. Knowing Mitch would be along any minute, she hurried into her den and booted up the laptop.

This time she sent a blanket email to everyone. She didn't have time for a chat and wasn't sure this was something to share on the blog.

Hey, everyone. You'll never believe this. Last night was beyond fantastic. Oh, man. I wish I'd known about younger men years ago. Of course, then I'd have been young too. I only embarrassed myself twice by letting my insecurities show but I got over it pretty quickly. Fortunately Mitch was kind enough not to chalk me up as a dork, because the sex was better than anything I could have imagined. And listen. He has a friend who could be his twin, who wants to join us in a ménage. A threesome! Ohmigod! Ohmigod! I sort of told them yes but now I don't know. Tell me what to do. Quick.

Autumn

The back door slammed and she heard Mitch calling to her from the kitchen.

"Coming," she shouted, closed down the computer and hurried from the room.

He had already poured coffee into a mug for himself but he put it on the counter and pulled her into his arms. His tongue tickled her ear and his warm breath was like a caress on her skin.

"I just want to be sure you know," he told her, "that including Randy is strictly your choice. If you say no, nothing will change between us."

"So what did you tell Randy?"

"That when you were ready he'd get his invitation. Again, that's strictly up to you."

"Did you tell him..." She bit her bottom lip. "I mean..."

Why was this such a problem to her? Why couldn't she keep her insecurities in her back pocket where they belonged?

"How old you are?" Mitch's face set in a hard expression. "I told you, that's not important. Not to me, not to Randy. What's important is you and who you are. And honey, you are hotter and better than women half your age. So can we forget about that for a while?"

"Yes. All right." She let out her breath. "If you say so, I believe it."

"I say so."

He pulled her t-shirt from the waistband of her jeans, slid his hands beneath it to her warm skin and cupped her breasts.

"You haven't told me how you like it with a younger man, you know," he teased.

"Maybe you'd better remind me."

His thumbs rasped over her nipples, already beaded into hard points. Autumn leaned into him, loving the feel of his hands on her. She wound her arms around his neck, then jerked back when she remembered they were standing in her kitchen.

"Ohmigod!" She took a step backward. "What am I doing? Any one of the men could walk in any time."

Mitch pulled her toward him again. "First of all, no one would dare just walk into this house. You're the owner, remember? The big boss? Secondly, I locked the door. So relax. I need something sweet with my coffee."

He put his hand beneath her buttocks and lifted her so she had to wrap her legs around his waist. Pressing his open mouth to hers, he carried her through the kitchen to the room she'd set up as her office. The top of her desk was littered with file folders and magazines Mitch had given her to read, plus the stack of budget printouts she'd been trying to go through. With a sweep of his hand he moved them all to one side and plunked her buttocks onto the recently polished wood.

"Mitch, what—"

But his mouth cut her off again, pressing against hers, his tongue exploring expertly as he pulled up her t-shirt and pushed her bra aside. Agile fingers pinched her nipples, teasing them until she thought for sure they would burst from fullness. Still claiming her mouth, he moved his hands to unsnap her jeans, lifted her with one hand while the other swept jeans and panties to her ankles.

"Hush," he said into her mouth when she tried to speak again.

He bent her knees, widening her thighs as much as he could with her boots still on and her clothing draped at her ankles. He bent his head and licked her already moist cunt, pausing to flick his tongue back and forth across her clit.

"I have to fuck you now," he said in a guttural voice, unzipping his jeans and pulling out his cock. "Jesus, Autumn, I've been as hard as a brick since we talked to Randy."

He yanked a condom from his pocket, ripped the foil and rolled the latex on before she even realized what he was doing. Then he was plunging inside her, seating himself with one hard, fast thrust. She clenched around him, shocked at how ready she was.

He rolled his hips and pushed hard and fast, no long and slow this time.

"Tell me," he rasped. "Tell me what you want me to do to you."

"I don't... I can't..." she gasped.

"You can, you can. I need to hear it. Say it, Autumn."

"Fuck me," she hissed, shocking herself that the words came out so easily. "Fuck me, Mitch."

He slid his hands beneath her ass and she wound her arms around his neck, steadying herself in her awkward position as he rammed home again and again. The climax built, then erupted with force, her entire body clenching and pulsing.

"That's it." The words ground out between gritted teeth. "Come for me, darlin'. Oh, god. I'm there. I'm there. I'm there."

He spurted into the condom, pulse after pulse of semen as her cunt muscles continued to milk him again and again. Her head felt back as aftershocks rippled through her, Mitch's mouth on her neck, the hollow of her throat, every place he could reach her.

At last he pulled back, his breath still coming in gasps. Pulling the condom off and wrapping it in his handkerchief, he put his shaft back into his jeans and zipped himself up. He stared at Autumn's pussy as if it were a bountiful feast and he a dying man. Then he leaned over, kissed her and helped her put herself together. When her clothes were in place again, he pulled her against him, hugging her tightly against his chest.

"You okay?" His voice was still uneven.

"Y-Yes, I think so." But she wasn't exactly sure. She'd never been ravaged on a desk before — or any other piece of furniture — and she was still assimilating the force of their frantic coupling.

I don't think I'll post this one for the girls to read. Whew!

He kissed her gently. "I think one of these days I won't be hard as a rock and ready to spill every time I set eyes on you but I can't say exactly when that will be."

"I'll take that as a compliment."

"As it was meant to be." He helped her slide off the desk.

"I wonder what the hands working out there think about what's going on."

Mitch cupped her chin and tilted her face up to his. "They have no idea what's going on. They think you are a woman committed to making Sweetgrass Ranch profitable again, to putting it in proper shape. That you didn't make this commitment lightly and they hope to impress you enough so you'll keep them on when the initial work's done."

"But they must suspect what's going on with us. Especially since I came out of your house with you this morning."

Don't let me blush. Don't let me blush.

"If they want to keep their jobs they won't think anything of it. Listen, Autumn. They've seen you work harder than a ranch hand since you got here and treat them fairly. That's all they care about." He touched his lips to hers in a brief caress. "Okay?"

She smiled back at him. "Definitely okay."

"Now I think we could both use some of that coffee."

* * * * *

Autumn stepped out of the old clawfoot tub and wrapped one of her fluffy new bath towels around herself, clouds of steam from the scented water still filling the bathroom. She broke the seal on a new bottle of jasmine lotion and massaged it into every inch and crevice of her body, taking special care with the cleft of her ass. She had a feeling Mitch would be paying particular attention to that area tonight.

The dark thrill ran through her again at the thought of his cock in her ass. The first time she'd read about it she'd squirmed in her bed, crossing her legs and squeezing her thighs at the arousal it incited in her. She'd tried to imagine what it would feel like, even considered buying one of the butt plugs the book described but had chickened out at the last minute. Now she was almost sorry she had.

Desiree Holt

I'm doing it. I'm really doing it. Ohmigod.

She'd brought the laptop into her room and left it open on the little side table. Still wrapped in the big towel, she sat down to scroll through the emails again.

From Edie: Two men? We should all be so lucky. I say go for it, girl.

From Cam: I say jump in with both feet. *giggle* And be sure to give us all the details.

From Rachel: Two young studs? Honey, if you turn it down you'll regret it forever. Don't forget. You're exploring new horizons. Take whatever comes, if you'll pardon the pun.

It was all the encouragement she needed. She smiled and closed the computer.

And even as she looked forward to the night she was thinking ahead of Randy Churchill joining them. When would that be? Had Mitch already made arrangements?

She'd found an old mirror in the attic, a cheval glass and she stood before it now, eyeing her naked body critically. She'd shaved her legs and under her arms but she knew a lot of women shaved their pubic hair. Did Mitch like curls covering a pussy or did he like it naked?

The naughty thought crept in out of nowhere.

I'll ask him. And if he wants to, I'll let him shave me.

Tiny spasms rocketed through her cunt just thinking about it.

She looked around her bedroom, eying it critically. Last night at Mitch's had been wonderful but tonight she wanted him here. In her house. In her room. And she'd told him so. If she was going to do this, she wanted it to be in her own home, on her turf. Somehow it made her feel more in control, even though that might be an illusion.

She'd opened a new package of sheets and pulled out a brand-new soft coverlet she'd bought on her manic shopping

54

trip. Chiding herself at the same time for overkill, she gently sprayed some of her jasmine scent over the sheets and plumped all the pillows. On the round antique table she'd rescued from the attic and placed in front of the wide window was a huge spray of lilies. Next to it was a bottle of bourbon and two tumblers. She'd get the ice later.

She'd debated about the drinks, thinking beer wouldn't set the right mood and she had no idea if Mitch drank wine. The bourbon seemed a good compromise.

Well, Autumn, who's seducing whom here?

Scenes from the night before teased at her mind, the two of them naked, Mitch whispering erotic words in her ear. Then the image of Randy Churchill popped into the picture and heat suffused her body. Could she go through with it, having sex with two men? She'd read enough ménage stories to be tempted by it. No, more than tempted. Anxious, at forty-one, to finally experience everything.

Mitch had told her he'd grab something to eat before he showered, so she'd swallowed a quick sandwich before her bath. Now she slipped a filmy, lacy gown over her head, one she'd bought before coming here as part of her Free Autumn plan. Checking herself from all angles in the mirror, she gave her shining hair a casual flip, moistened her lips and glanced around the room one last time just as she heard the back door open and close.

"Autumn?"

She heard Mitch's boots on the hardwood floor as he walked through the house.

"In here," she called. "In my bedroom."

He filled the doorway and the sight of him took her breath away. His dark hair lay in thick waves on his head and the shirt he was wearing was the exact vivid shade of blue as his eyes. Right now those eyes looked at her with such lust her knees wobbled.

"Wow is the only appropriate word I can think of," he said in a thick voice, those blue eyes taking in every inch of her. Then his gaze took in the rest of the room and his mouth turned up in a grin. "Exactly who's seducing whom here, anyway?"

"Maybe it will be a contest," she said, suddenly shy. Had she gone too far? Did he like his women less bold?

But his next words swept away her doubt.

"My kind of woman," he told her, strode into the room and lifted her into his arms.

He brushed his lips gently against hers, then licked the outline. Autumn let her tongue peep out and touched the tip of it to his. Shards of heat shot through her and she wound her arms around his neck, pressing her breasts against the soft cotton of his shirt.

"I feel your nipples," he whispered against her lips. "They're already hard. I wonder how wet you are."

He stood her on her feet, reached beneath her gown and softly probed her cunt. When he lifted his hand she saw his fingers glistening with the liquid of her arousal. Deliberately he licked each one, his eyes locked onto hers.

"I guess you've been looking forward to tonight as much as I have." He cupped her cheeks in his warm hands. "But tonight let's not rush things. I'm glad you wanted us to be here, in your room. I'm glad you set everything up this way." He winked. "Especially the bourbon. How about pouring us each a drink?"

When they each held a tumbler filled with ice and whiskey, he touched his glass to hers. "To exploring pleasure together."

"To pleasure." She lifted her glass and took a small sip, the liquor burning through her veins and warming her system. Not that she needed anything more to heat her up. She was already embarrassed at his knowledge of how ready for him she was.

He noticed the little radio she'd set on her bedside table. "How about a little music?" He snapped it on and fiddled with the dial until he found something slow and bluesy. Then he held out his arms and Autumn walked into them.

Just like at The Armadillo, they fit together perfectly. He rested his chin on her head which was tucked into his shoulder, and his hands moved lazily up and down her back. Their slow travel took them to the cheeks of her ass which he gripped gently in both hands, rhythmically squeezing them. His cock pressed into the softness of her belly, thick and hard and she couldn't help rubbing herself against it. They moved in place to the music, swaying as they teased each other.

One of Mitch's hands slid to the cleft of her buttocks, fingers rubbing the length of it through the sheer fabric of her gown. Somehow that was even sexier than if he'd been touching her bare skin. She pushed herself against him even harder and a little sound of pleasure burst from her throat.

"You like that, do you?" His warm, thick voice rolled over her. "Tonight we're going to find out just how much you like playing back there. I promise you, darlin', you won't believe the pleasure I'll bring you."

The music stopped and they picked up their drinks. Autumn took a healthy swallow of hers, blinking back the sudden tears it brought to her eyes."

"Easy, darlin'," Mitch chuckled, taking the drink from her. "Slow and easy, just like everything else tonight." He set both glasses on the table and eased her gown up over her head. "This is so pretty it's almost a shame to take it off but it's hiding the body I want to see. Besides, I've always wanted to dance naked." Amusement twinkled in his eyes. "Haven't you?"

"I-I don't think I've ever thought about it," she stammered, then had to squeeze her thighs together to contain the sudden pulsing in her cunt.

"I think this is as good a time as any to give it a try." He unbuttoned his shirt, pulled the tails from his waistband and tossed it over the little slipper chair. His eyes never left hers as he toed off his boots, unfastened his jeans and divested himself of them but not before reaching into one pocket for condoms which he dropped next to their drinks.

"Come here," he said, motioning to her.

She walked into his arms, pressing against him, skin to skin and he wrapped her in an embrace. His cock was so hard it was like a steel rod pressing against her, hot and urgent. The thick pelt of hair on his chest tickled her nipples, making them swell even more. She could feel the movement of each muscle in his thighs and his arms as they swayed to the beat. His hands did a little dance on her spine, tracing each bump on a downward journey to the cleft of her buttocks.

Autumn shivered as two fingers rubbed slowly from one end of the cleft to another.

"Like that?" Mitch murmured, plunging his fingers deeper.

"I... Yes," she breathed. *I love it.*

They continued to move to the music, his cock rubbing against her, his chest hair stimulating her breasts. His arms around her tightened, pressing her even closer, moving so the base of his shaft pressed against her clit. He moved his hips infinitesimally to create friction at that very spot and before she could realize it the muscles in her pussy quaked, the low throb of the pulse inside her built and the insides of her thighs were suddenly wet and slick.

As her body jerked with the spasms Mitch held her tight, supporting her, whispering to her, rubbing his body against hers.

"Ohmigod," she breathed, weak-kneed. I can't believe that just happened?"

He laughed softly. "Having an orgasm while you were dancing? How did it feel?"

"A-Amazing. Ohmigod," she repeated and leaned against him.

"You have no idea how much I love fucking you." His voice was low in her ear, his warm breath tickling her skin. "Last night we barely scratched the surface of the things I want to do to you. With you."

Her hands clutched his shoulders to steady herself. "Like what?"

"Well, maybe…like…this."

He danced her over to the bed and lowered her to the sheets, pulling her legs up and spreading them apart. He eased himself down to his knees, bent his head and, just as he had last night, placed an open-mouthed kiss directly onto the lips of her cunt.

Streaks of fire burned through her body, her hips jerking, her hands fisting at the electric feel of the contact.

Holding her in place with his big, warm hands, he licked her slit from end to end, pausing each time to flick his tongue at her clit and rim the opening of her vagina with the tip. Up, down, back and forth, teasing and tormenting. Low in her belly spasms began to gather and an icy-hot feeling raced over her skin.

He lifted his head for a moment, raising his eyes to her. "I thought about this all day today, darlin'. How sweet you tasted, how tasty this little pussy is. I couldn't wait to get my mouth on it again. Tonight I'm going to eat my way to heaven."

His tongue probed inside her vagina and Autumn fisted her hands in the sheets as he tongue-fucked her, then withdrew to stimulate her clit. Then the stiffened tongue was back inside her again, rasping the sensitive walls, reaching for the sweet spot that he knew drove her wild. Then back to her clit again.

Every time she reached the edge of orgasm, every time she felt herself about to crash over the edge, he pulled back, licked the insides of her thighs, her calves, her ankles. And then began again.

She lost count of how many times he took her up without letting her reach the peak. She knew only that she was a quivering, shaking mass of need when he shifted his head slightly and his tongue found the very tender skin between her vagina and her anus.

"Ohmigod," she screamed, bucking in his grasp.

When he touched that puckered opening with the tip of his tongue her body nearly arched off the bed.

"Come for me, darlin'. Do it now."

His thumbs held the lips of her cunt apart and his tongue continued to lick everywhere as she finally flew into space, shaking and convulsing, whirling in a black velvet void with fireworks exploding behind her eyelids. She tried to squeeze her thighs together, tried to urge him to fill her with his tongue or his fingers but he was determined to keep her open, expose her to his eyes.

"That's it," he urged. "Oh, Jesus, Autumn. I'll never get enough of watching that little pink pussy quiver and spasm. See your juices spilling out. That's it, darlin'. Oh, yeah."

When the last little twitch died away she was exhausted, her body limp, yet still far from satisfied. Mitch gave one final sweep with his tongue, then rose over her and lightly brushed his lips against hers.

"I'm dead," she told him, "but I'm not done. Can you believe that?"

He laughed, his breath tickling her. "That's the idea." His hand skimmed over her pubic curls. "You know these are gorgeous but I'll bet that sweet little pussy would look even better without them."

She gave him what she hoped was a seductive smile. "Maybe you'd like to do it for me."

He kissed her curls. "And maybe we'll save that treat until Randy joins us."

Heat sizzled through her as she imagined two men shaving her pussy and lavishing their attention on it. Two *younger* men full of testosterone with high-octane sex drives.

Mitch caught the expression on her face. "You like that thought, do you? I'll have to make a note of it." He lifted her to a sitting position. "Come on. I think you need another sip of your drink. I'm just getting started."

* * * * *

Autumn was ready to plead, beg, anything if Mitch would only let her come. They finished their drinks lying side by side on the bed, then he nudged her to her side, lifted one of her legs over his and slid two fingers in and out of her slick cunt while she moaned in his arms. One hand stole around to pinch and roll a nipple.

She worked hard to reach ecstasy but at the crucial moment he pulled his fingers free, rolled her to her stomach and pulled her to her knees. A sudden *snap!* told her he was rolling on a condom. Then, again using his thumbs to open her wide, he plunged into her waiting vagina and set up a slow, steady rhythm. Autumn pressed her forehead to her arms crossed in front of her, pushing her hips back against each thrust of Mitch's thick, hard cock.

Again she felt the beginning quakes in her vagina, felt the muscles twitch low in her belly, the icy-hot flame wash over her skin. And again, before she could crest, he pulled out. Flipping to his back, he took her with him, lifted her with his hands on her hips and eased her down on his throbbing cock.

When she looked into his eyes she could tell he was using every measure of control he had. She could tell he was determined to draw this out, to drive her to the absolute end of her limits, see how far he could push her. And in the back of her mind, she sensed he was working her to a fever pitch for what he had planned. That tonight he would teach her what it was like to be fucked in the ass.

Now he had her on her hands and knees again, pillows plumped beneath her for support, her body so aroused she was sure it would implode any minute. She moaned as Mitch slid first two then three fingers into her hungry pussy, gathering her moisture, then painting it on the tight ring of muscle at her anus.

She had reached a point where she didn't care which way he took her, as long as she could finally climax, finally give her throbbing body the release it so desperately needed. She was barely aware of the music still playing in the background, only of her own aching need, her out-of-control desire.

He pressed a kiss to the base of her spine, licked the spot with his tongue and murmured. "Hold on, darlin'. We're going for a wild ride."

The tip of one finger pressed against her anus, pushed, pushed, then made its way inside. Chills raced over her at this new intrusion and dark desire curled low in her belly. The tender tissues of her rectum clenched around his finger. She had just adjusted to it when a second finger worked its way in next to the first. Mitch worked them in a scissor fashion, little by little stretching her tight muscles.

"Easy, darlin'," he crooned. "Slow and easy. The last thing I want is to hurt you."

She adjusted to the initial fullness and began rocking back and forth on her knees, moving her hips in cadence with the tempo of his fingers.

"One more," he murmured, his deep voice resonating over her. "Take a deep breath and let it out slowly."

Autumn was so aroused she could barely process what he was saying. Still she managed to do what he said, taking in a deep breath, then letting it out in a whoosh as a third finger pressed inside her.

Mitch never varied the rhythm, moving his fingers at a steady, unhurried pace. By now Autumn was ready to shout at him, "Fuck me now. Right now."

When he withdrew his fingers she wanted to scream at the sudden loss. She thrust her hips back at him hard, begging for more.

Then Mitch's hands were on her hips, his thighs between hers spreading her wide.

"Take another deep breath, darlin'." His voice was so hoarse with need she almost didn't recognize it.

The head of his cock pressed against her tender opening, harder, firmer. She pulled in a deep breath and as she let it out Mitch pushed inside her, a slow, steady stroke until he filled her rectum completely. The initial discomfort disappeared at once and a clawing need came over her. All the teasing, the playing, bringing her to the edge but never turning her loose had driven her to a stage of rampant desire and animalistic need.

As Mitch began to move his shaft in and out of her ass, his balls slapping on the backs of her thighs, the dark ribbon of forbidden lust uncoiled inside her. She thrust her hips back hard, riding his cock as much as taking it, screaming her need, yelling for him to fuck her harder, harder.

When the explosion came it was like being shot into space on the tail of a rocket. Her pussy spasmed, her rectum clenched, every muscle in her body convulsed and she shook like a tree in the wind. She heard Mitch shouting her name as his shaft flexed and spurted inside the thin latex that felt like no barrier at all.

On and on it went, Mitch pounding into her, Autumn shrieking with ecstasy and pushing her hips back at him, the orgasm so prolonged it stole her breath.

Then it was over and she collapsed forward, Mitch on top of her, sweat-slicked skin sticking to skin, harsh breathing slicing the air, heartbeats so loud they sounded like percussion instruments. She wasn't sure she would ever be able to move again.

Autumn had no idea how long they lay there, the radio still playing in the background, their uneven breathing settling to a steady rhythm. Finally Mitch pulled himself from her body with obvious reluctance and went to dispose of the condom. When he came back to the bed she was still draped over the pillows. He lifted and turned her and lay down with her cradled in his arms. His lips rained gentle kisses on her face, her neck, the hollow of her throat. His hand stroked her back, gentling her.

"You okay?" he asked, his voice soft in her ear.

"Uh-huh." She barely had strength to answer him.

"I worked you pretty hard."

"'Sokay," she mumbled. "Liked it."

His laugh was low and sexy. "I knew you would. Autumn, I've been with a lot of women but I've never come like that before. Or enjoyed it so much."

She managed to raise her eyes to look at him. "Really?"

"Yes, really." He stroked her cheek. "You look like you're about to pass out but first we need to shower."

"Noooo," she wailed. "Just sleep."

"Shower first," he insisted, lifting her in his arms.

Standing in the clawfoot tub, he bathed her like a baby, washing her thoroughly and drying her with the towel she'd hung on the door.

At last she sank into blessed sleep, wondering if somehow she'd bitten off more than she could chew.

Chapter Five

ℰᴏ

Dear blog friends,

If anyone had ever told me sex could be exhilarating, rejuvenating and enthralling I'd have hit them with a frying pan. After so many years of men who thought of it as an exercise to gain relief, or who had to apologize for their lack of performance, or worse yet, for the entire episode concluding so fast I wasn't even sure it had happened, it is wonderful to find a man—yes, a young man *growl*—to whom it is an art. Now I know what the term performance magic means. There is definitely something to be said for younger men. Wait, make that a lot to be said.

Mitch has been with me in my bed every night since the first one. I am exhausted but energized by the time dawn arrives, when he leaves to go to his own house to protect me from prying eyes. I don't get many hours of sleep—I'm up with the chickens working my fool head off around here—but the sleep I do get is deep and refreshing.

Oh, girls, what a hunk of man he is. I wanted someone who could hardly keep their hands off me but I'm the one who can't stop touching him.

I am so very grateful that we all met up at the convention and formed this wonderful group. I would never have had the courage to do this without your support and I wish the same amazing results for all of you.

More later.

Autumn

* * * * *

For the next week Autumn worked side by side with Mitch, tackling every job he gave her. She spread hay in stalls, scrubbed the tack room, hosed out feed buckets, painted rails, whatever was called for. She was sending the message that she wasn't a hands-off owner and she could see the men developing a healthy respect for her. And she found herself settling more comfortably into her role as ranch owner than she'd ever expected, considering the stupid way it had come about.

She also spent some time with Randy, working in the barn with him to ready the tack room. She discovered he was bright, funny and as experienced in the business as Mitch. He made it his business, despite sharp looks from Mitch, to bring her cold bottles of water and make sure she took enough breaks. Sometimes they just sat on an old tack trunk and he told her about the days when he and Mitch rodeoed together and why they quit.

She loved the warm sound of his voice, the touch of humor as he poked fun at himself. And he seemed genuinely interested in her as he tactfully drew out her story and the big eBay fiasco. Autumn found him very easy to talk to. But the air between them was so sexually charged she almost told both men to climb into one of the stalls, strip off their clothes and they'd all go at it.

Again, her sense of self-control was all that saved her from what she knew would be making a fool of herself. The time would come for the three of them. She was beginning to hope it was soon.

Nights were spent in Mitch's arms, living out her fantasies and learning that the erotic romances she read didn't do justice to the reality of exhilarating sex. To her surprise, she also found a friendship forming between the two of them.

Autumn hoped it would be enough of a foundation for him to stay on as foreman once they got Sweetgrass into shape.

Nothing more had been mentioned about Randy joining them but he continued to show up every day for work and she often caught him eyeing her with curiosity.

When the day of the auction arrived, Autumn could sense the excitement vibrating from Mitch's body.

"This is a big deal to you, isn't it," she said as he wheeled the huge pickup down the highway.

"You could say," he said, trying to appear nonchalant. "There's just something about finding the right stock, the right breeding cows, the right bull. It's what can make or break a ranch."

"I have confidence in you," she told him. "No breaking allowed here."

The barn where the auction was held was packed with both lookers and buyers, men in jeans and shirts and others in western-cut suits. There were a fair number of women also, many of them bidders in their own right. Autumn was fascinated watching them, awed by the knowledge they seemed to have at what they were doing. She could feel the excitement humming around her like a living thing.

The air was a rich mixture of crowd sounds and animal scent. In the barn behind the wall erected at one side of the temporary ring she could hear the pawing and stamping of hooves on the dirt floor. The entire scene was exhilarating.

Mitch went over the program with her, marking the page with the two different lots they would bid on, one a backup to the other. When it was over and they successfully bid for the lot they wanted she was beside herself with excitement.

He walked her through the paperwork, introducing her to the people in charge and making arrangements for delivery of their cattle.

"This is great." She hugged his arm. "Totally fantastic."

Mitch laughed. "It's exciting, I'll agree. And we got a good lot to start the breeding program."

When he opened the truck door on the passenger side, she impulsively threw her arms around him and pressed her mouth to his. Almost automatically his tongue slipped through her lips into her mouth, finding hers and sliding against it. His arms pulled her tight against his body, the thickness of his cock pressing firmly against her even through his jeans.

He broke the kiss first, fighting to control his breathing. "I like your moves, darlin' but I say we take this some place a little more private."

Heat crept Autumn's cheeks and she extricated herself from him. "I'm sorry. I just got a little carried away." She turned to climb into the cab.

Mitch wrapped his fingers around one arm. "There's nothing to apologize for. Auctions get my blood pumped up too." He leaned his face close to hers. "But I've got a better idea how to work it off."

"Oh?" She arched an eyebrow. She'd been working just as hard as the men putting the buildings back together, sore and tired at the end of each day but not so sore that she and Mitch hadn't spent night after night performing every kind of sexual callisthenic possible. Mitch had introduced her to pleasures she didn't think had even been written about yet.

If she worried about anything, it was her growing feelings for the younger man, something she worked damn hard to conceal. And something she hadn't planned for when she'd set out on this...call it a mission for lack of a better word. She'd been looking for fun and adventure and the challenge of sex with a younger man. Her inner cougar had finally escaped its cage. Anything more than that wasn't in the picture.

Besides, she reminded herself, she hoped he would stay on as foreman. She knew jack shit about running a ranch and he seemed to have all the answers. A complicated relationship would alter the picture. No, great sex whenever they both wanted it was the answer. Absolutely. For sure.

"You didn't hear a word I said, did you?" Mitch's warm voice held the touch of a laugh.

Autumn shook herself, "Of course I did. Every word."

His laugh was rich and full. "Uh-huh. So what's your answer?"

She frowned. "To what?"

His hand reached over and cupped her chin, turning her face until it was mere inches from his. "I said, I thought this would be a good time to see if Randy can join us. What do you think?"

She swallowed, twice, her heart suddenly racing and her bones like jelly. "Tonight?" she squeaked.

"Uh-huh." He kissed her lips, a gentle touch. "If you don't want to, just tell me. No problem." His voice dropped a notch. "But I think you'd enjoy it."

All her pulses were throbbing with a sudden rush of need. Two instead of one? Be part of a ménage?

She looked him straight in the eye and said, "Call him."

"You sure?"

"Yes." *I think so.*

"All right." He pressed a kiss to her mouth again. "Let me make the call." He pulled his cell phone from his pocket and speed dialed a number. "Randy? Nine o'clock. And you'd better be on your best behavior." He snapped the phone shut and stuffed it back in his pocket. "All right, darlin'. Let's go home and get ready for tonight.

* * * * *

Dear bloggers,

Today I went to my first cattle auction and I can't believe how aroused I got looking at all those cows. Of course, by the time we left I was ready to tear off my clothes and Mitch's and jump his bones in the truck. I can hardly believe how bold I've gotten in such a short time.

Bypass, Texas is still...hot as hell and in the middle of no place. But not as hot as it gets when Mitch and I get together. I took everyone's advice and gave Mitch the go-ahead with Randy.

Tonight's the night! The three of us together!

Ohmigod! Ohmigod. I can't believe this is actually happening.

Autumn

Chewing on a fingernail, she opened her Instant Messenger and searched frantically to see if Rachel was on line. Yes! There she was.

Autumn clicked on her name and when the message box appeared, typed: Rachel! Help again! I've gotten myself into it all right.

Rachel: I just read the blog. So tonight's the big night?

Autumn: Uh-huh. I'm scared and nervous and so excited and aroused you wouldn't believe it.

Rachel: Why? I thought we agreed this was what you wanted. Part of your fantasies. Please don't tell me it's the age thing again.

Autumn: No. I've stopped worrying about whether he thinks I'm too old, figuring he wouldn't bring his friend in if he thought that. And Randy's eyes have been sending me hot messages. But...am I really doing the right thing?

Rachel: Sigh! We agreed to push the boundaries, right? If it feels comfortable, you need to go for it. And trust Mitch to control things. Between you and me, I wish I had the guts to be there in your place.

Autumn: Oh, Rachel. Your turn will come and I'll be right there for you too.

Rachel: Go for it, kiddo. Experience it all. Enjoy, enjoy.

Autumn: You're right. I'm making problems where there aren't any. Frankly, I never knew sex could be this much fun.

Rachel: Go get ready for your big night. And IM me in the morning!!!!!

Autumn signed off, her niggling fears set to rest, Rachel's straightforward practicality once again giving her a clear look at the picture.

* * * * *

The two men had undressed her with great care, trailing their fingers over every inch of her body as they exposed it. Now all three were naked in her bedroom. Autumn had finished a glass of wine while they were waiting for Randy, just enough to take the edge off her nerves. But when Randy walked in the door, pulled her to his hard body and probed her mouth with his tongue, the last of her anxiety faded away.

While his tongue was exploring every bit of her mouth, his hands cupping her head to give him the best access, Mitch came up behind her, pressing his erection against her ass through their clothing while his hands slipped around to her front and caressed her pussy through the thin fabric of her shorts.

His warm breath caressed her ear as his tongue licked the edge of it with delicate strokes. Her head was swimming and she barely registered the movement as Randy dropped his hands to the buttons on her blouse and opened them one by one. Mitch's hands slipped back to unfasten her bra and then her breasts were free, cupped in Randy's warm hands, his thumbs chafing her nipples.

His mouth had still never left hers, his tongue doing an erotic dance that made her nerve endings sizzle. Caught up in the maelstrom of sensation, she was hardly aware of their hands moving from place to place, their bodies shifting, until she realized that all three of them were completely naked.

Mitch bent to slide his forearms beneath her thighs and lifted her so her legs were spread wide, her pussy completely exposed to Randy's gaze and touch. Lust flared in his eyes as he eyed the feast laid out before him. One lean finger reached out and traced the length of her slit, then rubbed it up and down before licking the tip of the finger.

"Sweet," he breathed. "Like passion fruit."

"Take a real taste," Mitch encouraged.

Randy needed no more urging. Autumn reached up and behind her to clasp Mitch's neck, steadying herself as Randy bent to one knee, spread the lips of her cunt and proceeded to taste every inch of her juicy sex. His tongue was like a soft flame, heating her core. Mitch's cock rubbing against the crack of her ass only added fuel to her internal fire.

Autumn felt totally wanton being handled this way by two masculine, mouthwatering men. She hitched her hips forward as much as she could, pressing against Randy's tongue and his soft laugh rumbled through her body.

"I do believe she likes this, Mitchell. Let's all get a little more comfortable, shall we?"

Autumn felt her body being shifted and in a moment the three of them were lying on the bed, with her in the middle. Randy was still stimulating her pussy, now with his strong fingers, pinching and rubbing her clit. Mitch had moved his hands to her breasts, tugging on the nipples and lightly raking his fingernails over the hardened tips.

The liquid of her arousal was sticky on her thighs and she couldn't help the soft sighs rolling from her lips as the two men continued their erotic assault on her body with light but steady strokes. She opened her eyes to see Randy staring into them, his own bright with lust and need. His fingers moved faster in her pussy, three of them now, curled to rub against *the spot*, the beat of her pulses rising, her blood rushing through her veins.

Mitch's cock was fitted exactly to the cleft of her buttocks, so with each movement is moved against her, while his hands continued to tease her breasts.

The orgasm came with such suddenness it simply swept over her, shaking her in its grip. Randy's hand and fingers pressed and rubbed, Mitch's cocked pushed harder against her, his hands squeezing harder. When he bit down gently on the sensitive spot on her neck she could do nothing but let the explosion take her, reveling in the spasms that raced through her. The walls of her cunt flexed against Randy's fingers, milking them and her hips thrust in the small motion allowed by her position as she rode the storm that captured her.

They worked her gently until the last aftershock died away, placing soft kisses on every part of her body, soothing her, taking her down as gently as they could. She closed her eyes, sinking into the folds of black velvet.

* * * * *

Autumn lay back on her bed, a glass of wine pleasantly buzzing through her system, her hips propped upward by pillows, a towel beneath her. Two gloriously naked men knelt at her feet, each one straddling a leg. Telling her she needed to be sure to keep her hands out of the way, Mitch had wrapped a silk scarf around them and tied the cloth to a spoke of the headboard. She'd never felt so wanton in her life.

She wondered how many of the blog ladies would be in a situation like this.

At first she'd felt self-conscious with Randy but he and Mitch were so obviously comfortable with each other and so determined to put her at ease that it didn't take her long to relax into the erotic situation. Now he leaned down and kissed her ankle, then tickled the inside of one thigh with his tongue.

"I think you have to be the most delicious woman I have ever tasted," he told her. "I can't wait until we get to the really sweet stuff."

Naked, he was just as glorious as Mitch.

Well, almost.

But when he'd unselfconsciously shed his clothes, she couldn't help but notice the size and magnificence of his cock, the thickness of the curls surrounding the root, the sharp definition of the muscles in his body, the tautness of the muscles in his very fine ass. His lips, when he kissed her, were slightly rougher than Mitch's, not as full but he certainly knew how to use them. And his tongue.

Mitch rubbed a soft bath sponge over her mound in a slow, circling motion, like the swish of velvet against her skin. "Ready, darlin'?"

She took in a deep breath, let it out and nodded.

Mitch straddled her right thigh, lathering her curls with scented soap, while Randy shifted to pull her left leg further to the side. With the pillows beneath her, her cunt was wide open to them. She'd never thought to find herself in this position but it was so erotically stimulating she was afraid she might come just from the idea of it. Of two men able to see every inch of her pussy. Touch it. Stimulate it. Do whatever they wanted to do.

As if they'd done this together many times—and maybe they had—Randy held her still while Mitch shaved her. She had to bite her bottom lip hard to keep her inner muscles from quivering and her body from twitching in response. When Randy moved his hand to pull back her labia, his fingers pressing lightly on her sensitive skin and Mitch ran the razor over the soft surface she couldn't help the moan that escaped.

Randy chuckled. "Our girl likes this."

"Not half as much as we do," Mitch told him in a slightly hoarse voice.

Autumn forced herself with great difficulty to hold still as Randy manipulated her flesh and Mitch slowly removed all traces of hair. When Mitch moved from his position she thought he was finished, unprepared for Randy to circle both ankles with his fingers and lift her legs, pressing her knees into her chest.

"W-What's happening?" she asked. "What are you doing now?"

"Just a little bit of fine barbering, darlin'," Mitch told her.

Randy pressed one forearm to the backs of her thighs to keep her legs in place, then he and Mitch together separated the cheeks of her ass. The next thing she knew Mitch was carefully running the razor over the fine hairs surrounding her anus, his touch soft and meticulous.

Mitch raised his head and looked at her over her bent legs. "Just want to make sure we get everything." He winked at her.

She heard the swishing sound of water, then felt the touch of the bath sponge as they cleaned her every place Mitch had shaved. The clanking and tinkling sounds told her the basin and razor were being disposed of. Randy lowered her legs and spread them apart.

Mitch moved to the side of her bed next to her head, another silk scarf in his hand.

"I'm going to blindfold you, Autumn. Don't worry. Nothing will happen if you don't want it to. But if you can't see, your sense of touch, of feeling, will be that much sharper."

"Oh." She swallowed. "All right."

She held herself still as he placed the soft fabric across her eyes and tied it behind her head.

What am I getting myself into here? Am I making a mistake thinking I can take on these two young studs?

She was hardly prepared for what came next.

A tongue flicked against her clit while another licked her bare labia. Hands pulled her legs as wide as they could and twin tongues licked up and down each side of her cunt, over and over again. Lips—whose?—closed around her clit while two fingers slid simultaneously into her weeping pussy. In and out they pumped, in time to the sucking movement on her clit.

She heard tiny sounds slip through the air and realized they were coming from her. Her entire body was on fire, heated blood surging through her veins, pulses throbbing everywhere. She tried to clench her inner muscles around the fingers that were...almost touching the right place. Almost. Almost. She wriggled her hips as much as she could, trying to urge the fingers deeper.

A soft laugh vibrated against her cunt, the sensations echoing through her and intensifying her need.

Teeth grazed her clit, just enough to drive her closer to the edge and a third finger joined the other two inside her vagina. Each man held a thigh with the strong fingers of one hand so it was impossible for her to squeeze her legs together and relieve the building pleasure. Randy increased the tempo of his fingers on the other hand while Mitch bent forward and kept his mouth tormenting her clit. The sharp spiral inside her was rising higher and higher.

She tried to move her hips, to ride the fingers plundering her but the dual grip on her was too firm.

"Let it go, darlin'," Mitch told her, his voice deep and thick. "It's time. Let us see you come."

As if his words released the coil inside her, she exploded, spilling into their hands and mouth, inner muscles spasming and clenching, over and over again. She was in a deep, sensuous void, where nothing mattered except the orgasm gripping her. The high keening sound that sliced into her consciousness was hers, ignited by the intensity of the sensations washing over her.

At last the pulsing subsided and her muscles relaxed. She dragged air into her lungs, not sure she'd ever be able to breathe properly again. Two sets of hands released her wrists and removed the blindfold. Two warm, naked male bodies cuddled her, one on each side. Hands stroked her lightly, touching her breasts, her nipples, her navel and finally her newly shaved mound. Two mouths rained light kisses on her face, the texture of their lips like the brush of fabric on her skin.

Finally she opened her eyes to see both men smiling at her.

"Like the ride?" Randy asked, his eyes burning into hers even as a smile tilted up the corners of his mouth.

She shifted her gaze to Mitch and saw him watching her with equal intensity.

"I'd say she did." His voice was soft but she could hear the edge of lust in it. He bent down and kissed her mound, the tip of his tongue flicking once to catch her clit.

Autumn moaned and shifted slightly, trying to urge him to further intimacy but he pulled back with a short laugh.

"All that soft skin with nothing in the way," he murmured. "More beautiful than I ever expected."

"I'd say the lady deserves another glass of wine," Randy told him, sliding one arm beneath her to lift her to a sitting position, rearranging the pillows.

"Maybe I'd rather have some of your bourbon," she said breathlessly.

Mitch ran his fingers down the side of her cheek. "I know you loved it the other night, darlin' but we don't want to get you drunk." He kissed the tip of her nose. "Just pleasantly buzzed. And I was assured this was one of the best wines I could buy."

Autumn had a hard time imagining Mitch shopping for fine wine but the image aroused her almost as much as their touching did. She arranged herself comfortably on the pillow, accepted the chilled goblet and sipped at it as the two gloriously naked men toasted her with their bourbon.

She was sated and stimulated at the same time, the orgasm that had shaken her so only whetting her appetite for what was yet to some.

Wait until I email everyone about this!

Chapter Six

ᴇᴏ

The dildo that Mitch had slid carefully into her pussy was humming away on its lowest setting, enough to keep her on edge but not enough to allow her to climax. Which was just as well, since she was doing her best to concentrate on two very impressive cocks. Mitch knelt at one side of her, leaning forward so he could slide his shaft into her mouth. Randy was on the other side where her hand was busy stroking his hard, pulsing thickness. Autumn couldn't believe how aroused she was, her now-naked pussy dripping with the juices of her desire.

She closed her lips around Mitch's penis and sucked him as far into her mouth as she could, tilting her head back slightly to allow him to slide further down her throat. The thumb of her other hand found the drop of fluid beading from Randy's slit and rubbed it into the velvety skin. She heard him suck in his breath, felt the movement as he nudged his hips forward.

Two sets of fingers toyed with her nipples, pulling them, stretching them, rolling them. The humming of the vibrator echoed through her body, sparking delicate nerve endings and taking her to a place where all she could think of was satisfying her body's needs.

She'd never imagined, no matter what she'd read or how she and the blog women had discussed it, that wildly erotic feeling of servicing two cocks at the same time. Mitch was moving slowly beside her, gliding his swollen shaft in and out of her mouth, sucking in his breath whenever her small tongue licked at it or her teeth grazed it. Randy seemed to move in cadence with him, her fingers barely able to wrap around his thickness as she stroked him.

She sensed when the teasing reached a critical point. Both men increased their tempo, their breathing escalating, their cocks pulsing in her mouth and hands. Mitch picked up the remote to the dildo that he'd balanced on the flat of her stomach and pressed the button. Immediately the intensity of the vibrations increased.

"Damn it," Randy hissed between clenched teeth. "I'm going to come. Holy shit."

"Me too," Mitch ground out.

Now the vibrator reached its highest level, breaking something loose inside Autumn. As Randy spilled over her fingers, groaning and jerking, Mitch poured into her mouth and her own body convulsed, again and again. The three of them jerked and spasmed, Autumn riding the dildo as it drove her higher and higher, the men twitching in the last throes of orgasm.

Just at the moment when she was sure she couldn't stand it another minute, couldn't handle one more tremor, one more shudder racing through her, Mitch pulled back from her mouth and pressed the Off button on the dildo.

"Jesus!" Randy collapsed on the bed beside her. "Honey, you are one undiscovered treasure. The day you went trolling on eBay was a lucky one for us."

"Just remember whose party this is."

Mitch's voice held only a hint of humor. If Autumn didn't know better she'd think there was a note of jealousy in there. Of possession. But that was impossible. They were just...having fun. Right? She was enjoying her grand adventure with a young stud—make that two studs—and Mitch was her guide. Period.

But the kiss he placed on her lips was anything but casual, his fingers stroking her breast sending her some kind of message as he caressed her. When she looked up into his eyes, they were almost midnight blue, dark with some unreadable message.

Then, whatever it was disappeared. He brushed his lips against her and said, "I think we owe you a nice warm bath. You've earned it." He reached over her to poke his friend. "Come on, hotshot. Get your body moving."

* * * * *

The shower she'd taken with Mitch, which had kicked her libido into high gear, paled in comparison to being bathed by two very attentive men. The old clawfoot tub was filled with water into which one of them had dumped half the bottle of her jasmine bath beads and half the bottle of bubble bath. Mitch, insisting that she leave everything to them, brushed her hair into a high ponytail and tied it up with one of her scarves. Randy folded one of the big new bath towels and placed it behind her neck as they lowered her into the water.

With Mitch near her head and Randy by her feet, they began to lather her from her neck to her toes with the rich bath gel sitting on the counter. Firm fingers massaged every muscle, rubbing and kneading it until her limbs felt weak and loose. She had never believed ankles could be such an erogenous zone until Randy gave them his undivided attention, lifting her leg and resting her foot on the rim of the tub so he could reach every spot.

At the same time, Mitch was kneading her neck and her shoulders, rubbing his knuckles lightly against the spot where neck and shoulder joined and calling to her mind the delicate kisses he liked to place there. His strong hands worked the muscles of her arms until they fell limply to her sides, even manipulating her fingers. Another unknown erogenous zone!

By the time Mitch had shifted to her breasts and Randy to her cunt, she was enveloped in a great wave of lassitude, willing to let them do anything to her body if she could continue feeling so wonderful. Mitch massaged her breasts with expertise, rubbing her nipples until they peaked with desire. The movement of his hands was so light that her breasts ached for a harder touch.

One of Randy's hands drifted up between her thighs, nudging them easily apart and caressing the bare lips of her pussy. He tweaked her clit, tugging at it just enough for her to feel the pressure. His other hand held her hip while fingers slid easily into her cunt, stroking the quaking inner walls, his touch as light and delicate as Mitch's.

Autumn fell into a state of indolence, floating in the water that surrounded her like a cocoon. She was aware of the twin stimulations to her body but it wasn't enough to fire her nerves and drive her to the threshold of release, just enough to keep her hanging on a plane of great pleasure.

She had absolutely no idea how long she floated in nirvana, the two men working every muscle and tendon in her body, whispering erotic words to her. From somewhere Mitch had produced a fat scented candle in a holder—Mitch? With a candle?—and its floral scent teased at her nostrils and surrounded her with its warm aroma.

She startled slightly when Randy's fingers slipped from her pussy and drifted lower, pressing against her anus, pushing the tip of one finger inside. She tried to wriggle away but Mitch held her shoulder firmly, whispering in her ear and licking the edge of it with short, light strokes of his tongue.

Randy rubbed and pushed and scraped gently with his fingernail, sending icy-hot waves rushing through her body. Dark images swirled through her mind, ratcheting up the simmering need inside her.

"I think it's time to dry her off." Randy's voice was as deep as Mitch's and just as heavy with lust.

"I'd say you're right. She's completely relaxed."

They lifted her from the tub and stood her on a mat, drying her with towels, Randy patting down the last drops of moisture as Mitch released her hair and brushed it into loose waves. She closed her eyes, reveling in the attention, allowing herself to press limply against Mitch as he hoisted her into his arms and carried her to the bed.

Randy stretched out full-length beside her, his eyes glittering as he stroked his semihard cock. Autumn was pliant as Mitch kissed her, his tongue probing into her mouth, sweeping over her teeth, her tongue, the insides of her cheeks, sucking her tongue into his own wet cavern. When he placed her astride Randy she automatically reached for the other man's cock, closing her fingers over his and gliding up and down the thickness with him.

"Get him ready again, darlin'," Mitch urged, standing beside her and rubbing her back. "Go on. Take him in your mouth."

Autumn leaned forward, brushing Randy's fingers aside and lowering her mouth over the growing thickness. As she sucked him in deeper, her tongue playing over the surface, she reached between his thighs and cupped his balls, gently squeezing them then running the edge of her fingernails over them the way she'd read about in many of her books.

Randy jerked slightly. "Holy shit, Mitch. Did you teach her that?"

Mitch laughed softly. "If it's good, yes. If it's bad, no."

Autumn continued to work on Randy, feeling his cock thicken and grow firmer in her mouth as she stimulated his balls.

Suddenly he put his hands on either side of her face and pulled himself free of her wet lips. "Lift her up, Mitch. I want inside her pussy. Right now. I *need* to be inside all that tight, wet pink flesh."

Mitch's hands clamped down on her hips, lifted her until she was poised over Randy's cock. He held her as his friend sheathed himself, then lowered her as the man guided himself into her.

"Ride me, sweet thing," Randy rasped. "Clamp that little wet cunt right around me. Oh, yeah, just like that."

His words were as stimulating and arousing to Autumn as the feel of him inside her. She braced herself on his shoulders, her breasts swinging near his face. She sighed when a hand cupped one of them and guided a nipple to his mouth. She was so involved with the feeling of his lips and tongue on her hardened tip she almost didn't notice the feeling of something cool on her puckered anus. She started to pull back from Randy but he held her breasts tightly, his lips still firmly around her nipple.

"Easy, easy, darlin'," Mitch crooned, his finger busy at her hole. "Just a little soothing gel to make sure we don't hurt those luscious, sensitive tissues." His finger slipped inside her rectum, spreading the gel carefully, his touch setting off sparks in the tiny nerve endings lining the channel.

As Mitch probed and rubbed, Randy turned his attention to the other breast and nipple and Autumn slid her body up and down his now very rigid shaft. She cried out at the sudden loss of Mitch's finger inside her but then she heard the snap of latex and in another moment the head of his cock pressed against her.

"Lean forward," he commanded. "Bend forward as far as you can without letting Randy slip out of you."

She did as he asked, Randy now holding both breasts, her face close enough for him to press his mouth to hers.

"Oh, man, what a sight," Mitch breathed as he inched his penis inside her. "Those puffy pink lips around your cock, her juices coating your dick, and you sliding in and out of her."

Randy broke the kiss, his breath hitching. "Jesus, Mitch. You'll make me come before I want to."

Mitch's laugh was predatory. "I thought you had better control than that, buddy."

"Not when you're drawing hot pictures in my mind," Randy said through gritted teeth.

Mitch tightened his grip on Autumn's hips. "Breathe in, darlin'. Just like the other night."

Autumn sucked in a breath just as Randy's mouth latched onto a nipple again and pulled on it and Mitch thrust inside her rectum until his cock was completely inside.

"Ready?" Mitch asked.

"Damn straight," Randy answered.

They set up a coordinated rhythm that spoke of long practice. As one drove into her, the other pulled back. In, out, back, forth, so steadily she lost track of whose cock was whose. She was totally full, stretched to capacity, dark need racing through her, Randy's mouth on her nipple setting up tiny explosions inside her.

The climax hit her without warning, rippling through her, grabbing her muscles but the two men never ceased their movements.

"Man, I can feel her come," Randy gasped, pulling away from her breast. "Shit, Mitch. Put your fingers down there."

One hand left Autumn's hip and probed between her thighs, touching the stretched lips of her cunt that were quivering and pulsing.

"Can you feel it?" Randy asked.

"Oh, yeah." Mitch's voice was strained. "You bet I can. She's got you in a vise."

"I don't know how long I can last."

Their conversation barely registered with Autumn. She was wrapped in such a fog of lust very little penetrated fully. Except for the stiff, hard cocks inside her.

"I'm almost there," Mitch said. "Autumn? Autumn, can you hear me?"

"Mmm?" was all she could manage.

"Rub your clit. Do it now, darlin'. Reach down there and brush that little nub hard."

She fell forward again as her fingers stole between her thighs, easily finding her nub exposed, the flesh around it distended. Barely aware of what she was doing, she rubbed as he'd instructed, slowly at first, then harder and faster as the two men picked up the pace. The orgasm was building again, spiraling up from the pit of her stomach.

"Now!" Mitch shouted. "Right now!"

As both men exploded inside her, Autumn's orgasm roared through her like wildfire, burning her up, shaking her, pushing her from one plane to the next. Her pussy spasmed again and again, her hips rocking back and forth, riding first one man then the other. It seemed to go on forever, stretching her on a rack of desire that was beyond anything she'd ever felt. As if it had a mind of its own, her hand continued stimulating her clit, rubbing and rubbing, as the men shouted and pumped their semen inside the latex reservoirs.

She thought the tremors would never stop undulating through her. Even when the men were spent, their cocks no longer pulsing inside her, aftershocks continued to ripple through the walls of her cunt.

Her heart was crashing in her ears and she couldn't get enough air in her lungs. She fell forward onto Randy's chest, gasping for air, shivering in the aftermath of an orgasm so ferocious it drained every bit of her strength. She was only faintly aware of Mitch pulling back from her ass, then lifting her from Randy's body. Gentle hands placed her on her back on the bed. She heard murmuring as the voices moved away, then they were back, sponging her with a warm cloth, sliding her beneath the cool, crisp sheets.

"You think we worked her too hard?" she heard Randy ask, concern in his voice.

"I think it was just because she's never done this before," Mitch answered. "But she needs to rest now."

"Okay. I could use a little nap too. Which side of the bed do you want?"

There was a long silence and Autumn forced herself to awareness, curious as to what was happening. She opened her eyes slowly to see Mitch standing beside the bed, a strange expression on his face.

"Well?" Randy prodded. "I didn't think that was such a hard question."

Mitch let out a slow breath. "I think it would work better if you went on home tonight, buddy. Okay?"

That woke Autumn up. She glanced at Randy, standing there naked with his mouth open.

"Are you shitting me? What the hell's going on here?"

Mitch shrugged. "Just-just go on home, okay? We've had a great party here but it's over. For tonight."

Randy looked at Autumn as if to find some clue but she was as mystified as he was. Mitch had explained to her carefully exactly how the two men did this and the sleepover with morning sex was part of it. Finally he shrugged and reached for his clothes.

"Whatever you say, Mitchell. But you'll have to explain to me what's going on here, okay?"

"Tomorrow. I'll call you tomorrow."

Randy drained the last few drops of bourbon in his glass, tugged on his boots, gave Autumn one more look and stomped off out the door. The room was filled with silence broken only by the slamming of the front door and the revving of the engine of Randy's pickup.

Autumn hitched herself up on the pillows, tucking the sheet under her arms and stared at Mitch. "You want to tell me what just happened here?"

He slid under the sheet next to her, wrapped his arm around her and tugged her close so her head was resting on his shoulder. Idly his hand reached beneath the sheet and stroked her breast.

"I find myself in something of a dilemma, Autumn Kelley," he began. "I don't know quite what to make of it."

Oh, god, was he finally disappointed in her? Had she done something wrong tonight? Was he going to leave?

She tilted her head to look up at him. "What kind of dilemma?"

He cleared his throat. "I've spent my life being pretty much loose and free. Taking my work seriously but not my women."

Autumn clenched one of her hands into a fist. "Mitch, if you're trying to tell me I shouldn't expect anything more from you, it's all right. I understand."

"No. I don't think you do." He kissed the top of her head, his hand continuing to play with her breast and nipple. "For the first time in my life, I find myself wanting something more. A lot more. Except..."

"Except what?" she prompted.

"Except I don't know what *you* want. A romp in the hay with a boy toy? A chance to test your wings? The sex has been unbelievable but I think we've got something more than that going here, only..."

"Only what?" She sat up, pushing his hand away, the sheet falling to her waist. "God, will you spit it out already?"

"Except I don't know if you want someone younger than you hanging around on a more or less permanent basis. You might be happier with someone closer to your...interests."

She couldn't believe the look of apprehension on his face. Mitchell Brand worried? The sexiest man she'd ever met? The man who could take on the world? Autumn threw back the sheet, scrambled over Mitch's body and began pacing the floor, completely oblivious to the fact she was stark naked.

"Are you crazy?" She stopped next to him, her hands fisted on her hips. "I've had men closer to my *interests*, as you call it, until they bore me out of my skull. I can't believe that *you're* worried that I might care that you're younger than me." She resumed her pacing. "You're what I want. I just didn't want to presume anything. After all, you've been around and

I've..." she waved her arms, "been standing still. If anyone should be bored it's you."

"Autumn."

"Shut up. I'm just getting started." She had no idea where all this sass was coming from but she went with it. "I have never, ever heard anything so stupid in my life. I can't believe—"

As she moved near him again Mitch grabbed her arm and tumbled her on top of him, cradling her in his arms, kissing her until she was breathless.

"That's why I sent Randy home tonight. This was great. I know you enjoyed it and if you want to do it again we will. But like I said, the rules have changed. I want you to belong to *me*. I want there to be an us. A little icing on the cake now and then is all right but only now and then."

Her heart was beating triple time in her chest. "Are you saying what I think you're saying?"

"I'm asking you if you'll think I'm a freeloader if I tell you I want to stay. Forever. To build up this ranch with you. To take whatever the future brings for us."

She reached up and pressed her fingers to his lips. "Don't even use that word. I was so afraid when the basic work was done you were going to leave,"

In one smooth move he rolled her beneath him. Grabbing a condom from the nightstand he sheathed his cock and spread her legs.

"I'm not leaving," he told her. "This is where I'm staying. Right here."

And with one shift of his hips he slid home into her still-wet pussy.

* * * * *

Dear bloggers,

You absolutely won't believe what I'm going to tell you.

ASSUME THE POSITIONS

Mari Carr

&

Dedication

ॐ

This story is dedicated to the ladies of International Heat. Your support of my writing has been a godsend to me this past year. Jess, Joy, Jayne, Jambrea, Lexxie, Lila, Valerie, Viv, T and Rhian – you gals ROCK!

Author Note

ॐ

You'll find the women of Cougar Challenge and the Tempt the Cougar blog at www.temptthecougar.blogspot.com/

Trademarks Acknowledgement

ဢ

The author acknowledges the trademarked status and trademark owners of the following wordmarks mentioned in this work of fiction:

eBay: eBay Inc.

Friends: Warner Bros. Entertainment Inc.

L'Oréal: L'Oréal Societe Anonyme France

Milky Way: Mars Incorporated

Nerf: Hasbro Inc.

RomantiCon: Jasmine Jade Enterprises

Starbucks: Starbucks Corporation

Voldemort: JK Rowling

Chapter One

ஒ

Rachel Bridges stared at the computer screen and sighed. She was generally a happy-go-lucky kind of girl, but lately she couldn't fight back the brief spurts of depression that plagued her.

Since her friend Monica had issued that ridiculous dare — Cougar Challenge, she called it — more than a few of her online pals had actually gone out and found themselves younger men. Crap, a couple of the girls had actually hooked up with *two* younger men. Her friends were turning out to be fearless and adventurous, and Rachel couldn't help but be envious as she read about their sexual liaisons on the Tempt the Cougar blog they'd created together.

She'd met all but one of the women at RomantiCon, a conference for erotic romance novel fans. In one weekend, she'd formed a tighter bond with these women than with any friends she'd made in all of her thirty-seven years. Besides their shared love of hot books, they'd really connected personally as they shared their struggles to cope with the harsh realities of getting older. They'd been a godsend for Rachel at a time when loneliness and her own mortality had begun kicking her in the ass on a daily basis.

She clicked on her IM list, grateful to find Autumn online. Since buying a ranch on eBay and finding the hunkiest cowboy in Texas, her friend had been on the blog less and less. Having too much great sex all the time was clearly cutting into Autumn's computer time. Bitch.

Rachel: Hey.
Autumn: What's up, buttercup?

Rachel: My life sucks.

She was aware she was whining, but she didn't care. She was PMSing and the damn vending machine ate her last three quarters without giving her the Milky Way she wanted. Now her hip hurt from beating the machine and the stupid son of a bitch was still dangling there, taunting her from across the room.

Autumn: Why?

Rachel: I'm never going to be able to complete Monica's challenge. There's no way I can find a younger man to sleep with me. Hell, I can't find an old man to have sex with.

She'd never been into the club scene and she basically sucked at flirting. In fact, the entire concept of using her feminine wiles to attract the opposite sex struck her as downright silly. The few times she'd gone out to bars, she'd spent the entire time laughing at the antics of other women as they attempted to hook up. Her bizarre sense of humor clearly overshadowed every girly personality trait she possessed.

Her mother viewed her lack of relationships differently, saying she was far too practical for her own good and teasing her good-naturedly about the fact there wasn't a romantic bone in her whole body. There was probably a basis of truth in both theories.

Autumn: Men would love to sleep with you. You're pretty, successful, funny. Oh hell...where are you, sweetie?

Rachel stared around at the empty physical therapy office where she worked and grimaced.

Rachel: Work.

Autumn: That's what I thought. Get the hell out of there. It's Friday night. Get dolled up and hit a bar.

Rachel: I can't. I have a client coming in.

Autumn: Dammit, Rach. You're not even trying to find a guy. I hate to break it to you, but you aren't going to find Mr. Right by hiding out at work all the time. You've got to get out there and take some chances.

Rachel: I know, but hitting the pick-up scene again is just too damn depressing.

Autumn: I really think this lack of confidence is your ex-husband's fault. You're letting him win.

Rachel: Voldemort already won.

Autumn: LMAO. He'd shit himself if he knew that's how you referred to him.

Rachel: Truth hurts. Besides, can you blame me for being trigger shy? My whole life has been one big fucking cliché. Worked my ass off to support the shithead so he could attend medical school then dump me.

Autumn: He didn't deserve you.

Rachel: No, apparently he deserved his twenty-something blonde nurse. You do realize the only way I'm going to get the image of them screwing in our bed out of my mind is to scratch my eyes out.

Autumn: At least you kicked the bum out on his ass.

Rachel: Wasn't much of a kick. He wanted her, so he left. Catching them in the act just saved him the trouble of telling me.

After she'd divorced her husband, Rachel had pursued her own dreams, going back to school to work toward her physical therapy degree. For nearly six years, she'd managed

97

to work herself into oblivion in hopes of avoiding the concept of "getting out there". During the stressful time after her divorce, she'd turned to erotic romance as a means of escape. Curling up in bed with a hunky fictional character was a hell of a lot easier than dealing with a real flesh-and-blood man.

Autumn: Christ, Rachel. Don't you miss hot, sweaty, set-the-sheets-on-fire sex?

She rolled her eyes. The only man she'd ever had sex with—her ex-husband—had made reading the changes in tax laws seem exciting in comparison.

Rachel: Hard to miss what you never had.

Autumn: All the more reason to get out there.

Rachel: Yeah. I guess you're right. Thanks for the pep talk.

Autumn: Is that what this was? Because, sweetie, you don't seem much peppier. Guess it's a good thing I never went out for cheerleading in high school. Of course, with my lack of hips, I'd have spent the entire time cheering with that little skirt around my ankles. Nothing to hold it up.

Rachel grinned. Even through IMs, Autumn always managed to make her laugh.

Rachel: Talking to you always helps. Give Mitch a kiss for me.

Autumn: I will. Bye, sweetie.

She closed her computer rather than go back to the Cougar blog. Tonight, listening to all her friends chatter about their fun lives just deepened her depression. Hearing them talk about overcoming their problems and finding their dreams left her to wonder if there was something seriously wrong with her. She'd been dragged along with the Cougar Challenge and now they were expecting her to go out and have a fling with not just a man, but a younger man.

Shit.

She'd never be able to do that. She was too sensible to go around flirting with younger men who in all likelihood wouldn't even notice her pathetic efforts. She was more the gal-pal type than the "pick up a stranger in a bar" sort of woman.

She pulled out the tatty notebook she always carried with her and flipped through the pages until she found the list she was looking for. She'd started keeping lists back in high school and the habit had never gone away. Once she filled a notebook, she bought a new one, loading the pages with list after list on every subject under the sun. In the beginning they were a way to stay organized. As she got older, they'd begun to also serve the purpose of reminding her of various things as she tended to be more forgetful.

She found the page she was looking for and scanned her pitiful list of potential younger men once again. She'd been keeping a running list since the night Monica issued the challenge, adding and marking out names for months. Unfortunately, the list was as pitiful now as it had been when she'd started it. There were currently seven names on the page, but four of those had been scratched out for various reasons. The three remaining prospects weren't exactly thrilling. She leaned her head against her desk chair and fought back a groan. Apparently, she wasn't cougar material after all.

She glanced at the clock, closed her eyes and sighed. Ethan was late again. Officer Russell was her most disgruntled patient. As a physical therapist, she was used to treating people who preferred to ignore their injuries, who chose instead to carry on with their normal activities without regard for the fact they were doing themselves more harm. Ethan took the award for stubbornness.

For the past eight weeks, she'd worked with him as he recovered from a gunshot wound to his upper leg. If not for the police department's strict policy on the treatment of work-related injuries, she was certain Ethan would never have darkened her door, and it had taken more than a little bit of convincing on her part to get him to take the exercises and recovery strategy seriously.

If she had any feminine wiles at all, she'd be using the handsome twenty-eight-year-old officer to practice her seduction skills. But her work ethic prohibited her from becoming involved with a patient and her damn practicality prohibited basically everything else in regards to Ethan Russell.

"Whatcha doin', Doc? Sleeping?"

"Oh shit!" She jumped out of her chair, her heart racing at the sudden sound in the room. She hadn't heard Ethan walk in. There he stood, six feet four inches of mouth-watering perfection, with wavy dark brown hair and a smile that reduced her insides to utter mush. His hot-chocolate-colored gaze should be registered as lethal as his work-issued gun.

His grin at her alarm was remorseless. "Tsk, tsk, tsk. Napping on the clock," he teased.

She shook her head and ignored his comment. "You're late. Again."

He shrugged, unconcerned. "Caught a bad guy right at the end of shift. Lousy paperwork took awhile."

"You couldn't call?" she asked, aware her voice was snippy, but he'd truly frightened the hell out of her.

He looked at the clock that hung on the wall. "I'm only five minutes late, Rachel."

She gave him a crooked smile and acknowledged the truth of his words. "Sorry," she muttered. "Bad day."

"Lose a list or something?" he asked, gesturing toward her notebook. He'd teased her relentlessly about her list fetish ever since asking about the book one night. She'd foolishly shown him the thing and for some reason, he'd found her fervent list-keeping hysterical.

"Ha ha. No, Mr. Smart Ass, I didn't lose a list. I just don't happen to like the one I'm working on."

He quirked his eyebrows with interest and she cursed her loose tongue. The last thing she needed was to give the man another reason to ridicule her. He already had far too much fun at her expense. A fact, she had to admit, she sort of enjoyed. They seemed to share the same twisted sense of humor. In addition to being too hot for words, Ethan was funny and friendly and it hadn't exactly been a hardship to volunteer to stay late to accommodate his crazy work schedule.

"Forget it," she said quickly, hoping to deter his sudden interest.

"Let me see your list. Maybe I can help you with it." Ethan grabbed her notebook and she swiftly attempted to pull it out of his grasp. They struggled over the book for several seconds before she lost her grip.

"It's personal," she said loudly when he won their tug-of-war. Her protest was too late as he read the heading on the page.

"Potential Younger Men for Cougar Challenge?"

Rachel prayed to God he didn't know what "cougar" meant. She'd only learned of the term while reading her erotic romance novels. She'd been shocked to discover how much the idea of an older woman hooking up with a younger man turned her on, pushed her hot buttons.

"It's just something silly...something stupid, really. Give me back my notebook and we'll get started on your exercises."

Ethan ignored her and she watched as he scanned the list of names. When he closed the book with a snap, she flinched at the unfamiliar look on his face. She'd never seen him look so serious or…angry. "What are you doing, Rachel? What the hell is this list about?"

She took a step back, confused by his reaction. Over the course of the past two months, she'd felt a friendship forming between her and the young cop. As a result, she now found her fears, her anxiety over the challenge falling from her lips uncontrolled.

Even though she was sure she was making a mistake, she told him everything—from meeting her friends at the conference to the blog to the dare to sleep with a younger man. She didn't leave out a single detail and throughout her entire confession, Ethan was quiet. In the end, it was his silence that unnerved her more than his initial anger.

"So there," she said at last. "That should keep you busy in the teasing department for months. I'm an insane, horny-as-hell woman who's actually contemplating throwing herself at a younger man on a dare. And before you say anything, yes, I know…I'm old enough to know better." She walked away from him as she said the last, too embarrassed to face him.

She'd only made it two steps when he reached out and gripped her forearm, turning her back around. "Old enough to know better?" he asked. "You think you couldn't land a younger guy?"

"Maybe I could," she said, surprised to find him taking this conversation so seriously. "I mean, I don't think I'm unattractive, just sort of out of practice with the whole dating scene."

Ethan grinned and she spied the usual mischievous sparkle in his gaze that she'd grown accustomed to over the past few weeks. "Wish you'd mentioned this horny problem of yours earlier, Rach."

"It's not something a polite woman advertises," she said.

He continued pulling her toward him until they stood face-to-face, close enough that she could smell his skin, a pleasant combination of fresh shower, soap and—*yummy*—man. Rather than look up, she stared straight ahead, placing her line of vision at the top of his chest. There was no way she could look at his handsome face and not spend the rest of their session imagining him naked. He wore a tight T-shirt and she could just imagine what his bare pecs would look like. She swallowed heavily, her mouth watering at the thought.

"Isn't that a shame," Ethan added. "Advertisements like that sure would take a lot of the guess work out of dating."

"I haven't been doing a lot of dating since my divorce from Voldemort."

"Mm hmm." She felt certain if she hadn't been standing so closely, she wouldn't have heard the small, guttural sound—a growl?—that emanated from him. Did it make him angry to hear her mention her ex? "Look at me, Rachel," he said as she felt his gaze bore through the top of her head.

"I am," she said, her eyes remaining locked in place, several inches below his chin.

He reached down and gently forced her head back with firm fingers at her jaw. She took a deep breath and faced him. His head was cocked to the side, his lips painfully close to hers. An impractical woman would lean forward and initiate a kiss. A woman without any common sense would rise up on her tiptoes, close the gap separating them and take a nice, long taste of him. An adventurous woman—

Her mouth stroked his briefly and her mind struggled to understand how she'd gotten close enough for that touch. Had she moved?

Her lips brushed his again, but rather than move away, she continued to push closer.

Oh shit.

She was kissing Ethan. Her brain kicked into high gear.

Red alert! Abort! Abort!

103

Her practical side was practically screaming for her body to step away from the hot man. But apparently her body had its own agenda.

His fingers moved from her chin and along her cheek, taking up residence in her hair. His hand pulled her closer and he deepened the kiss, forcing her lips open with his, exploring her mouth with his tongue.

Holy crap. He was kissing her back. She wrapped her arms around his neck and struggled not to moan when his other hand traveled up and down her back, rubbing delicious patterns through her shirt that made her want to purr like a kitten.

They continued to kiss, but Rachel's racing mind kept fighting for the control her body had seized.

This is wrong. He's so far out of your league I'm not sure you can consider yourselves inhabitants of the same planet. He's a patient.

The last thought jarred her enough that she pushed away abruptly.

"Shit," Ethan muttered when she struggled out of his embrace. "I was wondering when that head of yours was going to get in the way."

"What?" she asked.

"You think too much," he replied.

"That's not true. I just don't think it's professional for me to be kissing you in the clinic."

He grinned. "But it would be okay if you kissed me outside? The door's right there. Let's go."

"It's not professional, period. I shouldn't have— It was wrong of me to—"

"Kiss me?" he supplied, and she could see he was enjoying her predicament far too much.

"Yes," she hissed.

"Did that overactive brain of yours happen to notice that I was kissing you back?"

Oh, her brain noticed — it just didn't want her to be happy. Meanwhile, every other major organ and nerve in her body was singing — big time. Her nipples were cutting through the satin material of her bra, her stomach was still doing happy flip-flops and she was noticing regions south of her waist reappearing after deserting her years ago.

She shrugged. Seemed like the easiest thing to do.

"Why wasn't my name on your list?" he asked.

She burst into laughter.

"I'm serious," he persisted when she continued to chuckle.

"You sound as if you're hurt by the omission," she said. "Is this some male ego switch I've triggered? I would think you'd be relieved. You don't have to worry about some sex-starved divorcee setting her sights on you. Trying to lure you into her lair." She raised her hands in a claw-like fashion and made a scary face.

He didn't smile at her joke, so she lowered her hands and shook her head. "I like you, Ethan. You've become a good friend these past couple of months and I wouldn't dream of annoying you like that."

"Annoying me? You think I'm not attracted to you? Sexually?" he asked, setting off her laughter again.

"Oh damn, now that *is* funny," she said between giggles. "Well, I guess I'll just have to say it. You're hot, Ethan. Super hot. And about a decade younger than me."

"I thought that was the point of this challenge of yours," he argued.

"Well, let's just say there're younger men and then there're younger men. In the world of women like me, you fall into the untouchable category."

He nodded, but she could see he didn't like her answer. "I didn't see that 'untouchable' thing holding you back a few minutes ago."

She sobered up at his scowling face. "As I said, I shouldn't have done that."

He was silent for several uncomfortable moments and she wished she could read his mind. "I've screwed up everything tonight, Ethan," she added, desperate to fill the void. "Can we just start this whole PT session over? I'll even let you sneak in and scare me again."

His face cleared suddenly and his cocky grin returned. She took a deep breath of relief—until his next words knocked it out of her again.

"Put my name on your list," he demanded. "The *top* of your list. And then mark out every name under it. You're going to follow through on that dare…with me."

Chapter Two

ஓ

Rachel stared at the ceiling in her bedroom the next morning, trying to wrap her head around Ethan's proposition. After his insistence that his name be added to her list—he'd waited until she'd picked up the pen and actually wrote it on the damn thing—they continued with their usual physical therapy routine as if nothing unusual had occurred. As he was leaving the clinic last night, he'd given her a quick peck on the cheek and told her he would be in touch. What the hell did that mean? In touch when? And what would he be touching?

She groaned as the same nagging feeling in the pit of her stomach returned. She'd tossed and turned all night with an ache that wouldn't go away until she'd dug out the vibrator Monica had sent all the cougar ladies for Christmas. Rachel had treated the gift as a joke, throwing the thing in her nightstand and never touching it again...until last night.

She squeezed her legs together tightly and debated going for round two with the wickedly fun toy. Just the mere thought of Ethan had her dying for sexual relief. This sudden, unfamiliar sex drive was going to put her in an insane asylum or break her Laundromat bank. The man had only kissed her, for God's sake, and yet she'd had to change her panties twice during the night, she'd gotten so wet...dreaming of Ethan and imagining all the things she wanted to do to him.

She was just reaching toward the nightstand for the vibrator when her phone rang. Screwed by the bell.

"Hello?" she said.

"Good morning." Ethan's deep voice shot through the telephone line like an electrical shock and she squirmed again at the juices his sexy, masculine tone produced. Shit, she was going to give up wearing panties altogether at this rate.

"Hiya. What's up?"

"Not you, by the sound of your voice. Have to admit I sort of saw you as an early-to-bed, early-to-rise kind of girl."

Well, he certainly had her pegged. Normally she was up at the crack of dawn. It was his fault her usual routine was out of whack.

"It's the weekend and I have nothing to do. Thought I'd give myself a nice, relaxing sleep-in."

Liar, liar, pants on fire.

She was about as relaxed as a stockbroker hopped up on Starbucks.

"Well, I wouldn't say you have nothing to do," he replied.

She paused for a moment and considered her schedule. Was she supposed to be somewhere? She didn't recall making any plans. Certainly none with Ethan. She'd sure as hell remember that. "I don't understand."

"There's a package outside your door. I want you to go get it. Your instructions are inside."

"Instructions?" she asked, her heart rate accelerating. Ethan had been by her place? This morning? Why oh why hadn't she heard him? He could have taken the place of the lousy vibrator.

"Don't sound so worried, Rachel. You'll like this assignment. It involves making a list."

She grinned at his joke. "You know, there's nothing wrong with making lists and being prepared. It wouldn't hurt you to be a little more organized—might actually prevent you from being late all the time." She could tease as well as the next person.

"Yeah, well. You won't have to worry about that tonight."

"Tonight?" she asked.

"I'll be at your place at seven sharp."

"You will?" She realized her voice had taken on a higher pitch with each consecutive question and she cleared her throat. "Why?"

"It's all in the package," he replied enigmatically. "And Rachel, wear something sexy. See you later."

He hung up the phone with a light chuckle before she could wrap her lips around the word goodbye. Her brain was actually still trying to process the "something sexy" comment. She didn't do sexy. She wouldn't know sexy if it bit her in the ass. Her mother had trained her well and she was quite firmly ensconced in the land of prim and proper.

Dammit.

She jumped out of bed and walked to her front door, not sure if she wanted to see what was in Ethan's surprise package or read his instructions.

Rachel opened the door and found a small square box neatly wrapped in brown paper. Carrying it into the living room, she dropped onto the couch to open it, grinning as she tore the paper. She loved presents.

She gasped when she lifted the lid on the box. Inside was a new copy of the *Kama Sutra*.

Holy shit.

She picked up the book and flipped through the pages, her mouth dropping open a little bit farther with each subsequent photographed pose.

An envelope dropped out of the front cover and she bent to retrieve it from the floor. Inside were Ethan's instructions, as promised. It was a sheet of paper much like the paper in her notebook. He'd numbered down the side column one to ten and had even supplied a heading.

Kama Sutra Positions I Want to Try with Ethan.

Holy, holy shit.

Time to call in reinforcements.

She grabbed her laptop from the coffee table and fired it up.

She sent an email to all the ladies on the Tempt the Cougar blog. She'd mentioned hot cop Ethan and a few of her racy fantasies involving the man in past posts and several of her friends had suggested him for her cougar experience. She'd always brushed off the suggestions, saying it was as unlikely as Donald Trump getting a decent haircut.

Subject: Help me!

Ethan wants to help me fulfill this damn cougar challenge—TONIGHT! He's serious about it too. What the hell am I supposed to do? He just gave me a copy of the *Kama Sutra* and told me to pick out some positions to try. Then he told me to wear something sexy. What the hell is that supposed to mean? I'm as sexy as the Queen of England. Oh my God. Kill me now. How did I let you girls talk me into this?

Monica popped up in a chat window almost immediately and Rachel laughed aloud at her friend's advice—so typically Mon.

Monica: OH. MY. GOD. If you do not do this you will regret it for the REST OF YOUR LIFE. First, pick some positions that don't require circus acrobat training. If he's totally hung, try the Clasping or Indrani positions. But my personal favorite? The Tigress. Rawrr. Um, Sam likes that one too.

Rachel: And the sexy part?

Monica: I hate it when men say that. How do you know what he thinks is sexy? I mean, maybe he totally digs the French maid thing. Or plain cotton underwear. If

I were you, I'd just open the door naked. I bet he won't object.

Rachel shook her head, feeling only a bit less freaked out. Monica was the queen of free spirits. She didn't have an inhibited bone in her body. Open the door naked. As if.

An email from Cam came next.

Subject: re: Help me!

What to do? Enjoy the heck out of it, honey! As far as the *Kama Sutra* goes...well, if it was me, I'd grab a mirror and try out positions to see which ones are the most flattering. But hey, that's me and my insecurities. Go for it. And post details tomorrow.

She closed the laptop and walked to the bathroom carrying the *Kama Sutra*. As she stood in front of the mirror, she looked at her reflection more closely than she had in a very, very long time. Shortly after her divorce, she'd stopped looking in mirrors completely. It had taken her several months to come to grips with the fact that Alex, her ex-husband, hadn't left her because of *her* problems, but because of his. He was a shallow, self-serving asshole who ranked image above love, honor and respect in order of importance.

She was much better off without him, and she'd even developed a nagging sense of pity for his new wife, Carolyn. A leopard didn't change his spots, and she wondered how much longer the bride behind door number two would shine bright enough for Alex to keep her around. Eventually Carolyn would be tossed aside for a newer model, and she actually felt sorry for the woman—to an extent.

Usually until she remembered finding the bitch in bed with her husband and then she just laughed with glee at the old "what goes around, comes around" saying.

Her reflection showed her just what she'd expected—a woman in desperate need of a dye job. The roots peeking out were grayer nowadays than the mousy brown of her youth. She checked beneath the sink and found a box of L'Oréal—light auburn. Thank the hair dye gods. At least she would be saved a trip to the drugstore today. Placing the box on the counter, she leaned forward, examining her face. She'd dodged wrinkles so far, although there were definite laugh lines forming around her brown eyes and full lips. She grinned ruefully.

Guess there's nothing wrong with lines formed by laughter.

Turning around, she looked in the full-length mirror that hung on the back of the door.

I'd grab a mirror and try out positions to see which ones are the most flattering.

Cam's words drifted back to her and she quickly crossed the line from mildly nervous to full-blown anxiety attack. Her hands shook so badly she nearly dropped the *Kama Sutra*.

Crap. She'd never be able to take her clothes off in front of Ethan. She'd seen him shirtless, wearing nothing but workout shorts during a few of their PT sessions, and to merely say the man was built was an insult to Mother Nature for blessing women everywhere with the image of his physique, his male perfection. Meanwhile, the fates had clearly been drunk the day they'd made her, putting excesses of everything…everywhere. Wide hips, huge breasts, fat ass. The only places they'd skimped on were her ankles and wrists.

She shrugged off the T-shirt and pajama shorts she was wearing and studied the profile of her shape.

Wonder if I can lose twenty pounds by seven o'clock tonight. Maybe she could find ten *Kama Sutra* positions that required the man to have his eyes closed.

Time to change the game plan.

Evasion tactics. Excuses. Outright lies if necessary. What to choose?

Professionalism. Ethics. Of course, it was so simple. The main reason she hadn't put Ethan's name on her list to begin with was because he was her patient. She couldn't have sex with a patient.

She rushed to the phone and called him.

"That didn't take long," he said dryly, rather than the customary hello.

"It would be unethical for me to have sex with a patient." She was proud of the strength and conviction in her voice. Hippocrates would have been impressed.

"I'm not your patient anymore," he answered calmly. "Before I called you this morning, I had my medical records transferred to Dr. Philips. He'll be doing the rest of my PT."

"You did? He will?" She dropped down on the couch, surprise turning her legs to jelly. Damn man had thought of everything.

"I only have a few more sessions until I satisfy the stupid workman's comp requirements anyway."

"Oh, well..." She wasn't sure what to say. A part of her was disappointed she wouldn't be finishing up his sessions. He was her happy dose of eye candy. She'd actually looked forward to going to work on days when he had an appointment. Of course, if he wasn't her patient, she didn't have to worry about facing him the morning after what was certain to be a fiasco.

"Have you made your list?" he asked.

"No," she replied.

"Get started on it. See you at seven." He hung up without the customary goodbye. She was going to have to talk to him about his lack of phone manners.

Returning to the bathroom, she picked up the *Kama Sutra* and studied the pictures again. She immediately found ten

113

positions that pushed all her hot buttons just to look at. Then she pictured herself as the woman, with Ethan as the man.

Aw hell. She was so screwed.

* * * * *

In the end, Rachel settled for what she prayed Ethan would consider sexy. She'd pulled the tags off a skimpy little black dress she had hanging in the back of her closet and underneath she'd put on the only bra and panty set she owned. The concept of matching undergarments just seemed bizarre to her, but this set was new and completely impractical from a comfort standpoint. It was also sexy as hell. It pushed her breasts up and the panties were cut low and actually looked kind of hot on her.

She'd bought the entire outfit on a whim once after she'd seen Voldemort out and about with the blonde bitch, but she'd never had the nerve to wear it out of the house. It showed way too much of her figure, way too many inches of cleavage. There was a fine line between sexy and trashy and she was never quite sure where it was. A fashion expert she was *not*, despite the fact she never missed an episode of *What Not to Wear*.

At seven o'clock on the dot, her doorbell rang. She took a deep breath as she opened the front door—awestruck by the sight of Ethan on her doorstep.

He was wearing new blue jeans and a dark green button-down shirt. He let out a catcall whistle and grinned. She felt herself blush at his appreciative look.

Then her gaze drifted down to enjoy every yummy inch of him, her eyes lingering on his muscular arms before taking in the image of his strong legs encased in the tight denim. His light chuckle forced her eyes back to his face.

"Are you going to invite me in or are we going to do this thing on the front porch?"

She rolled her eyes at his cocky tone. "I'm not so sure we're going to do any *thing* at all."

She closed the door as he walked past her, surprised when he turned and slowly pushed her forward, pressing her stomach against the wood and caging her in. She was completely surrounded by his body, his strength, and she shivered with desire when his lips brushed against her ear.

"Assume the position," he said, his voice husky, deep, sexy as hell. "Or should I say *positions*? We're going to do so many things tonight, Rachel, you'll need to keep a list to remember them all. Now are you going to play nice or do I need to whip out the handcuffs already?"

"You brought your handcuffs?" she asked breathlessly, the idea of being restrained one of her favorite fantasies.

He laughed softly. "Oh yeah, what kind of cop would I be if I traveled without them?"

His close proximity, the smell of his cologne, slowly eased her fears and she felt her inner minx emerging, ready to play. "What about your gun?" she asked. "Did you bring that too?" As she spoke she reached behind her, teasing his erection with her fingers to make her meaning clear.

He took her hand in his and pushed her palm firmly against the front placket of his jeans, letting her feel his undeniable arousal. "Oh yeah, baby. I brought the big gun tonight and believe me, it's loaded and ready to roll."

She wanted to giggle at his jest, but she couldn't spare the breath as her body fought to draw in any air that wasn't filled with his amazingly seductive scent.

He moved far enough away to turn her to face him. Once he had her in the position he wanted, he crowded her against the door and leaned down to kiss her.

She'd expected awkward conversation, a slow buildup, anything except the power of this moment. Ethan was kissing her, touching her with such need, such desire, she wanted to cry with the realization that she'd spent a lifetime without this feeling.

She pulled away for a second to suck in a breath. "God," she panted. "Too much."

"Not enough," he muttered, gripping her head in his hands, claiming her lips once more.

She pulled him closer, her fingers digging into the material of his shirt. He deepened the kiss and she struggled to process everything that was happening to her. Her blood felt as if it were literally boiling.

This can't be happening. Stuff like this doesn't happen to me.

"Stop thinking," he murmured against her lips. "Just let it happen."

Let it happen. Let it happen.

The words played in her mind like the chorus of her favorite song as his hands left her face to cup her breasts. Why she expected him to be gentle now after the intensity of his kisses, she didn't know, but when he roughly palmed her sensitive flesh, pinching her nipples through her dress, she had to break again for air.

"God, need...air," she muttered as he growled, unhappy at being denied her lips. His freshly shaven face rubbed against her cheek as he descended on her neck. Damn, she loved having her neck kissed. The sensation sent a tingling feeling clear down to her toes. His hands tightened on her breasts as he covered her skin with hot, wet kisses. "Oh yeah. Right there. More," she demanded, reaching up to run her hands through his soft, dark hair, wrapping her leg around his to pull him even closer.

Ethan pulled back at her words and she hissed.

"My fierce little kitten," he said, attempting to take a step away from her. She followed his retreat and he gave her a husky laugh that sent her hackles up, harsh words rising to her throat. He stopped her tirade with a finger against her lips.

"Hush, Doc. If we don't stop now, I'll take you against that door."

She shrugged. "Sounds like a plan to me," she said, yanking him close again.

"Not *my* plan," he said, untangling her fingers from his shirt and taking her hands into his. He pulled her toward the couch before seemingly changing his mind. "Where're the list and the book?"

"Bedroom," she admitted, foolishly thinking if she'd kept them out of sight, she could dissuade him from his seduction plans with a calm, reasonable conversation in her living room. She'd convinced herself all day that he'd eventually come to his senses and jilt her. Barring that, she'd made a list of all the reasons why they shouldn't embark on an affair.

As he tugged her quickly down the hallway to her bedroom, she scrambled to think of one of those damn reasons now.

Christ, she had a ton of them. What were they? Where the hell was her notebook?

Ah ha! The age difference.

"I'm way too old for you," she blurted out as they crossed the threshold into her bedroom. Mercifully, she knew how lame her willpower was and she'd changed the sheets and hidden the pile of discarded undies.

"Says who?" he asked, turning to pull the straps of her dress over her shoulders.

"Says me," she replied, swatting away his nimble fingers.

Undeterred by her pitiful attempts at evasion, he pulled the dress down to her waist while continuing to dodge her hands. When she realized she was practically naked from the waist up, she stood speechless for a moment as he gripped her waist and stared at her with a too-satisfied look on his face.

"Well?" she asked.

"Well what?"

"You know it's not too late to change your mind. I could always find another guy to 'do this thing' with me," she said, mimicking his words from the front porch.

He scoffed at her words, an honest-to-God scoff. "You try to find another younger guy and I'll be forced to beat the poor bastard to a pulp. This challenge is all mine."

She had to grin at his comment. It was so typically Ethan. Throughout his PT sessions, they'd had so many heart-to-heart discussions on such a wide variety of topics, she couldn't begin to remember a time when she hadn't felt as if she knew everything about him. He was open, honest and competitive as hell. Of course he would view this challenge as a game he wanted to play to win.

He reached out to tweak one of her nipples and she gasped, thrilled by the look of lust in his gaze.

"So you don't think I'm too old for you?" she asked again, foolishly needing his reassurance.

"I think you're hot as hell and I can't wait to fuck your brains out."

His words, so typically young and crude, caught her off-guard and she laughed. "Somehow I think I sort of proved a point on that one, but I'm not sure how."

"Give me your list and take off that dress. I want to see if your panties are as sexy as that bra." His face, his words, were too intent, too serious. She licked her lips, though not from nervousness but excitement. She'd worried about her body turning him off all day, but he genuinely seemed to like what he saw. She retrieved her *Kama Sutra* list, handing it to him before tackling the zipper on the side of the dress.

She studied his face as she shimmied out of the tight sheath. He didn't look up, but instead read each position she'd listed on the page. She wished she could see his eyes, see what he thought of her choices.

"Did you list these in any particular order?" he asked.

"No," she whispered, trying to stop herself from tackling him to the floor and having her wicked way with him. "Aren't you going to get undressed?" Her need must have sounded in her voice because he glanced up.

"Damn. I knew it," he murmured.

"Knew what?"

"Knew I'd never be able to escape the image of you standing there, just like that. You are so sexy, Rachel."

"You think so?" she asked, turning slowly in a circle, grinning seductively when his gaze darkened.

"Take off the underwear and lie on your back."

His deep voice was demanding and she suddenly understood why he was such a good police officer. Criminals must fall in line under his commanding presence. Before she could think of another item on her list of reasons to refuse him, she unhooked her bra and shed her panties.

"What are you going to do?" she asked, immediately rolling her eyes at the inane question. They were in her bedroom with a list of *Kama Sutra* positions. What the hell did she *think* they were going to do?

"I thought we'd split the bamboo first," he replied easily. She shivered as she recalled the picture of that position. She'd chosen it because it was a fairly easy one to perform and didn't require her to be Nadia Fucking Comaneci. Splitting the Bamboo was actually one of the least risqué of her choices. She simply needed to lie on her back while Ethan took her missionary style. The bamboo splitting was achieved when she lifted one leg straight up over Ethan's shoulder.

She wondered why he'd chosen that one at all. Then she stopped wondering and instead felt grateful for his thoughtfulness. Some of her other choices had taken every bit of her nerve just to write on the list. By starting simply, perhaps it would make it easier to work their way up to the much more challenging positions. Splitting the Bamboo would be an easy one for them to get to know each other.

He didn't move until she was in the proper place, then he stepped to the side of the bed. While she watched, he slowly unbuttoned his shirt. Each inch of bare skin revealed left her squirming and needy. He watched her movements with a pleased grin as he dropped the soft cotton to the floor.

His hands drifted down his stomach to the fastening of his jeans. As he worked at releasing the erection she could see clearly confined there, she gripped the sheets in her fists, fighting her body's overwhelming reaction to his sexy striptease.

"Hurry up," she whispered, not hesitating to issue a few demands of her own.

He shook his head and stopped undressing. "Are you wet?"

Heat crept to her face at his question. Her ex-husband's idea of dirty talk was wanting to know if she'd showered before coming to bed.

"Don't," he said, leaning over her, his hands on either side of her head. Though he covered her completely, no part of his body brushed against hers—more's the pity.

"Don't what?"

"Don't think. Not tonight. Give that lovely brain of yours the night off. Tonight is about the pleasures of flesh."

She nodded her agreement. "Pleasure sounds cool," she said, forcing a lightness into her voice that simply wasn't there. Every word, every move he made sunk her deeper into the well of need and desire.

He rose and repeated his question. "Are you wet?"

"Yes," she whispered.

"Show me." Her eyes must have betrayed her confusion as he clarified, "Open your legs and touch yourself. Let me see all that hot juice you've made just for me."

She spread her legs apart, slowly dragging her hands along her chest, toying briefly with her breasts and reveling in making Ethan do a bit of squirming as well. As her fingers made their way along her body, he resumed his undressing and she detected a definite increase in the speed with which he moved.

This is fun.

When her hands reached the hair covering her pussy, he pushed his pants down.

Officer Russell went commando.

He cleared his throat and raised his eyebrows, reminding her of her task. She dragged her hand along her slit, her fingers quickly covered with the glistening proof of her arousal.

He took his cock in his hand and she physically fought back a gasp at the sexy sight of him touching himself so intimately.

Clearly not all men were created equal and for a moment, she wondered if Ethan hadn't gotten her ex-husband's share of the booty as well. She chuckled to herself at the irony of that thought then quickly dismissed Alex from her mind as she watched Ethan pull his hand along his rock-hard, thick, long, unbelievably inviting cock.

"Wow," she muttered and Ethan grinned.

"You act as if you've never seen a dick before," he said lightly.

"Only one and it wasn't even half as big as —" She stopped talking and glanced up. Ethan's hand had stopped moving against his flesh and she wanted him to start again.

"Only one?"

She shrugged. "Um, yes?" she asked, not sure what it was about her confession that bothered him.

"You've only been with one man. Your ex-husband, right?"

"Of *course* my ex-husband," she replied.

"How long have you been divorced?"

For a man who'd previously been ready to skip the small talk and get right to business, he sure was killing the mood now.

"Six years."

His grin reappeared and his hand moved against his cock more roughly.

"Doesn't that hurt?" she asked, spellbound by the sexiness of his movements.

"No. I should warn you right now, I like my sex hard and sweaty."

As easily as that, he'd taken the temperature in the room back to something the equivalent of living on the sun.

He gestured to her hand with a nod. "Show me," he said, repeating his earlier demand. She ran her hand along the opening of her pussy, gasping at the feeling produced by just her fingers and his hot gaze. She lifted her hand to him. He took it in his own, pulling it toward his mouth.

She cried out when his tongue cleaned each digit, sucking them one by one into his warm mouth.

"God, Ethan. That is so hot."

He grinned. "You know what I like about you?"

She shook her head.

"Every thought you have, you say out loud."

"And you *like* this?" she asked with disbelief. Most people of her acquaintance found that little habit completely annoying.

"I never have to guess where I stand with you."

"That's not always a good thing, you know," she replied, and he laughed and shrugged as if unconcerned.

"Times like now, it's a very good thing. I want you to tell me exactly how you feel tonight. Maybe it would make it more fun if you added an 'oh yes' or a 'fuck me harder' or an 'Ethan, you're a God' to the end of every sentence."

She laughed. "I'll try to bear that in mind."

"We could always practice now," he added as he dropped to his knees on the floor and grabbed her thighs, pulling her closer to the edge of the bed. His hot breath caressed her aching flesh as he bent and she gasped when he placed a wet, open-mouth French kiss on her vagina.

"Holy shit," she muttered as he chuckled.

"That's not a bad variation either." He repeated the kiss, lingering this time, his tongue thrusting in and out of her pussy. She fought to remain still but her traitorous hips couldn't resist the temptation of following his mouth, his lips. His teeth teased her clit mercilessly until she cried out, "Fuck me, Ethan!"

He stood slowly and pulled a condom from the pocket of his discarded pants. He put it on while she fought the sensations pummeling her body, fighting for more.

"Oh God, please fuck me."

Standing beside the bed, he placed the head of his cock at her wet opening and she threw her head back against the mattress. "Get inside me. Get inside me," she demanded, unconcerned by her wayward tongue. It was clear she'd never be able to hide the truth of his effect on her body.

His push into her was too torturously slow, but every time she tried to lift her hips to take in more of him, he halted her with firm hands.

"Harder," she begged.

He shook his head, refusing her. He was big and filling her so perfectly, she knew she couldn't rest 'til she had every bit of him crammed inside.

"You said hard and sweaty," she taunted.

"Too tight," he said through gritted teeth. "Only halfway."

Her eyes widened at his words. *This* was only half?

"See why I'm going slow?" he asked, sweat running down his cheek. "Six years is a damn long time, Rachel."

He moved another inch forward and she gasped at the electrical shock that coursed through her body. "What the hell was that?"

He grinned. "Think I found your G-spot." He moved out a bit and hit the same spot. She cried out.

"Oh yeah," he said, rubbing along the same area until she was shaking, writhing, arching with the pleasurable sensations he was provoking inside her. "Christ, you're gorgeous."

She screamed as his strokes pushed her into the most powerful orgasm of her life.

"What the hell was *that*?" she repeated after several moments. Her body was completely sated, utterly replete, and she felt as if she were floating on air.

"Awesome," he whispered.

As she became more aware, she realized he was completely inside her and still hard as a rock. "You didn't come."

"I'm not finished. I believe you wanted to try a little something called Splitting the Bamboo."

He reached down to grip her right ankle, pulling her leg straight up until it rested on his shoulder. As he moved her into the position, she felt his cock push even farther inside, until he was so deep she wanted to cry with relief. This was how she wanted him. How she needed him.

"Ready?" he asked and she nodded with a grin. "Gotta warn you," he added. "After watching you come like that, I'm not sure I'm going to be able to hold back this time. My balls are about to burst."

She laughed and reached down with her left hand to cup his testicles. He sucked in a sharp breath at her tantalizing touch. "Oh Ethan, you're a God," she teased as she squeezed his balls.

He laughed only briefly before pulling nearly all the way out and slamming back inside her in one hard thrust. As quickly as that, her body responded and she felt another orgasm beginning to build. He paused for just a moment before repeating the motion. Each rough shove into her body was followed by a short respite. After five times, she realized he was still trying to hold back, still trying to make it last—for her.

"Fuck me," she said during yet another pause. He looked at her closely. "No more stopping. I want you to take me hard...now."

Her request released the dragon from his lair as Ethan gave her exactly what she asked for. On each thrust he stroked her G-spot, driving her so high she felt as if she were on top of the world. She was flying. She was soaring. For the first time in her life, she understood what all the fuss was about. Sex *rocked*!

"Come with me," he demanded and she dove from the cliff, not needing to be asked twice.

Chapter Three

Rachel wasn't certain how long she'd dozed, but when she awoke, she found herself facing her new best friend.

"Well hello there," she said to Ethan's very-awake, very-ready-to-play cock.

Ethan's chuckle came from somewhere around the region of her waist and his breath tickled the hair surrounding her mons.

"Congress of the Crow," he said.

"Ah." No other explanation was necessary. She'd placed that position at the bottom of her *Kama Sutra* list, although it was by no means her last choice. She'd often wondered what it would be like to do a sixty-nine with a man who wasn't so hung up on sanitary conditions that sex felt more like an experiment in cleanliness than something based on fulfilling basic desires and needs. Her ex had refused to participate in oral sex, calling it disgusting.

As she studied Ethan's well-endowed cock and actually felt her mouth water a bit at the prospect, disgust was the furthest concept from her mind. Yummy, exciting, forbidden in a very hot way all crossed her mind — then panic set in. "Um...Ethan?"

"Mm hmm?" he hummed as he dragged his tongue against her slit.

She sucked in a breath and for a moment forgot what she'd meant to say.

He stopped when she failed to reply. "Is something wrong, Rach?"

"I might need a little guidance on this one."

He rose up onto his elbow and looked at her over the mountain that sadly was her hip. "Are you sure you were married?" he asked.

"Of course I was married. Married and divorced. I have an album full of pictures that have been torn in half to prove it. I have six table settings of china instead of twelve. I have half a damn set of encyclopedias. What kind of question is that?"

"Which half of the encyclopedias?"

"A through L," she said with a giggle.

He laughed at her jest then shook his head. "I swear I've slept with virgins with more experience than you. You didn't know where your G-spot was. You admitted you'd never had an orgasm like that and now you're lying there telling me you've never given a blowjob."

She narrowed her eyes. "How many virgins have you slept with?"

He rolled his eyes. "That was a joke. Before you, none."

"I'm not a virgin," she said defensively.

"I'm not so sure. Follow my lead. Do what I do."

She scowled, uncertain how that could possibly work. "Don't mean to question you or anything, but you are aware of the fact I have an innie and you have an outie, aren't you?"

He laughed. "Shut up and pay attention." He leaned forward and took her clit between his lips. The sensation shot through her like a rocket.

"Oh my. I see," she murmured. Moving toward him, she opened her mouth and took the head of his cock inside.

He wiggled his tongue against her clit and after the small explosion stopped shaking the ground, she imitated his movement with her tongue against his cock. She found a tiny spot just beneath the head that seemed to produce the same earth-shattering response in him that his tongue did in her.

She'd just gotten her bearings when Ethan brought his teeth into play, lightly nipping her clit. She moaned, the head of his cock snugly encased in her mouth, and he groaned in response. They repeated the same routine several times until she wondered if she would be able to hold on for much longer. She'd never come so quickly or so easily in the past, but every move Ethan made produced such incredible feelings in her, she wondered about this new hair-trigger climax of hers. Had it always been there?

His tongue teased her clit once more before drifting down to the opening of her body. He began that lovely thrusting in and out he'd done earlier. Gripping the base of his large cock in her hand, she mimicked his movements, taking him farther and farther into her mouth with each pass. Soon, it became a battle of willpower. Rachel was desperate to hold back her own imminent orgasm until Ethan came. She wanted so badly to make this good for him.

He broke away after giving her several minutes of pleasure so good, it hurt. "If you don't want me to come in your mouth, you'd better stop now," he said breathlessly.

She shook her head while still sucking on his cock and he groaned loudly. "God, Rachel. That looks so fucking hot and feels—" His words ended abruptly as she felt his climax begin. She moved faster, her grip stronger as she remembered how tightly, how roughly he'd played with his own erection earlier. He wasn't kidding about liking it hard and sweaty.

His come spurted out, hitting her throat in hot, thick jets and she swallowed rapidly, amazed by how much there was. His body trembled slightly as his flow slowed and she softened her movements, dragging her tongue along his flesh more to soothe than arouse.

"God bless virgins," he murmured.

"Hmm?" she hummed, unwilling to give up his cock just yet.

"What you lack in experience you sure as hell make up for in enthusiasm. That was incredible."

His head rested against her thigh as he spoke and she released him slowly, not able to resist the grin fighting to claim her face. She'd given him a blowjob, brought the hottest man she'd ever met to his knees — well, figuratively. He thought she was incredible.

No sooner had the pleasure of that compliment crossed her mind than Ethan's mouth was on her pussy again. His tongue caressed her clit mercilessly as his fingers entered the play. He pushed two inside her, fucking her with them as he kissed, bit and tormented her clit. Within seconds, she was giving in to an orgasm that must have been hiding just around the corner. She screamed as it claimed her, her body shaking with delight.

Not only was she a quick climaxer, she was a screamer. Who knew?

She felt Ethan move on the bed, his arms coming around her waist, his sweet kisses on her cheek. She turned her head to return the gesture, his lips rubbing lightly against hers. She tried to find the words to express what she was feeling, how incredible the entire night had been, but there just didn't seem to be a way, a word that would cover it all. Even his "incredible" seemed lackluster in the face of what they'd done.

He moved a bit closer and deepened the kiss. For several minutes they lay side-by-side, content to merely explore each other's lips, tongue and teeth. Ethan's hands gently gripped the side of her face and his rough, calloused fingers softly stroked her cheeks. God, she loved the sincerity, the sweetness of that touch.

His hard cock brushed against her leg...

Hard cock? What the hell?

She broke free of the kiss. "Are you kidding me?" she asked.

His grin covered his entire gorgeous face. "Benefit of hooking up with a younger man, Doc. We're always ready to roll."

She laughed, reaching down to grip his erection in her hand. He jerked back, surprised by her impetuous touch. "Guess there are all sorts of benefits to be found tonight. I've waited thirty-seven years for a man to play sex games with. Twenty bucks says you conk out before me."

"You're on. Sit up."

She forced her muscles to obey, perfectly aware she'd never felt so pleasantly relaxed in her life. Ethan perched himself on the end of the bed, donned a condom and beckoned her over. "Milk and Water Embrace."

She moved faster at his words. She'd picked the sitting position originally because it meant Ethan would be behind her and less likely to see things she didn't want him to see.

"Sit on my lap. Face the mirror."

Well, hell. So much for that plan.

Damn man had put himself directly across from her dressing table, which pretty much gave him the best—or worst—seat in the house. He'd be able to see every nook and cranny. Of course, he'd already seen it all and hadn't run from the room screaming, so maybe this would be okay too. The position certainly had other definite, too-hot-for-words merits.

She lowered herself onto his lap. She'd expected him to move in for the kill immediately, but this one short evening with the man should have proven he never did what she thought he would. He pulled his erection toward his stomach when she made a move to guide it into her body.

"Not yet," he mumbled. "Just sit on my lap and spread your legs apart."

She glanced ahead and saw her body—*all* of her body.

"Better than watching a porno," he said, studying her face reflected in the mirror. "Way better."

She grinned and shrugged. "I've never seen one of those the whole way through. The one I saw was a bit icky."

He laughed. "They're probably all 'icky' when it comes right down to it. This won't be though," he said. "God, I'm going to love watching you come this way."

She sat down. She never seemed to win in their small physical skirmishes. His hands pulled her legs open as he put her knees over his to hold them in place. She kept her head lowered for a moment, not quite willing to look up and see the damage.

"Damn, you have no idea how hot that looks," he whispered into her ear.

She decided to take his word for it, keeping her eyes averted, choosing instead to watch the action through her limited vision rather than through the hi-def reflection offered by the mirror. The live action was overwhelming enough. His hands drifted along the inside of her thighs and she inhaled sharply when they paused just before touching her clit.

"What do you want?" he asked.

"You really have to ask?"

"I like when you talk dirty to me. Tell me what you want. Say all the naughty words."

Her mind whirled over all the things she'd really like to say to him, but she wasn't sure she'd have the nerve. Saying things in the heat of passion was a hell of a lot easier than throwing them out as foreplay. It seemed more forgivable if she was out of her head. Right now, she was far too cognizant and aware.

"We've got all night," he said softly.

Maybe *he* did, but her body was already well on its way to Hornier-than-Hell City.

"Touch me," she whispered when his hands continued to rest on her upper thighs.

"I am."

Bastard.

He clearly intended to make her work for this.

"Touch my clit," she said, not needing to look up to see that she was blushing furiously.

He rubbed her clit lightly.

"Harder," she added. "Pinch it."

He obeyed as she started squirming again. Man had her dangling like a worm on a hook every damn second.

"Oh yeah, just like that. Put a finger inside me. No, two…two fingers." She couldn't believe she was actually saying these things.

He complied again, slowly pushing two of his thick fingers inside her pussy. Guess it was true what they said. Big hands, big…

His fingers, once inside, stopped moving.

Asshole.

"Move them." And then before he asked her to elaborate, she added, "Hard and fast."

He began working his hand against her and she groaned at how good his touch felt. Her head fell back against his shoulder and before she thought better of it, her eyes landed on the reflection of him finger-fucking her in the mirror.

"See what I mean?" he asked, his eyes capturing hers in the mirror. "Fucking hot."

He was right. Well, sort of right. She could definitely pick out the flaws in her body—damn cellulite—but as a whole? Fucking hot.

His fingers continued to move but she was too captured by the image and she shook her head. "Not enough. I need you. Inside me."

"I am inside you."

"Not your fingers," she said.

"What then?"

Prick.

She caught his gaze in the mirror and held it for just a moment before speaking her heart's desire. "I want your cock. Inside me. Deep inside me. Now."

It was his turn to groan. "Lift up."

She obeyed, reaching between her legs to greedily snatch his cock in her hand before he could take it away from her again. She guided him to her opening and slowly sat down.

"Fuck," he whispered and she looked up to see his pained expression in the mirror.

"Am I hurting you?" she asked.

"Only in the best possible way. Ride me, Rachel. This one is your show."

Her show? She hadn't considered that when she'd picked out the position, but he was right. She could direct this one, taking him any way she wanted. Should she tease him with a long, slow ride, as he'd done to her earlier, or pound against his flesh the way she loved?

Decisions, decisions.

She stood up slowly, careful to keep the head of his cock nestled just inside. His hands supported her waist but he was true to his word. He wasn't taking control. She moved back down, leisurely, relishing his hushed curse. There was something very heady, very exciting about holding a man's passion in her hands. She repeated her easy lovemaking, even when his grip on her waist tightened.

"You're killing me," he muttered, his voice low and so sexy, her already hard nipples tightened even more.

"Tell me what you want," she said. Now it was her turn.

His chuckle was cut off abruptly as she sped up on her next return. "Goddammit, woman. I want you to fuck me. I want to watch those gorgeous tits of yours bounce as you pound yourself on my hard cock."

All hail the King of Dirty Talk.

"Tits?" she asked instead, feigning offense.

133

"Breasts, boobs, jugs. Jesus, Rachel. If you have an ounce of compassion in you, you'll move."

She laughed—and then she moved.

* * * * *

Ethan mindlessly clicked through the television channels as Rachel rested her head on his lap. After round four hundred and thirty-nine in the bedroom, the hunger in their stomachs finally surpassed the hunger in every other part of their bodies. She'd thrown on a T-shirt and panties despite Ethan's assurances he wouldn't mind watching her make sandwiches in the nude. She'd declined the offer, watching with shock as he walked to the kitchen stark naked. What must it feel like to be so comfortable in your own skin, she wondered? She knew for a fact she would never suffer such a fate. Her modesty was far too ingrained to be so easily overcome. Although with Ethan, she felt adventurous enough to consider trying it. Maybe next time.

Next time.

She sighed softly and closed her eyes. There wouldn't be a next time. She was in the midst of her very first, and likely only, one-night stand. She lazily stroked his thigh, her mind drifting aimlessly over that thought, fighting back the depression that accompanied it.

He'd stopped on a sports channel and was watching some basketball game recap. It had been a long time since she'd even seen a sporting event on TV, generally breezing through them straight to the repeats of her favorite sitcoms. Her fingers encountered his scar and she stopped, touching the puckered bit of flesh.

"How were you shot?" she asked, rising up on her elbow, suddenly aware she'd never asked him about the injury that had brought him into her life.

He glanced down and noticed where her attention had fallen. He muted the game and grimaced. "I was the first man on the scene at a breaking and entering. Instead of waiting for backup, I decided I could handle things alone."

"I take it that was a bad decision."

He nodded. "I knew another patrol car was on the way and would be there in five minutes, tops. I figured I'd get a head start. Snuck in the back door with my gun drawn and caught the two thieves red-handed, trying to lift the stereo."

"Sounds okay so far," she said.

"I didn't see the third guy come out of the kitchen. He pulled his gun as I turned to point mine at him. He was faster."

Her heart raced at the idea of Ethan being in such danger. Suddenly, his job as a hot cop didn't seem so cool.

"What happened then?"

"Backup arrived. They rounded up the bad guys and called the ambulance."

"You're lucky you weren't killed."

He grinned. "Tell me about it. Thing is they were just young guys. I think the one who pulled the trigger was as surprised he shot me as I was. They were thieves, not killers. Gotta tell you, though, there's nothing like getting shot to adjust a man's priorities in life."

"How so?" she asked, sitting up beside him. He pulled her legs across his lap and she fought against the growing arousal that struck any time he touched her. His gesture had been a friendly, innocent one, but it was taking all the concentration in her body to focus on his words and not on his hand draped across her thigh.

"Until my injury, my life was pretty simple. Work my ass off all week in a job I thought was the most important thing in the world. Then I'd get drunk and laid all weekend."

Well, that got her attention.

"Ah, a womanizer, eh?" she asked.

He narrowed his eyes but dismissed her teasing barb. "Yeah, well. I'm not proud of it, but there it is. If there's a pickup line out there, I can pretty much assure you, I've used it."

Giggling, she said, "Oh no, tell me you never tried the 'What's your sign, baby?' on someone."

His shoulders shook with his laughter. "God, Rach. You kill me sometimes. No, I never used that line. Think it sort of died out a generation or two before I was born."

"Damn. I knew it was just a matter of time before the age jokes came out. For your information, that line was passé for me too. Disco had pretty much died out before I hit elementary school. So what was your best pickup line?"

He rolled his eyes. "I'm too embarrassed to tell you."

"Now you have to. What was it?"

"How *you* doin'?" he said, in his best impersonation of Joey from *Friends.*

"Shut. Up. Please tell me women didn't actually fall for that."

"Hey, what can I say? I'd throw it out there just like that, laugh at the end, maybe flex the big guns," he flexed his muscles, "and they'd fall all over themselves around me."

"Good God. Cocky much?"

He shrugged good-naturedly before sobering up. "Like I said, I'm not exactly proud of it."

She looked closely at him and realized that what he said was true. "So what part of your life changed after the shooting?"

"All of it," he said softly. She studied his face, wishing she could read the expression there. Sadness? Regret? "I figured out there's a hell of a lot more to life than work and sex. That damn bullet made me realize I'm not immortal."

"Oh yes. That's a biggie—discovering your mortality. I have to admit that's probably one of the things I miss most about my younger days. In my twenties, I had all the time in the world. As I approach my forties, I realize I've squandered all of it."

"I don't know about that. I'd say you've put the last few hours to very good use."

She laughed. "So I have. Well then, what are the new priorities, Mr. Mortal?"

"I've decided that work is just a paycheck. Don't get me wrong. I still care about my job — hell, it's a calling really. I love being able to help people. I just make sure that when I leave the precinct, I leave. Not just physically, but mentally as well."

"Good for you. So am I to assume you've stopped the bar hopping too? Thrown the little black book away?"

He shook his head at her questions, chuckling. "Uh, Rachel. Generation alert. It's not really called a 'little black book' anymore."

"Shit," she grimaced. "Do I want to know the new lingo for it?"

"Probably not. I referred to it as my 'booty call list' and the numbers were stored in my cell, not a book."

"Gross."

He laughed and turned the sound on the television back up. She rested her head on his shoulder and considered what he'd told her. She'd spent so much of their time together wrapped up in her own feelings of inadequacy that she'd never considered the fact he had problems too. She'd looked at him and seen a guy who had his act together, a good job, good looks, great personality. It was funny to think that inside, he was just as lost as she was.

They were simply two people looking at the world through different eyes from where they'd originally started. His entire outlook on life had been shattered by that bullet. Sort of like how her ex-husband had destroyed her self-esteem, her plans for a future she'd thought was solid. Difference was, Ethan had moved on and she hadn't.

Autumn was right, she'd shut down after the divorce. Wasted six fucking years of her life, never taking a risk with her heart.

Now she'd jumped from the frying pan into the fire — because she was afraid she was going to fall hopelessly and madly in love with Ethan. And when that happened, she was destined to be destroyed again. Maybe this time the damage would be irrevocable.

"Ready to cry uncle?"

She jerked at his question, suddenly aware he'd turned the TV off and was looking at her.

"Sorry?" she asked, confused.

His fist engulfed his aroused cock, focusing her wavering attention very quickly.

"Yowza," she whispered.

"There's twenty bucks on the table. You ready to concede and get some sleep, or is the game still on?"

She grinned at his dare. "Are we still working from the *Kama Sutra* list?"

He shrugged. "I want to take you doggy style."

Nodding, she upped the ante. "Standing up. In the shower."

"God, I love your style," he muttered, rising and pulling her up.

"Really? Not too old-fashioned? Out of date?" she joked.

"You're perfect. Now take off that stupid T-shirt before I rip it off you."

She giggled as she started for the bathroom. Dragging the cotton material over her head, she dropped it in the hallway. Ethan was hot on her heels as she bent to turn on the water. He peeled her panties over her hips from behind and caressed her ass as she pretended to adjust the water temperature. Soon his caresses turned more daring as he dragged his fingers along her slit. She opened her legs to grant him better access, gripping the side of the tub for support.

His fingers explored her pussy, playing with the moisture he found there.

"Ever done any anal play?" he asked, drawing his fingers back to her hole.

She gasped when he wiggled the tip of one finger inside her anus.

"Jesus," she muttered. "I'd never given a blowjob before tonight, Ethan. What the hell do *you* think?" As she spoke, she pushed back against his finger, curiosity outpacing the tiny bit of panic emerging.

"I think I can't wait to expand your horizons. Get in." He slapped her ass playfully then helped her into the shower before following. The steam in the shower was nothing compared to the heat rising off her body from his provocative comment.

Damn, he was right. She would need a list to remember all the amazing things they were doing together. In one night, the man had more than made up for thirty-seven years lived as a virtual nun.

God bless sinning!

He pulled her back against his chest, his hands wrapping around to engulf her breasts. "I love how well you fit me."

"Fit you?"

"You're the perfect height to have sex with," he answered.

"Ah well, nice to know what your requirements are. No age hang-ups, but women must fall between the five-foot-six to five-foot-eight range."

"Guy's gotta have his principles. Not to sound completely shallow, but mine also include big tits and an ass that a man can sink his fingers into." He illustrated his point by palming the cheeks of her rear end and squeezing.

She rolled her eyes. "Nope, that didn't sound shallow at all. I think I want to get out of this shower now, caveman."

He chuckled. "I'm just teasing. I told you, I got rid of the booty call list. I'm not looking for easy hook-ups anymore."

"So what are you looking for now?" she asked, fairly certain he wasn't looking for a thirty-seven-year-old divorcee. Dammit.

"Someone fun to hang out with. A sweet woman with a good sense of humor and intelligence. Someone I wouldn't mind spending forever with."

Her breath caught in her chest as he spoke. She wanted the same things.

Well, not a woman.

She looked over her shoulder and gave him a quick kiss. "I think everyone wishes for someone like that," she said softly.

"Do *you*?" he asked.

She nodded and he offered her a sweet grin. Christ, was he thinking of *her*? He didn't give her time to ponder that thought.

"Turn around and put your hands on that wall. If I'm not inside you in thirty seconds, this won't end well."

Impatience. Now *that* was something she could understand. She turned, thrilled when he kept his word and pushed his cock inside her in one hard thrust. While she loved his foreplay, sometimes it was better to simply get down to business. He took her exactly the way she'd discovered she loved—hard and fast—and she sensed an urgency in him she'd never seen before. She met him thrust for thrust and her orgasm, as usual, built quickly as his position behind her ensured he hit her sweet spot on every pass.

"Oh. My. God," she cried as her climax crashed down on her. She knew from his breathing that Ethan was close as well.

"Fuck," he muttered as he pulled out quickly. She was shocked — until she felt hot jets of come landing on her back.

No condom. They'd forgotten and they'd almost made a whopper of a mistake.

"I'm so sorry, Rachel," he whispered as the water continued to pound on her sensitive skin.

"I forgot too." She turned and wrapped her arms around his waist. He moved her into the direct stream of the water, using his hands to rinse away his sperm. "No harm, no foul."

"I didn't want to pull out," he confessed.

"What?" she asked, surprised when his grip tightened.

"I realized on the first thrust I'd forgotten the condom. I couldn't make myself stop. I..."

She pulled away and tried to understand what he was saying, what he was trying to tell her. "It's pretty close to period time for me, so chances are good we would have been okay anyway." She wondered if he was feeling guilty for putting her at risk.

He shook his head. "The thing is...I don't think I would have minded if you'd gotten pregnant."

She jerked, pressing herself against the tiled wall at her back. "Well, *I* would have minded. I'm too damn old to have a baby."

He scowled. "You are not. Are you telling me you don't want kids?"

A pain shot through her heart at his question. She'd always, always wanted kids, but she'd given up on that dream long ago. "I wanted them, but Alex — According to him, it was never a good time. He was in medical school for years and then trying to build up the practice the years following that. Of course, by that time, unbeknownst to me, he was already looking ahead to the next wife."

"I'm sorry, Rachel. Your ex sounds like a grade-A prick."

She smiled sadly and shrugged. "That he is."

"I want kids," he said. She imagined him with a brood of boys, him wrestling with them in the living room, playing cops and robbers in the backyard with Nerf guns. Then she saw him sitting on the edge of a bed, reading a bedtime story to a little girl with dark hair like his. "I never thought much about it until I got shot. Now I think about it all the time."

"You'll be a wonderful father. Your kids will be the luckiest on earth."

"Maybe." He reached around her to turn off the water before helping her out. He dried her off before grabbing a towel for himself.

"Well, apart from the amazing sex, that was a pretty useless shower. I didn't scrub one inch of my body."

"I wouldn't say it was useless at all. I love talking to you," he answered. She had to agree. In just a few short minutes, she'd learned more intimate details about the man than she had in all the weeks of their budding friendship. She was shocked to discover how many dreams they shared.

"We'll try it again in the morning." He wrapped the towel around his waist. "I'll even wash your hair for you." She stared at him, trying to convince herself this night was truly real and not some elaborate fantasy she'd created in her mind.

Ethan was turning out to be very different from the man she'd thought him to be. It was disconcerting to realize her handsome playboy possessed a serious, thoughtful side. He'd never been as attractive to her as he was now, as he talked about falling in love and having kids. Suddenly there was a small part of her that was afraid to go to sleep, afraid she'd wake up in the morning to discover none of this had happened.

"There goes that head of yours again. Come on, Doc. Let's get some sleep."

Chapter Four

❧

"Good morning, sunshine."

Rachel opened her eyes and blinked hard against the bright light. She sat up as Ethan walked into the room with two cups of coffee. He'd put his clothes on, but had left his shirt unbuttoned so she had a crystal-clear view of abs she could bounce a penny on.

"It wasn't a dream," she mumbled as he handed her a mug of much-needed caffeine.

He shook his head with a big grin, seemingly pleased by her surprise at finding him there. "You sure are good for the ego, Rachel."

She attempted to shake herself awake, shake herself aware. "Yeah, well, don't go getting a big head about it or anything."

"As well as for keeping a man grounded. You're a woman of many talents and incredible beauty."

At his words, she panicked. Oh shit. There he was looking like Mr. Universe and she was sitting in bed, naked from the waist up with morning-after hair and no makeup. She hastily put her coffee on the nightstand and looked for any piece of clothing close enough for her to lay her hands on.

Of course, it probably didn't matter. Their night was over. The challenge completed. Prior to last night she would have been surprised to find him still in her apartment. Part of her would have expected him to simply leave a note saying thanks for the shits and giggles. Now that she knew him better, she knew he was enough of a gentleman to stick around and at least say his goodbyes in person. Her heart ached at the thought. She'd prefer the damn note.

"I need to get dressed," she said at last.

"Okay," he replied easily, sitting at the edge of the bed.

"I suppose you'll be going then."

"Going?" he asked.

"Yeah. I mean, the night's over. I completed my dare. Thank you very much, by the way. So I guess this is the part where I say 'It's been fun', right?"

He scowled. "You aren't serious?"

"That it was fun?"

"I suppose we should get this part out of the way or the rest of this relationship is gonna suck," he said.

She narrowed her eyes, wondering at his words and the sadness of his tone. "I don't know what you mean."

"Your ex-husband—" he began, but she cut him off.

"I don't want to talk about him."

"Then I guess you should have left old Voldemort out in the hall rather than dragging him into the bedroom with us," he said.

"What the hell are you talking about?" she asked angrily. She wasn't about to go into the dirty details of her decade-long disaster of a marriage. Ethan already knew too much.

"He clearly fucked with your head. Made you feel insignificant, maybe even a little stupid, right?"

She sucked in a painful breath at his astute comments. As always, when faced with a question she couldn't answer, she merely shrugged.

"He convinced you that men don't stick around, right?"

"I—" she began, but Ethan cut her off.

"Well, he was a dumbass," Ethan said hotly. "And you're a dumbass for believing any of that shit."

"Excuse me?"

"I said you're a dumbass."

"I'm a dumbass," she repeated louder.

"Yes," he replied, his voice rising as well.

She rose up on her knees and poked her finger in his chest. "Well, if *I'm* a dumbass, then you're a liar."

"Liar?"

"*Liar.* You lied to me. You lied about your intentions. What is this crap about a relationship?" she asked.

"What the hell did you think last night was about?" he asked.

"What I was supposed to think it was about. A one-night stand. You were helping me live that cougar fantasy." She pulled the sheet up to her neck to cover herself and wondered about the frustration on his face. She knew she hadn't messed that up. She'd have remembered if he'd even slightly insinuated they were entering into a relationship.

"Fuck," he muttered. "Yeah, that was what you were supposed to think. Christ, I've screwed this up."

She forced a grin, hating how lost and forlorn he looked, wishing she could put a smile back on his face. "Well, you've certainly screwed something, but I don't think it's this," she joked. He looked too intense, too serious. She just wanted her lovely, easygoing Ethan back.

Unfortunately her lame jest missed the mark.

"I've been trying to figure out a way to ask you out for weeks, but I knew you'd throw the patient/client thing and the age difference up in my face. When I saw that stupid list of names, that cougar challenge, I latched onto it," he admitted.

She stared at him, trying to process his comments. His lips were moving, but the words she was hearing simply couldn't be right. He wanted to date her? *Her?*

"You wanted to go out with me?" She closed her eyes and groaned at her stupid question.

"Why is that so fucking hard for you to believe, Rachel?" he yelled.

145

She jumped at his harsh tone, his angry face.

"Look at me," she said. "I'm too old. I'm divorced. I'm—"

"Come here," Ethan said, gripping her upper arm in his large hand and dragging her to the mirror attached to her dressing table. Her attempt to hold on to the sheet failed, and she wanted to crawl under the bed as her naked body came into view. "Tell me what you see."

She fought against closing her eyes and blocking the image, knowing Ethan wouldn't allow her even that small escape.

"I see me," she said, her voice laced with her usual smartass tone.

"And?"

"You," she added with a smirk she hoped hid the despair closing in on her.

"Cute, Rachel. Real cute. Jokes work for you, don't they? You don't want to be serious, don't want to handle any heavy stuff, so you laugh it all away. Does that help when you're in bed alone at night?"

"I don't have to stand here and listen to—"

"Yeah, actually you do, because I'm not leaving this house until you see in that mirror what I see."

"Is that right?" she asked, sarcasm dripping off her tongue. "And what exactly would that be, Ethan?"

"The hottest woman I've ever laid eyes on. The funniest, sweetest, most compassionate woman I've ever met. The physical therapist who's had me rock-hard and aching since the first damn day she made me do those stupid stretching exercises and the woman I'm going to make love to all day and most of tonight. We haven't even scratched the surface on that list."

"All day?" she whispered.

"And night," he repeated.

"Oh my."

He shook his head ruefully. "Hell, who am I kidding? I wanna fuck you every night and pretty much every day for as long as you'll have me. So does that answer your question?"

She stared at her reflection in the mirror. He saw all that? She recalled her perusal of her face just the day before. All she'd seen was a woman in need of a dye job and with flabby upper arms. She studied her face again, looking at herself through Ethan's eyes and suddenly the blinders of her pain, the hurt inflicted on her by her ex-husband's infidelity, fell away.

"I don't think I've ever seen all that."

"You're living on an island, Doc, and you've burned down every bridge to the mainland."

Had she done that? Yes, she had. Her gaze left her reflection and moved to his. She studied his dear, sweet face and realized he'd been building a bridge, trying to reach her since the first day they'd met. He'd offered her friendship and fantasy all rolled into one delicious package.

"Is this a bad time to say I'm sorry?" she asked.

He grinned. "I don't want an apology, Rachel. I just want you to trust me. Believe the words that I say without always waiting for the other shoe to drop."

"That's not going to be easy for me, you know?" she admitted.

"All I want you to do is try."

"I can do that. Ethan?"

"Yeah?" he asked.

"Kiss me."

He gave her a hot grin that oozed sexual intent. "Oh, I can do even better than that. Go lie down on the bed."

"So," she said, walking to the bed, "Indrani or the Lotus?"

"Both. They're a nice complement to each other." His answer was quick and sure as he pushed her to her back.

"You younger men, so greedy," she teased.

147

"Lucky you," he joked back.

"Lucky me." She grabbed his unbuttoned shirt and tugged him toward the bed, pulling him down on top of her. She pushed his shirt off his shoulders as he captured her lips in a kiss hot enough to set the room on fire. "Why do you have so many clothes on?" she murmured when they broke apart.

"Mistake," he replied between kisses. "Won't happen again." He rose briefly to shed his jeans and don a condom before leaning over her once more.

"You taste yummy," she murmured, savoring the oddly intoxicating combination of toothpaste and coffee.

"You haven't had your morning caffeine hit yet," he teased.

"Don't need it with you around. I feel amazingly energized."

"Lucky me," he said, mimicking her words.

"Lucky you. Now fuck me, Ethan."

He grinned evilly and she moaned. "Not so fast, Doc."

"Oh God, Ethan. I really don't think I can wait."

"Tough." He bent down to take one of her tightly budded nipples in his mouth, toying with the sensitive skin until she was squirming beneath him. She gripped his hair in her hands, torn between forcing the "fucking" issue and keeping his lips on her breast. Once he'd sensually tormented the first one to his satisfaction, he moved to the other breast, giving it the same heated attention. He sucked hard, sending a lightning bolt of need straight to her pussy. Her back arched against the bed and she whispered desperate pleas for relief, but his sole focus remained on her breasts, specifically her nipples, and she wondered if anyone had ever treated them with such adoration, such unrestrained need.

Soon his lips left her breasts and wandered down her stomach. She giggled when he thrust his tongue into her bellybutton playfully. Her laughter died in a hiss when his mouth landed on her clit, his tongue pressing forcefully. She fought back the climbing climax, not wanting to succumb so quickly. She was in heaven and ready to unpack her bags for a nice, long stay.

"More," she whispered breathlessly. Ethan answered her plea with actions rather than words, moving even farther down to plunge his talented tongue inside her pussy.

"I love the way you taste too," he said, looking up at her with a cocky grin that said he knew just how much he was turning her on. His tongue thrust inside her and again, she tamped down the need to give way to her orgasm.

After several moments, he replaced his tongue with his fingers, two of his long, thick digits stroking her higher and higher until she had no choice but to dive into the whirlpool of sensation.

"Holy shit," she cried out as he positioned himself above her once more, driving his cock into her as she was in the midst of her climax. His quick, hard thrust threw her into another orgasm, but he showed no mercy as he continued to move in and out, visiting that lovely G-spot he'd introduced her to last night.

"Indrani," he demanded on one retreat, gripping her legs and pulling them up until her knees were pressed along her sides. The position left her more gloriously vulnerable to his cock as he powered into her.

"Ethan," she cried as another climax began to emerge. He must have sensed her imminent eruption because he stopped moving.

"Wait for me, Rachel," he demanded.

"I'm not sure I can," she confessed and he grinned, kissing her lightly on the nose.

"Wait for me or I'll get out the handcuffs and keep you on the verge of an orgasm for the rest of the day."

"You wouldn't dare."

"Hell yeah I would and I'd have fun doing it."

"I'll wait for you," she reassured him quickly.

Ethan kissed her, returning to her body with a slow, tantalizing glide. "Don't worry, Doc. I'm pretty much a man on the edge. This won't take too much longer."

She laughed lightly at his confession. "Then I suppose we should try the Lotus."

Careful to keep his cock buried deep within her, he pushed his upper body away from her chest as she moved her legs inward, crossing them in front of her lotus style.

Both of them groaned as the position forced him in just a tiny bit farther.

"Hold on," he said, pulling out until just the head remained. He returned with a thrust that left her gasping. Over and over, he moved until she was screaming his name.

"Now," he said, and she plummeted into her climax, the sensations in her body struggling for supremacy, racking her body with more pleasure than she'd ever known.

"Damn that was good," Ethan said, helping her as she attempted to untangle her limbs, her legs feeling like wet noodles in the aftermath of her orgasm. "Honest to God, Rachel, I thought my balls were going to implode for a second. I don't think I've ever come that hard." He glanced down at his lower body while removing the used condom and Rachel laughed at the image he presented.

"Is it all still there?" she teased.

He grinned ruefully. "Doesn't hurt to take inventory every now and again. You seriously knocked my cock off."

She shook her head, pleased by his comment. "You sweet-talking fool."

"Yeah, well, I'm about to get a whole lot sweeter." As he spoke, he stood up and reached down to retrieve his jeans from the floor. She gasped when he pulled a pair of handcuffs out of the back pocket. "I'll let you decide who gets cuffed first."

"You'd let me put them on you?" she asked.

"If you wanted to," he said, placing the heavy metal in her hands.

She smiled seductively at the thought of all the things she wanted to try, a lifetime of fantasies and desires. And now she'd found the perfect partner in crime. Ethan's libido certainly seemed to rival her newly discovered one.

"Assume the position," she said, standing and swinging the handcuffs in her hand.

His gaze darkened with lust and she watched his erection come back to life.

"What are you going to do?" he asked as he stood, turning his back and placing his hands behind him. She clicked the cuffs in place, amazed by his acquiescence.

"I thought I could use a bit more practice on the blowjob concept."

"Practice does make perfect," he said, his rock-hard cock telling her without words how much he approved of her choice. She moved to face him and fondled his balls. He moaned at the touch before leaning forward to kiss her. "Just bear in mind that once you've had your turn, I get mine."

She felt a fresh rush of arousal streak through her body. "What will you do once you have me bound and at your mercy?"

He placed a light kiss on her cheek before whispering in her ear, "It's a surprise."

"I love surprises," she confessed.

"I love blowjobs," he said and she laughed briefly as she sank to her knees.

She glanced up at him, taking his cock in her hand. "Maybe this would be a bit more fun if you added a few comments to the play. I think 'Rachel, you're a goddess' or something to that effect would be nice."

"Rachel, you're a goddess," he said quickly. "Now suck my cock."

She laughed—and then she sucked.

Epilogue

♋

Thanks to Cam's suggestion, I will now be sharing expert advice on the Tempt the Cougar blog in regards to various *Kama Sutra* positions—LOL. Not quite sure when I crossed the line from horny divorcee to sex expert, but believe me, I'm loving it on this side of the tracks. Check back next week for my first installment!

* * * * *

Position of the week—Clasping

This position is achieved when the couple lies on their sides and the man spoons the woman from behind. It certainly helps if your guy is well endowed, like mine! Clasping is great for slow, deep, sensual lovemaking and extra special for the woman, as it leaves the man's hands free to explore other parts of her body as well.

Hey, gals. Ethan and I are really putting a dent in that *Kama Sutra* list he made me write. Oh, did I mention that I just keep adding to it? Hee hee. I still can't believe we've been going out for nearly a month! Last night, we ordered pizza in—you know how much my cooking sucks—and started watching a movie. Ethan whispered "Clasping" in my ear and before I knew it, we were naked on the living room floor, kissing and holding each other. I swear that man knows the positions better than I do. It was so incredibly romantic, simply lying in each other's arms, so close it was as if we were one person. Of course, the fact that he has a huge cock certainly helped.

LOL. He'd kill me if he knew all the things I share with you girls. Oh crap, there he is, beating on the door. Damn man never remembers his key.

Talk to you later.

* * * * *

Position of the week—Tigress

The one really puts the woman in control. It involves the man lying on his back while the woman sits on top facing away from him. Sort of like riding a horse backward, but what a ride, ladies! Talk about hitting all the hot spots. I had multiple orgasms with this one.

Grwrrr! Holy crap. Ethan showed up at my work yesterday and demanded that I take the rest of the day off. Said we were going somewhere special. We went out for a super-romantic lunch then he surprised me by booking a suite in the swankiest hotel in town. There was champagne and strawberries in the room and he'd even brought some romantic music and we slow danced! I was so hot for him by the time the music ended, I accidentally tore his shirt trying to undress him. We ended up on the floor as always and that was when I pushed him down on his back and gave him my personal brand of thank you in the form of the Tigress. Oh yeah, who's queen of the jungle now?

* * * * *

Position of the week—The Pair of Tongs

I looked at the picture of this one and just laughed. Talk about superhuman strength. Who makes this stuff up? In this position, the woman hangs off the bed sideways, supporting most of her weight on one arm.

The man straddles the woman's lower leg while holding her upper leg...well, up. Might have to lift weights for a few months (or years) to be able to achieve this one.

Well, you gals threw out the challenge and all I can say is we tried our best to do The Pair of Tongs position. Sweet Mary. I'm not sure who worked that position out, but God bless their upper-arm strength. Ethan tried to help me get in the right position and we even—sort of—held the pose for a few seconds before I started giggling uncontrollably. At that point, it went downhill fast. My arm gave out, Ethan tripped while trying to break my fall and we both fell onto the floor in a heap of naked body parts. I have to admit it will go down as my favorite pose regardless of the fact we never did it, because as we were sitting on the floor laughing our asses off—Ethan told me he loved me. He loves me!

SIN ON SKIN
Mari Freeman

෫෩

Dedication

§Ω

This book is for Samantha Kane. I raise a glass of Crystal Head Vodka to toast the coffee shop meetings, the phone bills, the road trips, the hotels and the conventions. You have whipped my lazy muse into submission more times than I can count. Thanks.

Acknowledgements

§Ω

The authors of the Cougar Challenge have been a hoot to work with. Each one put in the time and effort it takes to make a group project successful. Everyone did their part and did it on time. Cheers, ladies! I'm grateful to have shared this experience with such talented authors.

Author **N**ote

§Ω

You'll find the women of Cougar Challenge and the Tempt the Cougar blog at www.temptthecougar.blogspot.com

Trademarks Acknowledgement

The author acknowledges the trademarked status and trademark owners of the following wordmarks mentioned in this work of fiction:

Carolina Panthers: Panthers Football LLC

Crystal Head Vodka: Globefill Incorporated Corporation

iPod: Apple Inc.

Levi's: Levi Strauss & Co.

RomantiCon: Jasmine Jade Enterprises

Volvo: Aktiebolaget Volvo Corporation

Chapter One

ഇ

Stevie Jones got in her car and headed for home. She'd had to let two more bioengineers go today. Her friend Monica, who was the head of human resources, had offered to lay the guys off, but Stevie had needed to face them herself.

Most of them didn't like her. They called her the black-hearted bitch. She'd heard them. She was a tough, strict boss who stuck to procedure and ran a tight ship. Good for the pharmaceutical business but bad for the social life. Not that she would want to date any of those guys anyway. Work was work, and she didn't like any goofing off in the lab. Her tough policies got most drugs that came through her teams approved fast and clean.

Monica's mission over the last year had been to loosen Stevie up. She'd turned her on to these incredibly steamy erotic romances, where she'd found stories of women with sex lives Stevie never dreamed possible. Women in those stories had what they wanted—happiness with their partners. Something Stevie had never experienced. She'd always been a little take-it-or-leave-it when it came to sex.

Then Monica dragged her to RomantiCon, a conference for erotica readers and writers. They met several other women their age, all having a blast, drinking and ogling the cover models. Stevie had enjoyed the camaraderie. At the conference, her education or position didn't matter. She was just one of the girls.

The wildest of the bunch, Cam, started a blog as soon as she got back home. The Tempt the Cougar blog was another secret pleasure. The rest of the women were constantly posting pictures of hot younger men. Stevie had posted a few times, but it was mostly dirty jokes or spoofs about hot younger men.

Once home, she kicked off her shoes and grabbed a beer, taking a moment to scratch the cat on the head before turning on her home computer. She let some of the stress from the day slip away as she pulled up the Tempt the Cougar blog. Why she felt she wasn't worthy to participate more on the blog was beyond her. She should be able to jump right into it, wallow in her own sexuality. She wasn't afraid of it. She was around men all day. Yes, they were geeky, bioengineering types who were all brains and no butch. Sandal-wearing, whining liberals were not her type. Nope. She needed one of the alpha types in the erotic books. She doubted any of the single guys who worked for her had ever had sexual experiences like the ones she'd been reading. She doubted any of them had it in 'em.

But even with the blog, she usually felt outside everything. She looked at the latest post. Rachel had been online again, searching for images, and boy had she hit the jackpot. There were seven different shots of cops in various states of undress. But the last one caught Stevie's eye. He was thick, muscled, and the look in his eye said *I will cuff you up and use you all night long.*

She sighed. She'd never have the nerve to do the things these ladies had done. Monica had thrown the gauntlet down. A few weeks ago in a blog post, she'd taken their little obsession with younger men into the real word. Stevie remembered the post well.

"Let's do this! I challenge each of you, and me too, to go out there and find a younger man to make our fantasies come true. No more dreaming. Let's live, live, live!"

Stevie had laughed when she'd read it, not even bothering to answer the post. The rest of the group had. Some were excited, maybe a little frightened, but all were willing to take up the challenge. Stevie knew it would have to stay a fantasy for her. She wasn't that bad on the eyes or anything. Her hair was dirty blonde and hung to her shoulders with some natural wave. She didn't do much with it, but then, she was always working. No time to mess with appearances when you worked seventy hours a week or more. Her mother thought she was a bit on the thin side, and Monica always teased her about not having an ass. She wasn't horrible. But she still feared rejection.

When she dated, it was usually a disaster. Seemed most men really didn't want a strong, independent woman, even if they said they did. Not too many alpha males in her life. Lots of scientists, lots of accountants, but not one alpha werewolf running around Blake and Howell Pharmaceuticals.

Pity.

It seemed unless she found said werewolf, she was going to be alone for a while.

Stevie had been envious when she'd read the other women's adventures in Cougarland. She couldn't believe they'd each managed to do it. They'd all found younger men and fulfilled their fantasies. She had met these women, spent time with them; they weren't so different from her.

No. She'd fantasize about it, live vicariously through her friends, but she couldn't see herself actually rising to the challenge.

Monica was giving her a hard time, trying to convince her that she could do it too. Her friend had tried several different arguments, none of which were going to change Stevie's mind. She took another drink of beer and glanced over the latest comments. Rachel had found her younger man and gotten her fantasy cop all in one. Maybe *he* was a werewolf.

Her cell phone vibrated on the desk. It was Monica again. She ignored it. Monica had been increasingly pushing her to get out more. Her friend recently joked on the phone that when future archaeologists found Stevie's body, they'd know she was a homebody and a bookworm. No tattoos, not one piercing, not even her ears. They'd dig her up and find her sitting, ergonomically correct, in her computer chair, mummified, mouse in one hand and a copy of *Clinical Pharmacology Today* in the other.

Stevie looked at her reflection in the window across the room. Her hair hung unstyled, her glasses were riding on the end of her nose. She was wearing one of the five black skirts in her closet and one of probably a dozen white blouses. Stevie Jones was a nerd. Ten years of intense college courses and a very stressful job had taken their toll.

She looked around her living room. Beige surrounded her, soothed her. It wasn't as if she *couldn't* do something a little outside her comfort zone. She could. She'd driven past the Sin on Skin tattoo parlor every day for seven years. She'd thought about some ink. Had even considered designs.

She could do that. No fear of rejection there.

* * * * *

Before she changed her mind, Stevie was pulling into Sin on Skin's tiny parking lot. The air was cool as she stepped out of the car. A guy was sitting on a bench at the far side of the building, reading something from his cell phone. He nodded, barely looking up as she walked past him and through the door.

The tattoo would make Monica happy and fulfill the requirement of "getting out of the box" or whatever HR nonsense she was always pushing around the office.

"Hi. What can I do for you?"

Stevie headed over to a Goth-looking young girl with blond, pink and black hair, standing behind a glass case filled with jewelry for various piercings.

"Hey." Stevie glanced over the case. Some of the jewelry was so unusual she couldn't even imagine what had to be pierced to accommodate it. She shook her head. "I'd like to get a tattoo."

The girl had too many lip piercings for Stevie to count. "Do you have an appointment?"

Stevie looked around the reception area. Two empty couches sat in front of a huge TV playing some sort of skateboarding competition. The far wall had shelves and a table with large, open albums of the artists' work to help those undecided on designs. Not a soul besides her in the room.

"Do I need one right now?"

"Nah. Just wanted to know if you had someone already working on a design or something."

"Ah. Nope. Walk-ins welcome?"

The girl didn't even smile at the reference. "Um. Usually on a Friday night that would be a no, but you're way early. Let me see if Errol can do you."

Stevie glanced at her watch. Seven. Seven on a Friday night was way early to this crowd. She *was* getting old. Stevie paced over and flipped open the closest album on the table. The girl walked to the front and stuck her head out the door.

"Errol. I got a walk-in and no one's here yet. You want to take it or should I have her come back?"

There was more to the conversation that Stevie couldn't make out. She paged through the album. The work was fantastic. This artist used an incredible amount of detail and shadow to make the tattoos amazingly realistic.

"He'll be right with you." The girl still didn't smile. "If you need a soda or something, let me know. I'm Angel."

This girl was as far from an angel as one could get. Dressed in a short schoolgirl skirt and half-unbuttoned shirt, she sauntered away on extraordinarily high heels. Stevie would have considered it a Halloween costume, but this was a regular Friday night. "Thanks. I'm okay right now."

"That's Errol's book. Your lucky day. He's gonna do you."

Stevie barked out a small laugh. "I wish somebody would," she murmured. The girl gave her an unamused look over a clipboard.

"His stuff is beautiful." Stevie changed the subject, tapping her finger on a pencil drawing in one of the plastic sheet protectors. It was a wolf. Nothing much in particular stood out in the design. The artistry was what made it so incredible. The pencil lines looked more like brush strokes. The shading and the detail made the wolf appear alive on the page.

"Did that for a dude who never showed up to have it inked." The deep voice startled her. She hadn't heard him walk in. Stevie looked up. "Happens sometimes. I liked it."

"Errol, this is…what's your name, sweetie?" Angel asked as she snapped a clip over some papers on the tattered-looking clipboard. She pushed the board into Stevie's hands.

The guy who had been sitting out front stood before her. Stevie boldly eyed him from head to toe before realizing what she was doing. If he was *doing* her, she was a happy, happy lady. He gave her a knowing grin. They stood looking eye to eye for a moment.

Angel tapped the pen on the clipboard to bring Stevie's attention away from the artist and back to the task at hand. "I need you to fill this out. All of it. Sign the bottom of the second page. Have you had any alcohol today?"

"Um. No. I haven't." Stevie blushed. She'd been caught looking at him by the freaky girl.

Errol turned back to the album. "It's my policy not to ink anyone who's been drinking. I don't like clients with regrets in the morning."

Oh. Good. After that comment about somebody "doing her", Stevie assumed the overdone schoolgirl thought she was drunk. And then she'd given Errol such a bold once-over…

This guy was hot. Stevie knew she couldn't have been the first client to ogle him, but she hated that she'd been so obvious. Angel had to distract her—again—to get them all back on track. Embarrassed, she scribbled her name on the release forms.

Errol took the clipboard. "What do you want..." He looked down at the paper. "Stevie?"

Stevie inwardly laughed. His clean-shaven head, his slightly muscled arms and those dark, brooding eyes were what she wanted. After this week and all the talk on the blog, she wanted to be able to be like the other cougar women. She wanted to feel confident enough to convince this younger guy to let her have her way with him. She wanted to see just how much of his body was inked.

"An Ankh symbol," was the answer she managed to give aloud.

"This way." He started walking down a hallway covered in pictures of happy clients showing off their new tats. "The Egyptian symbol for eternal life. Nice." He turned down another hallway and pushed open the door to the last room. "My lair." He held the door for her.

As she walked past, she could smell his cologne, spicy and somewhat strong. It was as appealing as his full lips. Oh God. She was in trouble.

"What style are you thinking for the Ankh? Gothic? Celtic? Do you want ornamentation around it of any kind? Is there something in particular you're trying to express?"

The room held a chair that looked like it belonged in a dentist's office and a couple of stools. Like in the hallway, the walls were covered with more pictures of clients, a few random cartoons and other memorabilia. There were photos of Errol with friends or maybe family, she assumed, and an autographed photo with a couple of the Carolina Panther football players. He gathered up some papers, sat on a wheeled chair then pulled himself up to the drafting table in the corner.

"I think I want it fairly stark. Black and grays, like that wolf, and I'd like the cross to look like carved stone. Maybe have an aged, chipped look to it." He was drawing as she spoke. "In the loop at the top of the cross, I want a jewel."

"That black ink too? Some color would totally make that pop. It wouldn't need much."

Stevie titled her head. "I didn't think of that. I'm a little afraid of the color being too much on my skin." She felt a little embarrassed by her complete lack of a tan.

"Some emerald on that gorgeous, creamy skin would be hot." He didn't look up from the paper. Stevie felt herself blush.

"Where's it going and what size were you thinking?"

Wow. She was feeling like a schoolgirl herself. "Um. My hip." She put her hand on the top of her right butt cheek. "About an inch and a half tall."

"Hmm." He scribbled a little more. "I think you'll be happier if we go a little larger. Is there some purpose for the artwork, or statement you're trying to make? Anything that I can add in the details that will personalize it for you?"

She presumed most people were happy to tell him why they wanted a particular tat. She, on the other hand, was not ready to tell this hunky guy that she wanted to mark her membership in an exclusive club of sex-starved older women on a quest to find younger men. Well, that, and she'd always wanted one, and the Ankh was the best thing she'd thought of in a long time. She loved the symbol the publisher used, and it really would make a cool-looking design.

"Not really."

"Uh huh. It's okay to have personal reasons for your ink, baby. We all have them. But if you open up to me, I can make your experience so much better."

She'd bet he could. She'd have to spend the weekend looking up pictures of hot guys with tattoos so she could post one on the blog.

Errol continued to scribble as she sat on a stool. He reached over and started a boom box that housed his iPod. Not surprisingly, Stevie didn't recognize the band, but she did like the music. It reminded her of The Who in their early days.

"How's something like this?"

He handed her the translucent tracing paper. Stevie couldn't believe the detail for the short amount of time he had spent on the drawing.

He stood close to her so he could look over her shoulder as he spoke. "Of course, on you, it'll be much more intricate. But is the design what you're thinking?" Stevie inhaled his scent again. She could feel the heat of his body.

She thought of Monica and could hear her friend now. *"You mean you were that close to a sexy younger man and you didn't even try? Come on, Stevie."* She forced her concentration back to the design to take her mind off the man.

The Ankh was perfect. It had a three-dimensional feel that made it look like an ancient stone relic. He had included some wear around the bottom of the cross and a chip in one of the arms. In the loop that made the top of the cross was a gemstone with beams of light emitting both in front of the cross design and behind. Some vines wove from behind the base of the cross and reached out to the sides, giving the design more weight and depth than the Ankh would have held on its own.

"It's perfect." Stevie held it to her hip and looked in the full-length mirror by the door. Even though it was almost twice the size she had intended, it fit.

"All right. You ready?"

Stevie hesitated. She hadn't bothered to change after leaving work and still wore her black skirt, white shirt and scarf. What had she been thinking?

"Drop the skirt and let's put it in the right spot."

Stevie found herself a little excited at his command. She reached back and unzipped the skirt. She never wore hose anymore so at least she didn't have to fight those. She shimmied the skirt down a bit. He knelt behind her and pulled on the fabric, bringing it down a little farther.

"Do you want it more on the hip or more on the cheek?"

She looked over her shoulder to the mirror. He was on his knees, his hands holding the paper over her hip. He looked at her through the mirror. Were his eyes heated too? She wanted to drop the skirt and hold that drawing over her pussy right at this moment. But that was silly. She was getting carried away. He was doing his job. He'd seen a ton of stuff in this room Stevie couldn't even imagine. He was *not* getting excited over an older woman who thought she could replace a real adventure with a tamer trip to the Sin on Skin.

"A little lower." He slid the drawing down a little more. "That's good." If he only knew just how good. His fingers on her skin were exciting her.

After he transferred the image to his satisfaction, he had her stretch out on her stomach on the dentist chair, which he had reclined to a completely flat position.

"I'm going to need far more of that ass to show." He started pulling out supplies, leaving her with the dilemma of figuring out how *not* to completely expose herself.

Stevie couldn't think of a better alternative. She slid the skirt down and pulled her blouse up to the middle of her back. Her ass was almost completely exposed. At least she was keen enough to be wearing a thong and not granny panties today. She pulled them down and out of his way too. She took a deep breath and crossed her arms under her chin.

Directly in front of her was a picture of a girl with elaborate butterfly tattoos that covered both ass cheeks. Earlier, she'd seen a photo of a woman with a tat right on her mound. The photos reminded her that Errol didn't care about her ass anyway. Skin, any skin, was merely a canvas to him. Still, she couldn't help feeling self-conscious about lying half-naked in front of a stranger. If she wasn't attracted to the man it probably wouldn't matter, but she was. She closed her eyes.

"Here we go." The machine started up and he rubbed a thin layer of petroleum jelly over her skin. Stevie again tried to think clinically about the situation and not about how his hands were on her bare ass. She concentrated on the sound the machine was making. It reminded her of the high-pitched hum of the broken fluorescent light in the break room at work. He started with what felt like a couple of small lines and the sting of the needle wasn't nearly as bad as she'd thought it was going to be.

Errol drew a few more lines. "How we doing, Stevie?"

Stevie opened her eyes and realized that she faced a mirror so he could see her face and converse with her as he worked. "I'm good."

"I bet you are." He winked and went back to work.

Chapter Two

ॐ

Stevie blushed and looked off to the side. She couldn't help imagining how she might approach him sexually. How had Elizabeth and Cam done it? Monica had come out and simply told Sam she was looking to find a younger man to fulfill her fantasies.

Stevie felt some pressure on her back and glanced around. "You can relax," he said.

She hadn't realized her entire body was clenched, muscles taut. Probably because she felt like her ass was shoved in his face as he concentrated on his work. Oh, she wanted him concentrating on her, but not that way. She distracted herself with the pictures on the wall. More friends and more tat work.

"What do you do for a living, Stevie? I don't get a whole lot of women in suit skirts in here."

This she could talk about; get her mind off being exposed. She started in on her work bio. As she talked, she glanced at the shelf a little off to the left.

The photo prominently displayed there did not help her situation at all.

It was a picture of Errol. He was leaning against a brick wall wearing snug leather pants and motorcycle boots. A red leather vest hung open so she could see all the tats that adorned his upper body. The large tribal tat on his left side twisted and swirled over his shoulder and across his chest and down his torso. On his right side, a series of large skulls and a serpent wrapped around his shoulder and a very pretty pin-up girl covered his right biceps. Stevie could gain fifty pounds and still not have the curves that chick had. She looked past the pin-up girl to see he wore a thick leather bracelet on his wrist and two silver rings on the other hand. His head was tilted down but his dark eyes were looking back up at her from the photo with smoldering-hot desire.

She'd been having a hard enough time with attraction before the photo. But her mouth watered at the best part of the picture—he held up two large leather floggers, one in each hand. The kind of floggers she'd read about in her sexy stories. The kind men used to spank and pleasure submissive girls.

Somehow she still managed to talk pharmaceutical project management even as her imagination ran wild. She could easily see herself tied and bending to his will. The mental images her mind quickly created of playing with Errol and those floggers made her squirm.

"Easy, baby," Errol said and met her gaze in the mirror. "I don't want to mess up this beautiful ass." He glanced over to the picture and back to her and gave her a knowing look. She felt herself blush. "You play?"

"You mean with the...um. No." She needed to get up. She laughingly thought her pussy would be dripping on him soon if she didn't stop her brain from manufacturing fantasies of being tied down naked with his body hovering over hers.

Before she could change the subject back to pharmaceutical testing, he smiled and asked, "You want to though, don't you?" Stevie's mouth fell open and for the first time in years, a man had left her speechless. With a slight nod of his head, he started back to work on her skin. "I see it in your eyes."

He looked back up at her in the mirror. "High-powered businesswomen like you are often in the most need of submission."

Stevie didn't comment. She looked back at that stupid woman with all the butterflies flying out of her ass. She'd read several books about Domination and submission and had downloaded a couple more that were ready to be read. She *did* want it. Had wanted something like that for years, but she was worried about what that said about her state of mind. Did it make her weak? She'd shied away from anything but the books because she was fearful of the impact something like that might have on her life.

More than anything else, though, was the fact that Stevie Jones would never be able to let go like that. How could she be a strong, independent woman if she wanted to be submissive to a man?

He kept working as he spoke, easily looking from the mirror to her naked ass. "In charge all day at the office. Wrapped up in heavy responsibility and stifled by a business suit." He shook his head. "Your body is looking for release. Your mind needs the ability to let go. To let someone else take all the responsibility for your pleasure is a powerful draw."

It sounded like ecstasy. But she didn't think she could really do it. She couldn't give up that much control over anything. The stories were fiction. This was real life. Errol was a real Dom and Stevie Jones was a science geek.

"Don't shake your head, Stevie. You could explore that need, with some encouragement." He moved to change his angle and his arm brushed the naked skin on her ass. She could feel the cool vinyl cushion under her belly and the wetness beneath her pussy. She was having a hard time not fidgeting to work off some of the sexual tension they'd built up in the little room. It was getting hot and her skin stung where he worked. She gripped the chair, trying to think of the pain instead of how his gloved hand felt as held her skin tight.

He leaned closer to her. "It's not easy to submit, but then again, nothing worthwhile is easy." His words were almost a whisper, making his voice even sexier. "Come to my club tonight. I'll teach you how to unlock all the secrets your body holds."

"Club?" *Oh my God.* Stevie was about to explode. She glanced at his face in the picture. It was so strong. So *alpha.*

"I have a club for play parties."

Stevie rose on her elbows and turned her head to look at him. "You mean a dungeon?" Maybe he was a werewolf too.

"Something like that," he grinned. "But don't make it sound so creepy. You'd like it. It's nice enough for a sophisticated woman like you. Hold still."

She settled against the padded chair again, trying to imagine the playrooms she'd read about. They always sounded so exotic. She wanted to find out what one owned and operated by a tattoo artist looked like. Would it be a sparse dungeon or would he use his artistic abilities to make it sexy and sensual? She wanted to go. She *really* wanted to.

She gripped the edge of the chair again when he hit a spot that was a little more sensitive. He lifted the needle as his eyes met hers in the mirror. "Almost got the outline of the cross. You're doing great, Stevie." His fingers caressed the skin around the tender area. It was sweet that he was so conscious of her comfort, but she wasn't particularly worried about the pain.

Good God. Her arousal at the thought of submitting to Errol had almost made her forget she was getting a tattoo.

Why was she getting a tattoo again? Oh yeah. To overcome some fear of going out and making fantasies come true. Now here she was, face-to-face with that very fantasy. The rest of the girls had done it. They'd all stepped up and enjoyed their Cougar Challenge experience. Why couldn't she? Why not go for it?

Stevie gave him a little sexy smile in the mirror. "How old are you?"

He was adjusting something with the machine. "Thirty-two." He looked back to her, an eyebrow raised in question.

"Older than that," she said without embarrassment.

"Not giving it up, huh?" He smiled and began working again. "You can't be far off my age. Your skin is awesome."

Stevie's mind was racing faster than her blood pressure. She couldn't stop thinking about Errol's playroom. About him.

She kept glancing at the photograph while Errol worked away, not saying anything further that wasn't necessary to the tattooing process. She wanted to ask him a thousand questions. She wanted to know what submission was like in real life. Maybe the truth would scare her away from the things she was now considering. Putting herself in the position of submissive was easy when there were only her fantasies and a good book.

Stevie's sex life had been incredibly boring thus far. Her husband had been one of the lab geeks she met in graduate school. His idea of sex had been as hot as a yearly physical and included about that much contact. She'd always been the one to initiate anything. He would have rather been in the lab than the bed any day. The marriage ended over diverging career paths before she'd ever mentioned any of her desires or fantasies to her ex. She'd never mentioned them to anyone.

She'd pretty much written off sex as no big deal, all hype and no dividend. It wasn't until Monica managed to nag her enough to read one of the erotic novels that she'd even felt excited about what sex could be. Secretly, she'd read well over a dozen of them in the last few months. The books had managed to bring all her unlabeled desires to the surface.

Now her body and her brain were having a major disconnect. Her body *wanted*. All the time. She remembered some statistics about men thinking of sex every seven minutes. She was close to breaking that average. Hell, these days she masturbated more than most men. Her body was alive again after years of feeling that sex just wasn't worth the effort. Her body wanted her to play along with the Cougar Challenge and find someone who could fulfill the fantasies those sexy novels had reignited.

Her brain was a little more skeptical. Her brain knew that real life often let down hope and left expectations unfulfilled. She felt the want between her legs and wished it were otherwise. She would let him finish, go back to her life and be happy with the tattoo. That, she was sure, wouldn't be a disappointment. "It's all fantasy in those books anyway," she mumbled.

He stopped working. "Books about fantasies? Sounds good."

"Did I say that out loud?" She lifted her head and let it fall back against her arm. "I'm as much a dork as Monica accused me of being."

He started working again. "You've read BDSM books, huh?" His hand wiped away some extra ink. It was slow and deliberate, making Stevie think he was stroking rather than simply cleaning his work surface. God. Her imagination was getting away with her tonight. She needed a drink.

"Not really about BDSM. More like fiction that had it in there." She couldn't believe she was admitting it. "The content is probably absurdly inaccurate. You know romance..." She trailed off with a waving hand, hoping he'd drop the subject.

"Really? I've read a romance novel that got it pretty good. Submission is a little different for everyone. So is Dominance," he explained very nonchalantly. "What was it you found appealing, Stevie?" He didn't look up from the tat.

She hesitated to answer—but then figured if she answered his questions, maybe he'd answer a few for her. If she treated the subject clinically, took herself out of the fantasy, it could be an interesting conversation. Maybe she'd learn something that would calm her desire. "I think it's as you said. Strong women often have a hard time finding someone who's as strong as they are. The sexy werewolves in the stories are hard to come by in real life. So when women do find an alpha wolf, it's freeing to let go and not be responsible for the sexual aspects of the relationship."

"There are people who live their entire lives in that kind of Dom/sub relationship," Errol explained. "Not only as part of sexual expression. For some, the power exchange is 24/7. Food, clothes, jobs; the Dominant in the relationship makes all the decisions. The subs aren't responsible for any aspect of their own lives."

Stevie turned again to look directly at him. "Really?" She couldn't imagine that. "Not very sexy at all if you ask me."

He chuckled. "What you've read about is what some of us call a bedroom sub."

"Interesting. The stories I've read did include limits and safety issues, but nothing as extreme as turning an entire life over to a Dom." She relaxed, rested her chin on her arms again and then wondered…

"Do you have a sub like that? For whom you make all the decisions?"

"'For whom'?" He chuckled again. "First, not all subs are women." Stevie knew that but didn't interrupt him. "And no. I don't. I like to play, but I don't have a sub who's *mine,* or what we called 'collared', right now."

It *was* turning out to be an interesting conversation. "What's the dungeon like, Alpha Werewolf?"

"Wouldn't you like to know, closet sub?" He looked up at her. "You get turned on by the thought of a sexy, strong werewolf tying you up and having his way with you?"

Stevie looked away. Oh yeah. She did. She'd thought she could keep the conversation clinical. He was making that very hard. "I'm just trying to figure out if the books are accurate at all." If the words coming out of her mouth didn't ring true to *her,* she was sure Errol wasn't buying them.

"Tell you what. For research purposes, I'll run down a typical list of things one would ask a potential sub about limits. You tell me what yours are, from what you've read, and I'll tell you if your little books come from fantasy or reality."

"That's not necessary."

Her hip stung a bit as he wiped away extra ink. She wanted to know and then again, she didn't. She liked this new fantasy of playing with Errol. She could use it, blog about it and masturbate to it. If he told her she wasn't up to snuff to be a sub, she'd be disappointed.

"No, but it could be fun. For example—have you ever been spanked, Stevie? Has anyone reddened this ass before?"

She felt the hitch in her own voice when she answered. "No."

"Been tied up?" She shook her head. "Blindfolded?" Again she shook her head. She was beginning to feel embarrassed by her lack of playful experiences.

He turned to the machine and began changing out some piece of his equipment. His back was to her when the next words came out of his mouth. "Ever had anal sex?"

She didn't answer.

"Have you ever touched yourself there?"

She had after reading one of the books and was surprised at how much she'd enjoyed the sensation. She still didn't answer.

"So, some anal play would be permissible, but you're not ready for actual anal penetration?"

Stevie laughed. Now he was the one being clinical.

"I'll take that as a yes." He turned back to her. "How about public play? Was there anything about that in your books?"

She nodded. "Yes, there was."

He again stroked her. "You know, if you make me drag all this out, this tat is going to be huge. If you need to, close your eyes and let the answers just come out. They're words at this point, Stevie. They only power they have is the power to excite you right this minute. You're already there, so have some fun with it. I promise not to do anything but ink you."

She made eye contact with him again. His gaze was steady, his expression serious. He wanted her to trust him. For a second, she thought he might be genuinely interested in what her needs would be if *they* played.

It couldn't be. She was a decade older than him and surely with all his connections at the club, he would never be interested in a science geek. He would more likely be playing with someone like Angel. Stevie brought herself back to the conversation. He was teasing her to pass the time as he worked. That's all. She could enjoy it as well. She nodded.

He worked for a moment before asking another question. "Do you like the idea of being in a playroom, of being watched or playing with more than one person?"

She closed her eyes and took in a fortifying breath. "Yes. The idea of it." But the actuality of being that bold was beyond her. "I'm reasonably sure I couldn't do it though."

"Why not? In your own fantasies, are the characters all men or both men and women?"

"In the fantasies, men and women." But they were just that—fantasies. Even so, she was getting incredibly hot saying it out loud. She'd never voiced anything about her sexual desires before.

He patted her lower back. "Where do you think your pain threshold would be? High, low, somewhere in between?" He pinched her bare thigh and left his hand there.

The slick, smooth feel of the glove added to the mental images of him dancing through her head. Was this guy for real?

She laughed again. She was happy he'd pinched her. Now she knew she wasn't dreaming. At this moment, if she had the inclination, she could play with a sexy, young alpha werewolf. But she was getting the idea that maybe she wasn't ready for the wolf. "Probably the lowest."

"You'll be surprised." He rubbed that spot again.

It sounded as if the wolf was ready for her.

Chapter Three

ജ

Stevie threw the gym bag in her car and hopped in. She didn't look back at her condo, she didn't hesitate and she wasn't changing her mind. Nope. She was going. No reservations. Errol had extended the formal invitation when he finished the tattoo and the teasing conversation about her limits and she'd accepted. A quick trip to the house to clean up and get some clothes and she was on her way.

She glanced at the navigation system as the female voice instructed her to make the next left. She let out a nervous giggle. That would be the first of many instructions she'd receive in the next few hours and probably the easiest to follow.

Her mind was moving faster than the car. Being the scientist, she wanted to understand why she had decided *now* was the time to try this. Was it the blog? Had she spent too much time living vicariously though her friends? She didn't think so because until today, she was quite certain this would remain fantasy.

But here she was, driving to Errol's club.

Errol. She'd been attracted to him from the moment she saw him. He had been kind and teasing, and yet he could demand her attention with a look. Was she more attracted to him than she was letting herself believe? She found herself worrying if she would be good enough for him. Would he be interested in her beyond the playing?

She shook her head. She was just nervous over the situation, as she should be. She was about to pull onto the club's street. He'd dubbed his tattoo parlor Sin on Skin and she felt as if her tat and her experience with him reflected the name. She shuddered at the name of the club.

Sin City.

The address belonged to the last of four businesses in a commercial office complex. She pulled her Volvo station wagon into a spot right at the door of a nondescript building. Gray brick sides and a single blacked-out glass entry door gave Stevie no clue what lay ahead. Stevie snickered to herself over the very vanilla, innocuous white letters that served as a sign for the club. The letters were only about two inches high and looked more like the lettering you would expect on an office inside a building, not a sign on a front door.

Sin City sat near an insurance agency and cat adoption center. Evidently Errol wanted nothing brash or showy to catch unwanted attention. There were no other cars in the parking lot this long after business hours on a Friday. She checked her watch as she got out of the car. Was she early? It was almost ten.

She heard the telltale sound of a door unlocking before it swung outward. Errol stood in the doorway. He didn't look surprised that she'd shown up. He smiled and gestured for her to come inside.

Errol ushered her past the empty front office. "On a party night, someone would be here checking memberships. We're members only."

Stevie swallowed. She could smell that cologne again. He took her bag and she immediately wished he hadn't; clinging to the handle had been comforting. She wasn't exactly afraid, more like apprehensive and aroused over all the different sensations and emotions she was experiencing. At least she was feeling something.

Errol headed down a long hall. If he noticed her nervous condition, he didn't comment. Stevie figured there wasn't much she would do over the next few hours he wouldn't notice and respond to.

"There are a few rules. Most everybody knows everybody else. We never talk about other members outside these walls and I will never pass any boundaries you set. You say when. Red. Yellow. Green. Just like stop lights. You clear on that?"

She nodded.

"In here, it's *Sir* from now on."

Dang. She knew that. Not that the fictional scenarios from her erotic stories were going to give her all the info she needed for the real experience, but she hoped some of it was close. Errol had promised she could leave at any moment, and he would stop at any time. He'd given her all his contact information and his driver's license number, all of which she'd sent to Monica in an email. Monica wouldn't see it until she got home from another wild date with her younger man, Sam—and judging by the stories Monica had shared on the blog, it'd be late tonight—but she'd have it.

Stevie wasn't worried. She trusted her gut, and her gut had decided to trust Errol. Why, she wasn't so sure. She liked the way he'd eased her into the earlier discussion. He was light and charming. He seemed to understand what she needed more than she did. She needed to know if she could let go. She needed to feel sexy. Hell, she needed to *feel*.

They entered a large lounge area with a couple of dark red suede sofas and a large-screen TV. All very modern. Bright abstract artwork adorned the walls.

"Did you bring the uniform I requested?"

Stevie nodded, her throat suddenly dry.

They followed a second short hallway to another door. Stepping through it, she saw what looked like a hotel suite. "This is my private area. You can change back here then we'll talk. Wine or beer?"

Stevie didn't really need to change. The uniform consisted of black high heels, thigh-high stockings and a black thong, so it was all under her clothes. She only needed to strip. "Wine."

There was a bathroom, a large bed, and a sitting area with a credenza and another TV. She managed a few steps farther into the suite, stopping short of the bed. Errol followed behind her and over to the credenza where there was a couple wine bottles sitting on a black lacquer tray. The colors in the room were muted grays and blacks, with very masculine, boxy geometric designs coordinating the fabrics in the sitting area with the bed linens. Off to her right was another closed door.

Stevie let her skirt fall to the ground. She took a big breath and stepped out if it. Even knowing Errol was behind her and fully dressed, that didn't seem so hard. After all, he'd already been rather intimate with her naked backside. It was removing the shirt and bra that was a bit more intimidating. Her fingers shook as she fumbled with the buttons. The shirt hit the floor. She twisted the front-clasping bra and unhooked it.

This was it. She was forty-four. He was thirty-two. She was skinny and very white. He was muscular and tan. If he rejected her after seeing her naked, she would die of embarrassment. She straightened her back. But worse, if she chickened out she would never forgive herself. She dropped the bra.

"This can come off now." He peeled away the small bandage that covered her tattoo. "You told me your limits, but what do you want out of submission, Stevie?" His voice was close. She covered her small breasts with her hands and stood where she was, still facing the far wall. No mirror to use as a buffer here.

He reached around and offered her the drink. She took the glass and a quick gulp of the sweet wine. "I'm not sure how to answer that."

"Well. Some subs want to be spanked—hit—hard. It's about the pain. It's about taking it for their master. But I don't see you as the type. As a matter of fact, I don't think the pain is what you're all hot and bothered by at all. Is it?"

It wasn't, but she wasn't at all sure how Errol understood that with as little conversation as they had managed when setting up this meeting back at the tattoo parlor. They'd talked about her limits, but not her needs.

He whispered in her ear, "Tell me what you *think* you want. It's been a long time since I've played with a newbie. I want to understand you."

She was already wet. Standing open and vulnerable in nothing but heels and a thong, his presence behind her, looming, was sexy in itself. Stevie had found her alpha werewolf. "Why do you want to play with *me*?" She was glad she couldn't see his face.

His breath was warm against her ear. "You're a strong, intelligent woman, Stevie. Why wouldn't I?" His hand ran gently down her left side. "A strong female who can submit is far more interesting than a mindless girl who throws herself under your flogger because she has no sense of herself. I don't want a woman who needs me to form her completely. I want what every man wants—a beautiful, smart partner. I just want her to *want* to give."

Stevie fidgeted with the glass, trying to understand the difference.

He ran a finger down her spine, tracing the outline of each bone. "Think of it this way—in your office, do you like working with people who challenge you and themselves, people who push the envelope and make things happen? Or the yes-men type who are predictable and wimpy?"

That she understood.

"So, what is it Stevie needs?"

She wasn't sure what to say. Wasn't sure how to verbalize it. She tried to think back to the characters in the stories and what had most appealed to her from their experiences. What had made her so hot?

"Honesty will get you exactly what you want. Maybe not exactly how you thought you wanted it, but the truth will help you."

His voice made her want a lot of things. But how did she voice them without sounding like a slut? She took another drink

"I want to be completely sexual, with no hangs-up, no fears." She looked at the floor. "No accountability for the success of the experience. I want to be the object of the experience. I want sex to feel like something other than a chore."

"You want to be a slut?" He walked past her, not looking her over yet, no judgment in his voice. "You want your body to be the instrument of pleasure for others? Is it that simple? We can start there."

She looked down again. He was right, of course. It wasn't that simple, but he'd given her something to play with.

"Say it for me, Stevie. Tell me what you want."

She took a deep breath. Yes. That was exactly what she wanted to be. "I want to be a slut."

In no particular hurry, he turned to her. A wily smile came across his face. His eyes moved hungrily up her body, stopping at her chest. She held the glass in both hands so her arms were covering her breasts His glance darted to her eyes and he expectantly raised his eyebrows. It was an unspoken order. Stevie dropped her hands to her side.

"That's my girl."

The praise was for more than simply anticipating his demand, it was also for her appearance. His eyes were heated and his jaw tense. This young, hot man wasn't looking at her as if she were old or skinny. It was clear Errol liked what he saw.

"Through the next door is the playroom. We'll start with a little intro to submission for you, my executive slut. That's what you want? To be played with and used and have no need to moralize or worry about internal inhibitions? For me to take the responsibility for you being a dirty girl?"

He pushed open the door to her right. She walked past him into the next room and he pointed to a small bench at the far end. "Walk to the bench. Bend over it and put your hands by the cuffs."

Stevie was surprised at her lack of fear. The fact that he was fully clothed and standing there watching her as she walked away almost naked was so sexy. It made her *feel* sexy. She couldn't remember ever feeling particularly sexy when she was naked.

The room was dim and larger than she'd anticipated. The walls were dark, with near life-sized photos of nude, highly tattooed men and women every six feet or so. A couple of long racks with lots of hooks holding the tools of Errol's nighttime trade graced the walls on opposite sides of the room. Light flickered from artificial candles in sconces on the walls. The sensual lighting made her skin look warm and inviting.

She strutted without looking back, glancing at the unusual furnishings placed around the room. Some she recognized from her favorite erotic stories. There were three different benches for various spanking positions and in the far corner was a large St. Andrew's Cross. She passed a tall metal cage and a swing that hung from the ceiling, and every piece of equipment had plenty of space around it. There were beanbag chairs and large wedge-shaped cushions scattered everywhere. She figured when this place was full, it could accommodate close to fifty people.

She stopped at the bench Errol had indicated. It was almost waist high and at least three feet in depth—to support her upper body, she guessed—with a kneeling platform. Like most of the equipment, soft black leather covered both the bench and the platform. Supple green-leather cuffs were attached to chains fastened to the edge of the bench farthest from her. Stevie bent forward. Her naked stomach shivered from the cold of the leather as she lowered her torso to rest her head on the bench, a couple inches from the cuffs. Her arms were bent, her hands next to the cuffs. Her legs had naturally spread to avoid the kneeling platform, her feet firmly planted on either side. Her ass was open and exposed and so was her pussy.

Music started playing in the background, but she still heard Errol's approach from behind. "Now, tomorrow night," he said as he moved in front of her and knelt so they would be eye to eye, "there'll be a party here."

He'd removed his shirt. Stevie looked over his muscled chest and could now see the entire tribal design. It covered his left shoulder and snaked across his chest, appearing alive and moving in the low lighting. She caught the smell of fresh soap. "This room will be full of players and voyeurs." He buckled the first cuff on her small wrist and looked her over with hungry eyes. As he spoke, he ran his fingers down her free arm. The gentleness of his touch made her wonder if the books had been correct.

He got the second buckle latched and tested the chains with a little tug. "How are you, Stevie?" He looked her in the eye. The lengths of chain allowed her to reach far enough forward to touch the design on his shoulder as he knelt in front of her.

"I'm okay," she said as she traced one of the designs. Okay was an understatement. She felt the leather of the cuffs on her wrists and it was as if, by fastening those simple restraints, Errol had set her free of all her hangs-ups. She didn't care if her boobs were too small or if she was over forty. Laugh lines didn't matter here. She didn't care about budgeting initiatives or maintaining quality testing standards. She wanted his hands on her now.

He walked around to her side. "Red. Yellow. Green. You don't say anything else unless I ask for something more specific." His hand landed sharply on her ass. Not hard, but it had a sting. Stevie trembled.

"Yes Sir," she replied as he rubbed the same spot to soothe. His fingers were coming very close to her pussy. She tried to raise her rear, to get them there, but she was on her toes already in the heels.

"I like the intimacy of bare-hand spanking. I like to feel the reaction of the skin under my hand, the warmth it creates." She wiggled to get him to move again. "I see you do too." He smacked again, a little farther down, getting thigh and ass. Stevie gripped the short chains the cuffs were attached to. Her entire body was alive at the moment.

Errol reached down and ran his fingers up the inside of her silk-covered thigh. "How we doing?"

"Green!" she gasped. The time spent in the tattoo parlor, the time spent driving home and back here had made her horny beyond belief.

He pulled the thong over her ass. She lifted one leg at a time so he could slip the panties off. His fingers lightly brushed her pussy.

"You have a very lovely kitty, my executive slut." Two fingers slid into the folds, slipping around and easily finding her clit. "From your little books, you know the rule about asking permission to come, I presume?"

For a half second she regretted telling Errol about reading the books. Then again, giving him that secret was how he'd known of her interest. It was how he'd known she was aware of what she'd agreed to, how she was able to discuss her limitations before ever leaving the tattoo parlor. It was how she had managed to find herself tied down by this sexy man. "Yes."

A harder slap landed on her thigh. The unexpected sting made her body rock forward and she lost her footing, stumbling to balance with her feet spread around the kneeling pad. She immediately corrected her mistake. "Yes Sir."

"Lift your ass back up for me." His fingers returned to her aching pussy and started to rub her clit, making it hard to comply. She situated her feet so her ass was high in the air. With his free hand, he pulled open a drawer on the side of the bench. He moved some things around and then placed a small vibrator, a tube of lube and a butt plug on the bench. He reached back in before tossing a couple condoms beside her as well.

The attention to her clit didn't stop. She wanted to come so badly. "I need to come, Sir."

His fingers stopped. "Huh. That didn't sound much like asking permission, slut. It sounded like an executive order from some bossy blonde." He leaned down, brushed her hair away from her ear and kissed her gently on the cheek. "Remember, Stevie, this is about you submitting to me. It is my responsibility to make all the decisions. You come or not…" He stood back up and picked up the butt plug from the table. "It's up to me." He rolled it across the small of her back.

He returned to fingering her clit. "Next time, I stop and leave you here." She felt him pick up the small toy on her back. She'd had very little experience with ass play and had told him so in their "limits" conversation, but she'd said it was okay to try some. She hadn't expected him to go there so soon.

He rubbed the soft toy in her juices, using it to tease her clit. Her thighs were starting to tremble with the need to come. She felt sweat forming on her belly where it rested on the leather bench. He dipped the butt plug into her pussy and twisted it around, pulling it out and rubbing it around the rim of her back hole, the unusual sensation making her pussy clench. Then he squeezed a generous amount of lube onto her ass, the cold liquid running down the folds of her pussy and onto her thigh.

Then he slid the plug into her ass. No easing, no teasing — he pushed it all the way home.

"Holy Toledo!" Stevie said and tightened her muscles to lessen the sensation. The burning in her ass intensified the yearning in her pussy.

He walked around in front of her. "Hold it in." She nodded her head. Speaking wasn't a good idea right this moment. Her body was on fire. He was standing directly in front of her with his jeans hanging loose on his hips. "Unbutton the jeans."

Stevie struggled to reach him and work the buttons on his jeans. Had to be button-fly Levi's. Even though she had a bit of length on the chains, she had to stretch until she managed the task. His head and chest were bare of hair, but there was a small trail of soft black hair that led down his abdomen. His cock was still hidden from view by the denim that lingered on his hips. The short chains were attached to the bench mere inches apart and even with the extra play in the chains, it wouldn't allow her arms to open wide enough to push the jeans any farther down. But she tried getting a hand full of fabric and pulling at the denim anyway.

"Easy. You might catch something important there." He pushed the jeans a little farther down. The head of a wolf tattoo peeked from his left hip. It was the one from his album. He'd said he liked it back at the parlor. Evidently he liked it a lot.

Looks like I found my alpha werewolf!

Chapter Four

∾

"What do you want, slut? And tell me in the most vulgar vocabulary your higher-educated mind can manufacture."

She looked up at him. Oh my. He wanted her to talk dirty. It'd been hard enough just to say "slut". Now he wanted her to be vulgar.

"You're blushing. You are the most interesting woman, Stevie." He sweetly brushed her cheek with his fingers and wiggled his hips. His pants shifted a little bit lower. The wolf was showing some serious teeth. Her gaze followed the line of black hair that led down from his navel, teasing her. "Tell me."

She wanted to see him, to touch him. "I want to, um. I want to see you naked." The intense heat from her ass and pussy had made it all the way to her face. She felt the rush, and she hadn't even said what she'd wanted to say. She wanted to let go. She wanted to be the slut.

"I'm sure you do. But that's not what my little executive slut really wants, is it?" He dropped the pants. His cock sprang free. It was smooth and hung slightly to the left and he wasn't even all the way hard. She wanted to get him there. "Tell me or we stop, Stevie. You're mine while you're here." He reached over her, putting his cock right in her face as he nudged the plug.

She squirmed. "Sir."

He wiggled the plug back and forth. "Tell me." He rubbed his cock against her lips.

"I want to suck you," she stammered. Why was this so hard? She was tied naked. He was wiggling a butt plug in her ass. What were a few naughty words at this point? He slapped her ass again, right over the plug.

"Last chance." He stood, his cock now raging hard and right in front of her face. He reached to pull up his jeans.

Stevie looked away, every muscle in her body taut. She was breathing hard out of anxiousness. Had the music gotten louder? Until she'd been spread and tied and opened to him, she'd had no idea how deeply she'd been repressing her own sexual desires, her own needs. She wanted him. She wanted *this*.

"I want to suck your cock. I want it in my mouth while I have the plug in my ass. I want you to use me." The words were freeing. Her body relaxed.

With no comment on her statement, he rubbed his cock against her lips. The reward was giving her what she wanted. She fought to take him into her mouth, but he teased her by pulling just out of her reach. The position was awkward. She heard herself let out a whimper.

He again rewarded her with his cock, only this time, he let her have it all. She took him into her mouth, letting him press to the back of her throat, and she didn't care. When he eased back some, she hungrily licked and nibbled at his cock, enjoying the feel of his skin on her lips, the taste of him.

Errol moved and groaned. He held her head and fucked her face. "Suck it hard. That's it, Stevie." She looked up to see that his head was tilted back, eyes closed. "So good," he murmured. Each command made her greedy. Greedy for his appreciation. He was enjoying her, appreciating her for the pleasure her body was giving him.

She slowed her efforts when she felt his hands fumbling with the chain on one of her cuffs. "Don't stop until I tell you." She went about her labor, taking a moment to lick around the base of his cock and trying to suck one of his balls into her mouth. The angle was hard, and she couldn't manage it.

Her second hand came free from the chains but both still wore the cuffs. "Stand up."

She pouted her regret. "Yes Sir." As she stood, she realized her neck was stiff from the extended time in that position. He kicked off his boots and the jeans that had been in a sexy pile at his feet. Even if she hadn't realized her neck was stiff, he had, and he rubbed her shoulders as he guided her to her right.

She found herself in front of a huge square frame with ropes strung from side to side and top to bottom at varying angles, making a web. Also something she recognized from the erotic novels. "You can drop the shoes if you need to."

"Green," she said without much thought. She wore those heels all day long, five days a week. She needed to come really badly, but her feet were fine.

"Good." He clipped the cuffs to the ropes, slightly above her head but not fully extended. With the play of the ropes and the position of the clips, she could move her arms a little. "Spread your legs." She complied with the order.

He put his finger on the plug and gave it a wiggle. The action sent a new wave of pleasure through her body. "I need to come. Please."

He sauntered naked around the frame. "Well. That was almost a request and not an order, but not quite." He walked to the wall and grabbed a red leather bag from a series of pegs that held floggers, riding crops and a few things she didn't have a clue about. He reached for one of those mystery objects. It was a spanking device, she was sure. It looked like a bundle of switches. She fidgeted a bit.

"I think, Stevie, that you are very much enjoying yourself." He walked toward her with a very sexy smile. He dropped the bundle of switches on the floor and hung the bag from a hook on the frame. He was still on the opposite side of the web, gazing at her front, which was completely exposed through the ropes. Oh boy, was she enjoying herself.

Her breasts were pushed through the web where she leaned against it and he bent his head, running his tongue around her nipple and sucking it. The warmth and the sight of him there was hot. Her little nipples tightened into beads and he twisted one. The slight pinch made her suck in her breath and she felt her body quiver.

"So responsive," he praised.

To tease her, he took his time digging around in that red bag, mumbling to himself too softly for her to make anything out over the music. A set of nipple clamps and a blindfold were finally pulled from the bag. "We're getting to the good part, Stevie. You ready to really be a slut for me?"

She had to swallow. If what they had already done wasn't the good part, she wasn't sure she'd survive the rest. She looked down to his still very erect cock.

She wanted the good part.

"Green." She gripped the ropes and tried not to giggle in her excited state. He reached through the ropes and tossed the blindfold over her shoulder. She felt the toy in her ass with every slight movement of her body and watched as he closed a clamp on one of her nipples. Stevie whimpered again. The pressure on that tender tissue was overwhelming when added to the other sensations. She gripped the ropes tightly. After a second the pain settled into an additional sensual assault on her nervous system. Her ass, her pussy and now her nipple were all sending the same message to her brain. *Come.*

He walked around the frame and tied the blindfold around her eyes. The loss of vision was more like adding a sensation than taking one away. She tried to listen, to know what was coming next, to anticipate. "Sexy Stevie." He ran one finger over her ass and down to her pussy. Stevie held her breath. "You're made for this. You give so well the first time out."

She *felt* as if she was made for it. But she'd seen some of the severe whips and canes on the wall. Would she need to go that far to enjoy the experience? She didn't like the thought of that so much.

He fingered her clit again. "You've been a very good slut so far. I'd love to show you off." He leaned in close enough that she could feel his breath on her cheek. "I think my little executive slut would like that too." He licked her ear and let his breath tickle her. "I think you'd love to have an audience as you let yourself be used."

His words tickled her imagination. She knew she wasn't ready for that kind of play, but it made her feel good to hear his praise. Stevie shivered at the mental image created as his breath brushed her ears and his finger flicked her clit. The idea of being watched was much more appealing than the whips. She imagined people there now, watching her, imagined leaning over with her pussy exposed and her ass plugged.

"Maybe you want to be the party toy for a night, open and exposed to whomever I let play with you."

She could take no more. "May I come?"

"Already?" He moved away from her ear so he could play with the plug again and wiggle it some more. "Hold it for me."

She was dancing on her toes, squeezing all her muscles, working not to come. She felt his fingers leave her and she gasped at the loss of sensation. The nipple clamp came off and the surge of pain that followed from the blood returning to her flesh added yet another type of intense heat she'd never experienced. "Please!" She knew she sounded desperate, but she was. "Please, Sir."

"Stick your ass high and spread those legs as far as you can." Stevie almost collapsed when she felt him kneel behind her. He spread her cheeks and pulled her pussy to his lips. Stevie tried to hold it. She did. She wanted it to be his decision, but she couldn't.

"Errol!"

The orgasm started. She felt the muscles of her pussy tighten and a wave rush through her. He pulled out the plug, adding what felt like an additional orgasm to the experience.

She gripped the ropes as tight as she could to hold herself up so he could keep licking her. She screamed at the pleasure of the mix of sensations. She couldn't see anything. All she could do was feel. And she felt everything in that stinging nipple, in her ass and in her pussy all at the same time. She felt the coarseness of the ropes in her hands, her weight pressing on the balls of her feet. Her pulse seemed to thump with the beat of the music.

Stevie stood trembling, holding the ropes for support, breath ragged.

Errol tsked at her from behind. "Oh, my little executive slut, you came without permission." She strained to turn, to see him, but the blindfold was still in place. She felt him lean over her and unclip the cuffs. "Back to the spanking table with you. Lose the shoes." She kicked them off and he led her across the room by the arm. She stumbled over the kneeling bench. "Kneel this time."

Her knees found the top of the kneeling platform. She let her upper body fall over the bench, wrists at the edge, ready to be fastened. Errol brushed and lightly tapped her upper thighs with the bundle of switches. Maybe they were bamboo, she had no clue, but the sound of them hitting her skin reminded her of a snare drum. She shuddered, not sure if it was from fear he would overdo it or the remaining excitement from an incredible orgasm.

"This is one of my favorite little toys, Stevie. Not to worry. It's not as aggressive as it seems."

Errol tapped lightly up and down her thighs with the unusual flogger. No pain, just a new sensation added to her blindfolded world. Then the raining down of the switches intensified, as if Errol were warming up to something stronger. As he got closer to her exposed pussy, she found herself leaning toward it, tilting her hips to expose herself even more.

A sudden change in sensation shocked her when he used his hand and slapped her pussy. Several fast slaps made her push her knees off the bench to stand. She burned. She throbbed. It felt as if electricity flowed from her clit to her brain.

"Down." His order was stern.

She kneeled again, reaching for the chains she knew were there. He may not have bound her, but she needed something to grasp, something to ground her in reality. He slapped her pussy once again. The shock of the sting on her lips was lessened but she had the thrill of not knowing *when* he'd slap her again—and she didn't care.

He rubbed her clit. Stevie pushed against his hand, wanting him inside her. Wanting to be fucked, if only by his fingers.

"You want something?" he asked as he dipped two fingers inside her wet folds. "You ready to be fucked?"

"Yes Sir," she said with enthusiasm.

He pulled his fingers away. "I'm not ready yet, Stevie. I want to play with your lovely body a little more. I have a few more things I want to do to that pussy."

Stevie groaned aloud. No way could she take much more of this without coming again. "I still have to show you what happens to little executive sluts who come without permission."

The bamboo landed hard on her ass. She jumped and yelped. That one was *not* a little playful slap. He'd stung her good. She felt herself blush—she was bent over, asking for whatever he dished out. She was being a slut. And she was so turned on by the freedom of not caring about anything, by only feeling, by not being responsible for his pleasure or her own.

Again he swung and let the switches bite her tender skin, this time on the backs of her thighs. Immediately, Errol rubbed the offended areas to soothe her burning skin. The opposing sensations of the sting and the gentle caress were exaggerated by the inability to see him or the room or anticipate what his next action might be.

"Bad little sluts get punished, Stevie," his teasing voice said close to her ear. His warm body was leaning over her, his chest against her back. "But you didn't try to avoid the pain, you didn't let go of the chains even though you could. Very nice. You still okay?"

Stevie knew he had stayed well within her limits. It was her first real test. She'd done it. She loved the tone of his voice as he praised her. She loved the feeling of being the object of his attentions. She felt wanted and cared for. He'd done all those things for her — she hoped this was doing something for him as well. "Green."

"The pain level, is it at your limit?"

She nodded her head in agreement. Errol moved away from her. "You are a very good little slut. Your ass is the prettiest shade of pink. It makes the emerald in the Ankh stand out even more." She heard the distinctive hum of a vibrator and wiggled in fear. If he used that, she'd come again. She already wanted to.

She felt the slow vibration on her inner thigh and stilled. His other hand started to caress the skin around her still-sensitive ass. The vibrator was making small circles on the tender, sensitive skin of her upper thigh, moving closer to her pussy. The fingers of his other hand were making the same circles, inching closer to her ass. She gripped the chains harder.

The sensation, the anticipation, the darkness was memorizing. It made her shift her weight, tilt her hips and push her pussy closer to the sensation, wanting.

"I think you should come play with us tomorrow, Stevie." He touched the vibrator to her clit.

"Please, Sir! May I come?" The thought of being in this position with others watching jacked up her need for release. She wanted it *now*.

"Tomorrow? Of course you can. Right now? No." Two slippery fingers pressed into her ass.

"Oh! Please," she pleaded, raising her head but not pulling away from the ecstasy her body was experiencing.

"My friend Eva and her sub are my special guests tomorrow night, Stevie. We could make you the play toy for the night. Spread you out as the buffet. You could submit to the three of us. Imagine the sensations, the knowledge that people are watching you."

Her currently hyped-up imagination took no time to create an image of three people using her body for pleasure. That mental image added to the vibration on her sensitive clit and the sensation of his fingers stretching her tender opening. "Please, Sir!"

"Finally. Yes, Stevie. Come." He pulled his fingers away from her ass and added pressure to the vibrator, rubbing it across her clit.

At his command, her muscles tensed further and she let the sensations assaulting her body do their magic. She came, whimpering and wanting.

She lay panting across the bench when she heard the telltale sound of a ripping condom package. "Tell me what you want, slut. Tell me." A few seconds later, his hands grasped her hips. She felt his cock slide between her thighs, nudging to gain entry.

"Oh God! Fuck me. Fuck me, please."

He pressed in a little bit at a time. The teasing wasn't going to stop with his penetration. Stevie was amazed at his self-control. He'd held back through everything, managing his needs as well as hers. She remembered the sultry look in his eyes in that photo at Sin on Skin. She imagined him looking at her like that now as he stood behind her, looking down on his artwork.

He pulled back and then fucked her hard. No longer holding back his needs. He pounded, grunting at his pleasure. Stevie tried to match him, to push back and return his fervor, but he wanted control over that as well. Holding her hips so she couldn't do anything but take, he dropped the pace to a slow, grinding, circular rhythm. She felt every bit of him as he moved inside her. His cock was as fabulous as she had imagined it would be when she'd briefly sampled it with her lips.

After all the teasing and tormenting, this slow, sensual fuck was perfect. She dropped the chains and gripped the leather at the edge of the bench to try to keep herself from moving. She felt his shaft as it slid in and out of her very sensitive pussy. She was going to come a third time.

"Sir..."

"Yes, Stevie. Come, baby." He ground even harder. She could feel his thighs as they rubbed the inside of hers. She tried to hold off a little bit, but she burst again.

"Errol!"

He came when she did, growling when her muscles tightened around his cock. He slid in and out slowly a few more times after he came.

Stevie was exhausted. Errol helped her to stand and removed the blindfold.

"Hi." His smile made him look boyish.

"Hi."

"You okay?" He walked her to the bedroom where she'd dropped her clothes and eased her onto the bed. He crawled in beside her and started to remove the cuffs.

"You were so sexy in there, Stevie."

She smiled as he got the first cuff off. "Yeah, but I'm guessing that was small time compared to what you're used to." Since he owned the joint, she was sure he normally played far more hardcore than she would ever be able to do.

"It's not about extremes. Not always. Not for everyone. For me...I want a strong woman I can have a life with who happens to be submissive in nature. I like you. I like that you're here and participating so freely with someone you just met. They say just showing up is eighty percent of life. And sexy Stevie, you showed up in a big way today." He smiled gently, his fingers caressing her face.

She tried to snuggle up to him and felt the burn of her new tattoo. He'd managed to brush it a bit in all the excitement. "I think you scratched my tattoo at the end there. It stings a little."

He gave her an incredulous look. "Is that *all* that stings?"

"What else would sting?" She laughed, unable to keep a straight face. He chuckled with her. Man, he was cute when he smiled.

He squeezed her ass. "I'll have to make sure you don't ask that question next time."

* * * * *

"Do you actually live here?" She was heading to the bathroom for a shower. The building may have been on an office park, but he had created a comfortable space that resembled a studio apartment or luxe hotel suite.

"Nah. I like to stay here when the parties run late. It's a perk of owning the place. But a full apartment was against the zoning rules. No kitchen." He was buttoning up his shirt, getting ready to run out and get them some food from the bar and grill down the street.

"The complex management doesn't mind the parties?"

"I own all the buildings. Bought the land cheap a few years back and went in with a developer to build. I've got a couple office parks across the north side of the city," he said, to her surprise. He picked up his keys and threw her a black T-shirt and a wink. "I'll be right back."

Stevie took a warm shower, careful of the new tattoo. She thought back over all the emotions she had experienced with Errol. She wondered if, had she found out about this submission stuff earlier in her life, things would have been different. She'd never been very open in the bedroom. No one had known what she needed, not even her. She'd primarily been left unfulfilled by her sexual relationships and so had her lovers.

She'd enjoyed the play with Errol and she wanted to do it again, but she wanted…more. Tonight had been an awakening, and she had the Cougar Challenge to thank. Monica would be so impressed. She now knew this is what they'd all needed, to be awakened, to believe that forty was not fatal, to know that sex could get better from here. And for Stevie, she was going to make sure the sex got *much* better.

Errol's descriptions of party play came back to her, his teasing whispers about being a toy for his friends. She was aroused by the idea. She'd told him in their limits discussion that she'd not ever been with a woman. She'd never considered it. Though she'd also admitted to fantasizing about both men and women…

Right now, it was downright hot just to imagine. She wanted to try it. Wanted to experience all of it. She wanted this weekend to bust her skinny ass out of her self-imposed shell. She'd already made up her mind while she was hanging from the spider web.

When she stepped from the bathroom, Errol was arranging food on a coffee table. She was wearing his shirt and had a towel wrapped around her hair. She felt remarkably alive and awake. She didn't even worry about having no makeup on.

"He was shutting down but I talked him into cold sandwiches. I got us roast beef and turkey. You pick." He handed her a cold bottle of water.

The roast beef was a monstrosity and overflowing with mushrooms, onions and peppers. The much smaller turkey sandwich had only lettuce and tomato. "I'm guessing you like the hot stuff." She laughed as she plopped down on the red suede loveseat. "I'll take the turkey."

"You noticed that, huh?"

Oh yes, she had. "About tomorrow night…" She left the statement hanging, not exactly sure what she wanted to ask first.

"Tomorrow night is a real party, baby. I don't think you know what that means. I was teasing you in there, trying to get your imagination involved. I wanted you thinking even further out of the box than you were feeling." He took a huge bite of his sandwich.

She swallowed her much smaller taste. She hadn't realized how hungry she was until she'd started eating. "Exactly." Stevie dabbed her chin with a napkin. "I knew that—which is why now, after thinking it through, I want to do it." She wanted it for herself and she wanted to show Errol that she could do more than just "show up".

He leaned forward and caressed her knee. "Have you *really* thought it through? Have you considered that someone from that executive cabinet where you work might be here? Or even better—what if Eva is a coworker? Have you thought about that?"

Stevie almost spit out the tomato she was chewing in laughter. Only three women worked for her. None would be here.

"Don't be so quick to laugh, Stevie. *You're* here, and I bet none of your employees could imagine that. We've had what I call when-worlds-collide moments at parties, and it ain't pretty."

"So how does everyone else handle that?"

"If someone really cares, they wear a mask. But usually you start with smaller parties and a select group. Tomorrow's an open free-for-all. There'll be people at every piece of equipment and plenty of voyeurs hanging around to watch or join in." He watched her carefully, intensely, as he took another bite.

Stevie admired the muscles in his arm move as he tried to remove some stray crumbs from the sofa. She mulled over the ramifications of being found out as a submissive in a sex club. He was right. It was a serious consideration.

"So. I wear a mask. I want to play with you and your friends, Errol. Please?" She propped her hand on her hips to show her confidence and waited for a response.

He let out a sigh, his slight smile amused. "It's more than that. Eva may not want to play with a newbie. You're not exactly what she would consider a trained submissive."

She snuggled up to Errol, loving the solid feel of his body next to hers. She ran her fingers along the tribal tattoo on his shoulder, outlining the curves and swirls. "You could talk to her. I bet she'll do it if you ask her."

He looked up to the ceiling and grinned. "You're not a very good sub, Stevie."

She pouted, feeling very amused at how sexy and womanly she felt at the moment. Would this feel the same with anyone else? She doubted it. "Why not? I asked. I didn't give you an order."

He laughed. "Not exactly."

She pouted again and ran her hand across his thigh, down over his cock and gave a playful squeeze to his balls. "Please, Sir. May I play with your friends tomorrow night?"

Chapter Five

ဆ

"You asked for it. You ready for this?"

"We'll see." Stevie was more nervous than she had anticipated.

He popped her on her naked ass. "No 'we'll sees' here, baby. Your actions tonight represent my reputation. Eva may have agreed to your limits, but she'll play much differently than me. I'm in voyeur mode tonight. I'll be along for the pleasure of watching you get fucked and teased."

Stevie was naked, barefoot and already aroused. It was part of the conditions Eva had set. The rest of which Errol wouldn't tell her. He was in black leather pants and a retro rock T-shirt. His wristbands, rings and tats made him look tough and unforgiving. For all she knew, around others, that was exactly how he acted.

He moved in closer, face-to-face. He looked a little concerned. "You still have your red, yellow, green. Okay?" Stevie nodded her understanding. "Always stand with your feet slightly spread and your eyes down when you're not following a specific order. Make your body available to her." Stevie took the position he described. "I've done everything I can to make sure this will be a good night for you. What happens now, what you take from it, is up to you."

Stevie wondered exactly how it was up to her when she would essentially be the sex toy for a woman she'd never met. She wiggled her toes on the carpet and took a deep breath. If she wanted out, now would be the last time to change her mind. She looked at the closed door in front of her. In a few minutes, Domme Eva and her sub, Bill, would come though it. Other than that, Stevie had no idea what was going to happen this evening. She didn't make a single plan. No one had conferred with her on the details. She'd made no decisions. The only thing she needed to do was show up.

There was a tap at the door. It opened without Errol extending an invitation—and Eva walked in.

Stevie couldn't help but look up she came though the door. Eva wore a super-short black leather skirt with a matching corset that cinched in her waist with several shiny buckles. Her ample breasts threatened to spill over the top. She was a tall, curvy woman and the thigh-high platform leather boots exaggerated the look. Her face was round and very attractive. Her makeup was dark and dramatic. Eva matched the image Stevie had in her head and the stereotypes she'd seen in the media.

Bill walked in behind her. Stevie had imagined a thin, frail man who Eva would dominate and keep as a slave. Instead, Bill was as likely to have his picture posted on the Tempt the Cougar blog as Errol. Maybe more. He was a few inches shorter than Errol, but thickly muscled. His light brown hair was a bit long and shaggy. He had to be much younger than Errol, by the look of him.

Stevie glanced back to Eva. She was probably in her early thirties.

Wow. Stevie was about to have the ultimate cougar experience. She looked back to the floor when she realized that she was making eye contact with Eva.

Eva walked over to her. "She's prettier than I expected." She paraded around Stevie. Bill had stopped right in front her and Stevie felt the heated rush of blood going to her cheeks. She was standing naked in front of two total strangers and a man she met only the day before. Her body was humming with anticipation. All thoughts of backing out were gone. "But she needs to be shaved."

Eva sauntered to the credenza against the wall and started to pour herself a drink. "I'm going to have Bill shave you then I have a costume for you." She motioned for Bill. He had a bag Stevie hadn't noticed before and headed to the bathroom. Stevie stood frozen to her spot. "Go on, girl. I want that thing nice and smooth. Don't worry. Bill is very good with his hands. You'll see."

Errol gave her a gentle push to get her feet moving. "I forgot to tell you that Eva likes the costumes." Stevie highly doubted he forgot to tell her anything. His sly smile confirmed her suspicions. "Take what you need from the experience," he whispered.

She had no clue what that meant.

In the bathroom, Bill already had the water running in the tub and the soap and razor out. He was stripping as she entered. The muscles of his ass were tight, the globes round and clad in a bright green G-string. His shoulders flexed as he lowered himself into the tub with his back to the fixtures. Kneeling on the hard porcelain, he held out a hand. She took it and Bill guided her to sit on the ledge at the back of the tub. He was looking at her breasts as he kneaded the bar of soap, making a handful of lather. Stevie was holding her knees together, wondering if she should introduce herself before she let this man shave her pussy.

Bill pushed open her knees and went to work applying a generous amount of the slick lather. That answered that question. She blushed when he looked up and gave her a smile as his big fingers rubbed the suds over her clit. She knew she was already wet. The sweet-scented soap was making her even slicker. Bill rinsed his hands and expertly started to shave. He maneuvered her thighs and tugged on her skin in all the right places, preventing even the slightest nick.

She watched the concentration on his face as he worked. This was serious business to him. Did he appreciate the situation at all? Was he enjoying her in this position or was this some insane punishment from Eva? When his fingers again brushed over her pussy, Stevie moaned.

He stopped, closed his eyes and took a steadying breath.

So he was aroused. She looked down. His little G-string was insufficient to contain his excitement. Stevie found herself licking her lips at the thought of his cock in her mouth. She *was* an executive slut.

Losing her sense of mortification and gaining some confidence, Stevie tried to imagine telling Monica about this. She almost laughed out loud. What would the group think of her sitting spread out on a tub with a young stud between her legs, shaving her kitty while a Dom and Domme were waiting in the other room? They probably wouldn't believe it. She wasn't sure *she* believed it.

"Rinse," Bill said. Stevie hadn't been sure if he was going to speak at all or not. She lowered herself into the water enough to rinse the remaining soap. He'd not shaved her completely. He'd left a little hair on top, but her pussy was otherwise clean as whistle. Stevie reached to feel her own skin. He caught her hand to stop her. "Only if Ms. Eva says you can."

After they dried, Bill fished from the bag the tiny scraps of fabric that made up her costume. She was so nervous that she made a mess of the thing as she attempted to untangle the pieces. Bill ended up taking it from her and laying it out on the counter. It was something close to a harem girl get-up. She had a very short, shimmering teal skirt that would barely be long enough to cover her ass. It had beads and coins hanging around the waist. There was a headband to hold her hair off her face and help keep the veil in place. The veil was to act as the mask Errol had requested to keep her identity unknown to the rest of the crowd. The shimmering teal fabric was soft against her cheeks and covered her nose and mouth.

She looked in the mirror as Bill attached several longer sheer scarves to the waist of her skirt. The teal in the veil made her eyes gleam a vibrant green. She felt like a sheik's sexy slave girl.

Bill's costume was easy to put on, considering it was only two armbands around his biceps and a chunky green collar.

He finished securing the veil and gave her one last look-over. "I'm going to enjoy this."

The seriousness in his eyes didn't match the giddy feeling Stevie was having a hard time controlling. She knew she should be frightened, but the time with Bill had made her excited and very horny. She assumed that was the intention. A small introduction to having her body touched by strangers.

"It's time, little ones," Eva said. Stevie glanced up to see Errol and Eva both standing just outside the bathroom door. She had no clue if they'd watched the entire scene or not. She had been pretty wrapped up in watching Bill and the careful undertaking of his responsibilities.

Bill stepped from the room. Stevie followed and stopped next to him in the position Errol had told her to take when awaiting instructions. Eva pulled the little skirt higher on her hips. "I want that lovely pussy exposed. Nice job, Bill," she said as she reached down and stroked Stevie's pussy as if to inspect her.

Stevie about jumped out of her skin when she felt Eva's fingers brush across her freshly shaved mound. The only woman who'd ever touched her there was her doctor—and this was no office visit. Stevie took a deep breath to calm her nerves.

"Take her to the center bench and wait for us," Eva said as she walked back over to where Errol was leaning against the credenza, watching.

"Yes Ma'am." Bill nodded and gathered the bag before leading Stevie into the playroom. The lights were lower than they had been the night before. Couples were already playing at the cross and a young woman was suspended on the swing. More people were sitting in chairs around the room talking, as if they were at a cocktail party. Most everyone took a moment to eye her as Bill led her to the center of the room. He pushed her to her knees then knelt beside her with his own legs spread a little, clasping his hands behind his back. Stevie followed suit.

They waited in the middle of the room. Stevie couldn't stand the anticipation.

She glanced surreptitiously around the room again. A woman was tied to the spider web as Stevie had been the night before. The woman was very curvy, many might even consider her overweight, but in that position, with her large round breasts pushing through the ropes, her shapely legs spread and her ass tilted up in the air, she was incredibly sexy. The man lashing her ass with a long leather flogger was certainly enjoying her.

At one of the spanking benches, a man about Stevie's age had been tied. A much younger woman was really working on his ass with a paddle. His cheeks were bright red, his hard cock dancing between his thighs. Each time the paddle landed, his body jerked. The girl, dressed much like Angel had been, reached down and stroked his cock and said something to him Stevie couldn't hear. Whatever it was, he arched his back and stuck his ass higher.

Stevie felt a moment of self-consciousness. Errol would probably prefer to play with these more experienced women. He'd been wonderfully gentle and accommodating to her level of experience, but looking at the woman hanging from the swing with a vibrator strapped to her pussy, Stevie realized she might be in over her head—both with this adventure *and* Errol.

Eva appeared before her. Stevie didn't dare look up. "Stand," Eva said, her voice clear and stern over the music. "Face away from Bill." Stevie did so. "Bend over and put your hands on your knees." Stevie looked past Eva to see Errol standing behind her. He winked and gave her a little smile and a nod. Heat rushed back in and replaced the nervous anxiety.

Stevie felt a little uncomfortable being bent over with her ass and pussy right in Bill's face. Eva fished a crop out of her bag and placed the business end of it between Stevie's shoulder blades. She rolled the handle, letting the little leather fob dance along Stevie's back, tickling her and causing her to arch. Then she stepped to Stevie's side, out of her line of vision. "Errol, I know you don't like to be the second Dom, so tell me. Are you playing or just watching your new toy?"

"I'll join in where I like, if you don't mind." Errol also moved to stand somewhere behind Stevie. She couldn't see him. She couldn't see any of them as she looked forward.

"Don't want to take any orders, do you?"

He chuckled. "Not from you, Eva. I may lose all sense of myself and end up tied to the cross and at the end of your whip."

"No danger there, I'm sure." Eva's crop started little light taps on the side of Stevie's thigh. "You've never had a submissive bone in your body." The taps led up to Stevie's butt cheek. The little skirt was nothing more than a belt in this position. "Bill. Is she wet yet?" Stevie felt fingers probe her pussy and her back tightened. She tilted her hips to push her throbbing pussy greedily toward the sensation. She'd been wet for what seemed like two days.

"Yes Ma'am. Nice and swollen too."

"Huh." Eva walked around in front of Stevie again. "Get a couple of toys out," she said to Bill. She tilted Stevie's face up so she could look at her. "You see, Bill spent most of the afternoon with a large plug in his ass. It's not one of his favorite things. He did it for the reward of getting to play with you tonight. Bill will be using you as his own personal slave girl. Of course, I'll be directing him so he doesn't rush through and let you come too soon."

Eva's gaze fell on something behind her. "That's a good place to start, Bill. Even the playing field."

Stevie looked back and saw Bill covering a butt plug with lube before Eva tapped her chin with the crop, forcing her gaze forward once more. She felt Bill's thick finger dip back into her pussy and then swirl around her ass. She sucked in a breath and her knees bent as his finger slid in. She knew she whimpered, but didn't care. She pictured herself as others saw her, bent over, Bill playing with her and Errol watching, waiting to join in at his whim.

Bill took little time pulling out his finger and replacing it with a plug that was larger than the one Errol had used. The spreading, full sensation was acute. Stevie grit her teeth and hoped the pain would subside quickly and become the pleasurable sensation it had been the night before.

Bill wiggled the plug to give her yet another sensation. "Stand straight, slave girl," Eva ordered. Eva wasn't going to give her time to grow accustomed to the plug at all.

Stevie stood on shaky legs. Her ass was on fire. "Bill's going to attach some much-needed bling to those pert little titties of yours. Turn to face him." Stevie did so. Bill's meaty hands on her breasts were rough as he twisted and pulled her nipples until they were peaked before attaching a clamp to each one. They weren't as tight as the clamp Errol had used, but still added to the mounting thrills assaulting her body.

"Lift your arms over your head." Bill gave the instruction. She was low sub on the totem pole, so she followed his order, holding her hands together over her head. He was playing with her stinging breasts, licking her nipples and tugging at the clamps.

Eva tapped the crop on the tender skin of her inner thighs to get her to open her legs. The woman's long, slender fingers start to rub her pussy from behind. She thought the room started to spin; her entire body felt engaged. She smelled some kind of sage incense in the room and felt the presence of the other players moving about but had no care as to what they saw or thought of her. Her attention was on Errol and his reaction to her situation.

"Lay her on the bench." Errol's voice sounded heated as he issued the command. She doubted her werewolf would be out of the scene much longer. Bill scooped her up and placed her on her back on the nearby bench. This one was a little more than knee high and slightly wider than she was. Bill placed her feet on the ground and tied her ankles to the legs of the bench.

Then he pulled her toward him, pushing her legs open, leaving her pussy and ass accessible. Her hands were left free for the moment and the bench was short enough that her head almost hung off the other end.

"Can I taste her?" Bill also sounded gruff and needy.

Stevie heard several sharp slaps of the crop. Bill rolled his eyes and moaned. Stevie suspected this was a very mild evening for him.

"Me first, you greedy little boy," Eva snapped.

Stevie moaned at the thought of anyone licking her at this moment—she wanted Eva's red lips on her. She whimpered at the thought and thrust her pussy up, begging to be touched.

"Tell her what you want, slut." Errol's voice was in her ear. Bill moved to kneel on one side of her, his hand caressing the bottom of one breast. Errol slid to her other side. "Tell her like a good little slut." She was going to come before anyone even touched her aching pussy again.

"I want you to lick my pussy, Ma'am." She was writhing. "Please. Lick my pussy." The words embarrassed her. "I want your mouth on me."

Stevie closed her eyes as she felt Eva's hands caress the inside of her thighs, inching closer and closer. Eva bit her inner thigh, only inches from her pussy, and wiggled the anal plug at the same time. Stevie cried out.

"Oh, Errol. She's so fucking hot," Eva said—before her tongue pushed into Stevie's folds, forcing her to grip the edges of the bench. Errol squeezed one of her breasts, flicking the nipple, adding to the torture of the clamp as Eva worked on her, flicking her clit with a pierced tongue.

"I can't. I have to come. Please. Eva! May I come?"

Eva backed off. "The new ones take so long to learn to hold back." She kissed her tummy. The crop stung her thigh with three rapid strokes. "Bill, show her how you can deny yourself. Fuck her mouth but do not come."

Bill rose to his feet and swung one leg over the bench, straddling her. She felt his thighs brush against her shoulders as Errol wrapped his hands in Stevie's hair to hold her head still. Bill maneuvered his cock under the veil, teasing her lips. She opened her mouth for him—he was thick. She had little control over the speed or depth to which he penetrated her mouth. The taste of a condom distracted her for a moment, but she got past it and enjoyed the fact that she was sucking Bill's cock. He was enjoying *her*.

And Errol was watching.

Errol stroked her hair. "How do you feel, Stevie?" Eva started to tap Stevie's pussy with her crop. "You've got strangers fucking you, sucking you, and all you can do is lie there and take it."

On cue, Eva poked her tongue back into her throbbing pussy. Stevie could only imagine what it looked like to have a woman licking her. She tried to answer around Bill's cock, but it came out as a garbled moan. How he held back his own orgasm, she'd never understand. She was managing, but that wouldn't last much longer. Her thighs were trembling with the need to release.

Bill pulled back to let her answer. "Green! May I come? Please?" Stevie was tightening every muscle in her body to hold back. She knew this was supposed to be about them, about what the Dominant wanted, but she was enjoying herself too much to care right this minute. Errol had been right—she was *not* a good submissive.

"Do you like it, Stevie?" he asked.

She hadn't a clue why he was asking her that. Of course she liked it. Maybe the barrage of sensations was preventing her from thinking clearly. Eva's pace quickened. The crop hitting her clit started to feel like a vibrator. Stevie felt like she was going to explode. "Please!"

Eva pulled away. "Not yet, slave girl."

Everything stopped. Everyone stopped. Stevie thought she was going to cry. She lay loose and limp, panting from the exertion of holding back. Stevie felt her ankles being untied then Bill helped her sit up.

Eva was kneeling in front of her with a knowing smile, stroking Stevie's breasts. "Hold on, blondie. We need to get these things off." Stevie didn't register the meaning of the Domme's statement fast enough. Eva pinched open the clamps that had been on her nipples far too long and pain seared through her breasts as the blood returned.

Eva leaned forward and took one of the aching nipples into her mouth. Her hand gently massaged the other. The pain eased quickly and Stevie looked down at the woman nibbling on her breast.

The sight of it was more erotic than she could ever have imagined.

She glanced around the room as Eva licked her way to Stevie's other aching nipple. It was now full, each station busy with people playing. Observers dotted the floor and the beanbag chairs. Off to her left side, there were two men and a woman watching their play. She felt herself blush and closed her eyes.

"Open your eyes, Stevie," Errol said as he slipped off his jeans and sat behind her, reached around to finger her clit. "What is it you need from this? What do you need from us?"

She tried to clear her head as Eva and Errol both kept pushing her closer and closer to her breaking point. "I thought Doms did what they wanted to subs. That it was all about your pleasure, your needs."

He bit her on the shoulder. "Yes, that's the myth, isn't it? The ultimate is to get you to submit to your own desires as well as mine. You're uptight. You're closed off to most people. You ignore your own sexual desires in real life. I'm guessing you ignore much of anything that's not work related. We haven't had enough time for me to understand your needs completely, so I'm asking."

Why did she ignore her own desires? What had caused her to close off the emotional side of herself for years? It wasn't as simple as blaming the hours in the lab or the time spent at home staying on top of the newest technologies. She didn't hide from life for the sake of work. She used work to hide from life. She'd always been an all-or-nothing kind of girl—and somewhere along the way, her career had become the "all" and her personal life had been left with the "nothing".

"She's not ready, Errol. But I am." Eva's words brought her back to the moment. Her body hadn't gone off with her thoughts. It was still ramped up and ready to come. Eva reclined on the floor and spread her boot-clad legs. Her skirt was pulled up and her pussy was spread open in front of Stevie.

Her own desires faded quickly when she realized she wanted to explore the curvy woman. She wanted to feel her, to make her squirm.

Stevie glanced up to find Bill standing over to the side stroking his own cock. Poor thing was probably ready to bust.

"He's fine," Eva said. "Not to worry. You have something to attend to right here. I want those sweet lips on my cunt. I want to see your eyes as you taste a woman for the first time."

Stevie shuddered at the harshness of her demand. Errol whispered, "You are so sexy, Stevie," in her ear...

And that was it. Stevie went to her knees in front of Eva's pussy. The woman was propped up on her elbows looking down her body at Stevie. She ran her hand down the soft skin of Eva's thigh, enjoying the supple texture. Eva was as wet as Stevie. She traced the outline of the woman's outer lips with two fingers. She looked up to give Eva what she had asked for, direct eye contact. Stevie wanted to see Eva's reaction to her as well.

When she ran her fingers over Eva's clit, the Domme arched and threw her head back. So much for eye contact.

Stevie removed the irritating veil, tentatively leaned forward and touched the tip of her tongue to Eva's swollen folds. Stevie had tasted her own juices before, from the lips of others, from her fingers after masturbating, but this was something entirely different. This was another woman's pussy. The taste was stronger, saltier—and incredibly sexy.

Errol wiggled the plug in Stevie's ass. She'd almost forgotten about it, but the movement brought her attention back to her own body as well. "Eat her, slut. She gets hers before you get yours," he said.

Stevie *needed* to come, so she plunged her tongue into Eva's pussy—and more eagerly than she would have ever imagined. She pulled back and flicked the woman's swollen clit with a sharply pointed tongue. She pushed two fingers in Eva's pussy and stroked her as she licked. She felt Eva's hips push forward, her thighs tighten around her head. Eva was going to come. *Stevie* was making her come.

Errol pulled out the anal plug suddenly and she moaned against Eva's clit as Errol pushed his cock into Stevie's tormented pussy. She desperately wanted to come. She wanted Eva to come. She pushed a third finger into the Domme. It was enough.

Eva gripped her head and growled, "Yes!"

Stevie arched, pulling away from Eva's throbbing pussy to pay attention to her own aching, gluttonous need to be fucked—to be fucked by Errol. He pushed in slow and easy then stayed buried deep for a moment before pulling back just as slowly. Stevie wished he didn't have a condom on. She wanted to feel his skin. She dug her fingers into the carpet, squeezing her muscles, trying not to come right away.

Eva scooted to the side and motioned Bill back into the activities. Stevie saw that his balls were tight and red from a cock ring, his shaft straining as he helped Eva to her feet. The woman ordered him to recline on the bench and he groaned as she slid a condom over his cock. She retrieved her crop and mounted Bill's shaft without another word. She rode him hard, pinching his nipples and reaching around to tap his swollen balls with her crop. He let out a small yelp each time the crop landed. Bill gripped the edge of the bench above his head and pumped upward, giving her all he had. His muscled flexed, the veins in his arms bloated, exaggerating his bodybuilder physique.

Stevie's attention was brought back to her own body when Errol reached around and started to rub her clit. "Have you figured it out yet?"

"Please, Sir. I need to come."

He let his fingers slip away and he pushed in deep, grinding in circles without pulling back, his cock twisting and rubbing her insides. She cried out loudly, wanting him as deep as he could go, pushing back against him. "Please!" she pleaded.

"Yes, Stevie. Come."

He pulled back and shoved into her two more times before she exploded. Her body, racked with tension from the evening's activities, shook with the intensity of the orgasm. Errol's fingers dug into her skin as he gripped her hips. He ground his cock into her, moving his hips in a circular motion. When Stevie looked back, he stopped, pulled out and flipped her over before sliding back in. He looked into her eyes while he fucked her. He didn't seem interested in what was going on around them. He bent to take her lips, forcing a deep, heated kiss from her. "I'm there, baby," he rasped on her lips.

Stevie tightened all her muscles to grip his cock, to give him as much as she could as he came. He pushed in and groaned. She felt every muscle in his body contract and then slowly relax.

After several minutes, he rolled off her. He gathered her up and settled into a nearby beanbag chair, Stevie cradled on his lap. His body felt so warm. His hand traced the new tattoo he'd created on her body and Stevie knew that wasn't the only thing from Errol that would have a lasting impression.

"This Ankh...it's the symbol of life, Stevie. I think you chose it for more than one reason," he said as he pulled her headband off.

Yes, she now knew why she was here. Stevie caressed Errol's chest and watched Bill come. His collar looked ready to bust under the pressure of his tightened neck muscles. It should have felt strange to watch the couple fuck. It didn't. "I needed a catalyst," she said.

"I'm hoping it's a spark to light a new fire in you."

She nodded. She couldn't remember why she had decided to shut herself away in that biology lab. She'd had no horrible relationship, no real reason to spend her life alone, to lead a life as sterile the lab itself. She'd just quit trying, taken the path of least resistance. It took initiative to be happy. She had needed to put herself out there and find reasons to celebrate, people to enjoy.

She trusted herself. She could trust *him*. Errol could help her explore this part of her life. She'd gone to get a tattoo and taken a giant leap. Stevie looked around the room.

Boy, had she closed her eyes and leapt.

"Thank you," she said against Errol's chest. This wasn't the real lifestyle kind of experience. He'd played sensual Dom for her and his friends had done the same, to help push her out of her own way.

"You're welcome. For what exactly? So I know to do it again."

"For playing with me. For somehow knowing what I needed. I know I'm not a real submissive like those girls." She gave a nod of the head to indicate two girls who were strung up and covered with clothespins.

"This is different for everybody, Stevie." He kissed her forehead. "Being a Dominant is taking control and working an experience or a relationship so that you and your submissive both get what you need. If it was just about me hitting you, that would be a very toxic relationship. Real BDSM is not about pain or time commitment or extremes." He lightly gripped her chin so he could look into her eyes. "I'm looking for a relationship, not a punching bag."

Stevie's heart skipped a beat. "I didn't hurt the alpha werewolf's reputation by being a bedroom submissive?"

He chuckled again, his chest moving with his laughter. "No. My rep will stand. I'd love to explore this further with you — if that's something you'd like to do."

Stevie knew she wanted to see him again but hadn't allowed herself to think past this weekend. "I think I'd like to play with the wolf as much as possible and see what happens."

Epilogue

ॐ

Stevie finished typing the brief rundown of her activities over the past two nights and how they had opened her eyes. The Cougars had been right. It was okay for them all to have a fulfilling life and a few fantasies. Age didn't matter. She was now ready to explore what life had to offer. She was ready to feel something real again, and she had the Tempt the Cougar girls to thank for it.

So, there you have it. I had two younger men and one younger woman...or rather, they had *me*. LOL

Stevie smiled as she walked to the fridge for a beer, knowing the replies would be rolling in fast. There was a ding to indicate a new post before she could even make it back to her desk.

As expected, Cam, who put together the blog in the first place, was the first to post a comment.

You sneaky thing! All this time there was a wild woman lurking beneath that cool and quiet exterior! Sooooo... Ahem, any details you want to add to that little bomb???

Sunset, who was the second Cougar to pass the challenge, chimed in with her post only a few moments later.

Oh, you had *them*, baby! Congratulations! And I hope it brings you as much fulfillment as it did me. Now we know what to get you for Christmas. So what color do you prefer for your handcuffs?

And Monica's post came at the same time Stevie's cell phone rang. *Gee, she didn't even let me scan her post first,* Stevie thought as she reached for the phone while reading her best friend's remarks.

It's about damn time. I was afraid your hootchie couldn't cootchie anymore. You know what they say, use it or lose it. BTW, can we call you Slave Girl now? 'Cause that works for me on so many different levels. *grin*

CAM'S HOLIDAY
Ciana Stone

ഔ

Dedication

℘

To the writers of the Cougar Challenge series. You gals are not only talented authors, but smart, fun women I'm proud to know and call friends. Thanks for all the fun!

Author Note

℘

You'll find the women of *Cougar Challenge* and the Tempt the Cougar blog at www.temptthecougar.blogspot.com.

Trademarks Acknowledgement

℘

The author acknowledges the trademarked status and trademark owners of the following wordmarks mentioned in this work of fiction:

Google: Google, Inc.

iPhone: Apple, Inc.

iPod: Apple, Inc.

Stairmaster: Nautilus, Inc.

Chapter One

ဢ

Tempt the Cougar Blog

From Cam: Sometimes I really hate you, Monica. Well, not you. But that damn challenge you issued. Okay, so not even that. I hate that I'm a freaking coward who can't screw up her courage, get out there, and try to meet someone. What the heck's up with me? There was a time when I had gonads.

Sigh.

I did join a gym today. Okay, not exactly a walk on the wild side, but hey, there's bound to be men, right? And I signed up for a personal trainer. At least that way I won't be floundering around all alone while I'm scoping out the clientele.

And I swear, if I see a likely candidate for an adventure I'll rope him and drag him home with me.

But for now, I'm waiting on my first session with the trainer. I hope I'm able to move tomorrow!

Hugs, Cam.

Camille finished her blog entry and tapped on the *Publish Post* button. Her friends probably felt sorry for her. All six of them had found men—young men who made them feel sexy and vital again. She wondered if she was going to be the "odd man out", the one who couldn't find a guy.

At the moment, she wasn't sure why she'd joined this gym or signed up for a personal trainer. Maybe it had something to do with her ex-husband cheating on her with a woman half her age who had no jiggly bits except her exceedingly large breast implants. Maybe it was because she was feeling insecure about her body. Or maybe it was because all of her friends had guys and she had no one, and didn't have a clue how to go about meeting men. At least not young, sexy men.

Cam's self-confidence had pretty much been in the toilet since that day she found her husband Dan in bed with a younger woman. If the blow of him cheating on her was not enough, the gut-punch she felt when he moved out of their home the next day and into an uptown penthouse *with* the bimbo left her flattened.

Had it not been for the women she met at RomantiCon, a convention for erotic romance readers, she would have closed the blinds, locked the doors and wallowed in her misery.

"Camille?"

The deep male voice had her glancing up from her iPhone. *Holy mother of God!* "Yes?"

"Lee Holiday. Your trainer. I hope I haven't kept you waiting long."

Wow. Double wow. She'd expected muscles. Maybe even lots of muscles. What she hadn't expected was a freaking god. Silky, dark hair that nearly brushed his shoulders, eyes that rivaled the blue of the Carolina sky and a body that had her eyes threatening to bug out of her head.

Cam shoved her phone into her gym bag. "No, not at all. I was a bit early."

"Mind if I sit?"

"Please."

He took a seat beside her. "Before I can create a regimen for you, we're going to need to go through a short assessment to determine your current level of fitness. And I'll need to know what fitness goals you have. But I'd like to take a bit of time today to let you ask questions and decide if I'm the right trainer for you. Do you have any questions?"

"Not really. I wasn't expecting—"

Fuck! Coming at her was none other than the poster-girl for breast implants who had broken up her marriage. Kandy.

She'd run into Kandy a couple of times since the divorce, both times at fundraisers. And both times Kandy had made a point of commenting on how Cam was always alone. She'd even had the nerve to ask Cam if she'd like to be set up with someone so she didn't always have to attend social events alone.

Cam had imagined multiple and diverse ways she'd like to terminate the woman. But right now, Kandy was headed toward her and Cam was not about to go through a repeat performance of "poor Cam, always alone".

"Sorry about this," she blurted right before she leaned forward, clamped her hands on either side of Lee Holiday's face, and planted her lips securely on his.

"Camille?" Kandy squealed.

Cam started to break away from the completely inappropriate kiss, but Lee Holiday wrapped one muscular arm around her and pulled her right off her chair and onto his lap, slanting his mouth over hers and turning her knees to jelly as his tongue plundered her mouth.

"Camille?" Kandy's voice filtered in through the haze of lust that had Camille unable to form a coherent thought. Good god, could the man kiss!

Lee released her and gave her a sexy smirk when she swayed slightly.

"Oh my god!" Kandy wiggled up beside her. "I can't believe it's you! I mean I didn't think you worked out. Oh my god, Danny will *not* believe it when I tell him!"

Danny? Oh ugh. "Kandy." It took every ounce of control Cam possessed to utter the woman's name without adding expletives before and after.

"Hi," Kandy cooed at Lee Holiday. "I'm Kandy. With a K."

"Lee Holiday."

"So, you're—friends with Cam?"

"Actually, Lee is my lover." Cam almost looked around to see who the hell had spoken. Had those words actually come from her lips?

"You have *got* to be kidding!" Kandy screeched loud enough to draw the curious glance of others at nearby tables. Oblivious to everything and everyone save herself, she ran her eyes over Lee appreciatively. "You and...and Cam?" She giggled as she looked at Cam. "Aren't you a little...mature for him, Cammie?"

"Actually, I think she's just perfect," Lee answered.

"Oh, Danny is *so* not going to believe this!" Kandy's eyes narrowed fractionally then she smiled. "Cammie, you *are* bringing Lee to the fundraiser next weekend, aren't you?"

Cam felt like the proverbial deer caught in the headlights of an oncoming semi.

"Of course I'm escorting her." Lee once again saved her from coming up with a convenient lie.

"Really?" Kandy didn't seem to buy it.

"Really," Lee assured her and nuzzled Cam's neck. "Honey, if we're going to get a workout in we need to get moving."

"What? Oh! Oh yes."

"Nice to meet you," Lee nodded to Kandy as he put his hands on Cam's waist, guiding her to her feet.

Cam was mute as Lee steered her in the direction of the gym.

"You too," Kandy called after them. "See you later!"

Cam felt Lee's hand tighten on her waist as he steered her from the juice bar and into the gym. It was like a brand, searing her even through the layers of clothing. What had she done? And how in hell was she going to even look at him? Talk about a bad first impression!

"I'm going to assume that Kandy with a K is not one of your favorite people?"

"Not exactly." She dared a look up at him. "Look, I owe you an apology. Kandy is... well, it's a long story so let's just say she's something of a thorn in my side. Which doesn't excuse my behavior at all and I'll completely understand if you want to rethink being my trainer."

"Are you kidding? And miss escorting you to the fundraiser and meeting the mysterious Danny?"

Cam grimaced. "You do *not* have to attend the event."

"Oh but I do."

"Why?"

"Let's just say that I'm curious and leave it at that. For now."

Cam felt a tingle of excitement. Was that look on his face what she thought it was? Was Lee Holiday attracted to her?

Suddenly the idea of attending the fundraiser had a lot more appeal.

* * * * *

Tempt the Cougar Blog

From Cam: Well, I sure can't make fun of men anymore about thinking with their little heads. I swear all I could do was wonder if he'd be half as good in bed as I imagine. The damn man totally destroyed my concentration. All I could think about was that kiss. Oh god, what a kiss! I bet he thinks I'm the most uncoordinated, clumsy woman on the planet. I couldn't even think about working out and made some lame excuse about having an appointment I couldn't miss. But damn, I can't wait for the next workout. I might not be getting any, but I sure as hell am having some good fantasies about it.

Cam leaned back and stared at the screen. Lee Holiday was, by far, the sexiest man she had seen in a long, long time. But it was more than his appearance. An aura of power and an unspoken promise of pleasure seemed to hover around him like an intoxicating cloud. She'd never felt anything like it and her first meeting with him was one of the most sexually charged events she'd experienced in a long time.

Fortunately, she'd be prepared for his charisma when it came time for the next workout and maybe she'd make it through the exercises without seeming like a clumsy oaf. At least she hoped so. Impressing Lee Holiday was now at the top of her priority list.

* * * * *

Lee checked the clock in his office. Looked like Camille wasn't going to show for her next session. Shame. There was something about her that really appealed to him. That wasn't an everyday occurrence. He saw a lot of women, got hit on by a lot of them but rarely did one intrigue him. Camille did.

Disappointment reared its head and he shoved it aside. It just wasn't meant to be that he get to know the woman behind those big smoky eyes.

A knock on the door had him turning.

"Am I too late?" The object of his thoughts peered up at him as he opened the door.

Lee grinned. The last time he'd seen her she was wearing baggy sweatpants, a man's t-shirt that reached halfway down her thighs and her hair twisted into a knot on top of her head.

The woman gazing up at him now had a fresh-faced, scrubbed look. Long rich brown hair pulled up in a ponytail, a tank top, and gym shorts that displayed firm muscular legs. Only the eyes were the same. Smoky blue that seemed to look right inside him. He hoped that it was simply an illusion. It wouldn't be good for his reputation for her to know what he was thinking at the moment. That instead of training her in physical fitness, he'd far rather get physical with her in a very intimate way.

"Not at all, Ms. Stockton," he replied and held the door for her to enter.

"Please, call me Cam. And I'm sorry to be late. I got caught up in...well, never mind. I am sorry."

Their eyes met and he was surprised at the spike of excitement that flared inside him. It wasn't his imagination. There was something happening here. Would they act on it? He hoped so, but wasn't going to rush into it. The journey toward satisfaction was far too enjoyable.

"Are you ready?"

"For?"

Her question gave him pause. That low sexy voice of hers was modulated perfectly to make the word sound sexual and hot.

"Well, that depends."

Cam felt her insides literally tingle. Unless she was way off the mark, the attraction was mutual. That both excited her and made her nervous. It had been quite a while since she'd experienced anything like this. A very long time since she'd been adept at the single life. She wasn't sure she remembered all the rules to the attraction game.

And truth be told, she'd never been very good at playing games. Maybe part of shedding her old life and rediscovering herself was to let go of the behavior patterns she adopted when she married and get back to the Cam who existed before marriage. That Cam wasn't shy about speaking her mind, about shooting straight from the hip.

But what if he took offense? That question gave her pause. Until she heard her friend Edie in her head. *So what if he does? If he doesn't like you for who you are then he's not for you. You're through living to please a man, Cam. Time to please yourself.*

A sudden rush of courage had her looking up into his eyes.

"Mr. Holiday—"

"Lee."

"Lee," she said with a smile. "I'm not one for games so I'll tell you straight out. You're hot. Damn hot. And yes, there're a lot of things I can think of that I'd love to do with you or to you. A whole lot. But we don't know each other and despite the fact that you're the most lickably divine man I've met in a long time, I don't jump between the sheets fast. I'm one of those old-fashioned gals. I need to get to know a man a little before I take him to bed. And then there's the little matter of the age difference."

The smile he gave her was enough to have her blood race. "I appreciate your candor. And I admit there are a lot of things I'd rather be doing with you right now other than working out. But I respect a woman who doesn't move too fast. And I like the flirtation phase. Jumping past it seems like a waste."

He paused for a split second. "And as far as age goes, I don't think I'm too old for you, Cam. In fact, I'd say the age difference is just about perfect."

Cam laughed. "And you're quite the flatterer too. Look, we both know I'm...older. You don't have to pretend otherwise."

"I wasn't. Okay, I was flirting, but with honesty."

For one split second Cam wondered if she'd finally met Mr. Right. Then she quickly discarded the notion. It was way too early for such thoughts. Besides, as he said, the flirtation phase shouldn't be rushed.

"Well, in that case, how about flirting me into better shape?"

"Honey, your shape looks fantastic to me."

"Well the not-so-good parts are artfully hidden."

"Yeah? Let's see."

"See?"

"Yeah, take off your tank top. You're wearing a sports bra. If you want to get the maximum results we have to know what to work on."

Cam shrugged and stripped off her tank top. If her body was going to turn him off, might as well go ahead and find out.

Lee looked her up and down and walked slowly around her. "Good muscle tone. If you want a six-pack I can help you get there, but I don't really think it'd be the best look for you. You're not a tall woman. Too much muscle mass and it'll make you look shorter and—"

"Stumpy?"

"Well that isn't exactly the word I was searching for, but yeah, in a way. I think you want to stick with toning and maybe a little definition but not too much."

"So, you think you can do me better than I can do myself?"

The smile he gave her let her know that he didn't mind a little sass in the attitude, and the double entendre didn't go over his head.

"I promise you that I can do you much better than you can do yourself."

"Big promises," she teased.

"Iron-clad, money-back guarantee."

At the raise of her eyebrow and a sassy smirk, he smiled. "Honestly, I think you look damn good the way you are. However, I'm professionally obliged to say I can get you into even better shape. If I say no, then you might not come back."

His answer thrilled her. Knowing that he was interested in spending time with her, even if it was in the gym, was exciting.

"Well then, I'm all yours."

Lee titled his head back, closed his eyes and groaned. "Oh honey, please don't put it that way or you'll make me eat my words about enjoying the flirtation."

"Purely in a fitness sort of way," she added with a chuckle.

"Right. Okay. Putting my professional hat back on. So I can best determine what level to start you why don't you tell me what your current fitness regimen is?"

"Well, I run every day. About five miles. I do weight training—nothing serious. Minimal I suppose, just enough to stay toned, and I do yoga."

"What style yoga?"

"I really like Baron Baptiste's power yoga style the best."

Lee smiled and nodded. "Like to personalize it to fit you?"

"Exactly."

"Okay, then why don't we start with a little cardio warm-up? Say twenty minutes?"

"Sounds good."

He led her to the cardio center and gestured toward the rows of elliptical walkers, treadmills, stationary bikes and Stairmasters. "Take your pick."

Cam chose one of the elliptical walkers, a model that provided upper as well as lower body exercise. Lee got on one beside her and in silence they started their warm-up.

She couldn't help glancing over at him. Dressed in a tank top and shorts, he was very easy on the eyes. He had the look of a gymnast, strong and fit with muscles in all the right places, but none of the bulk of a bodybuilder. It was sexy and sleek and fit him well.

His eyes met hers when her gaze moved to his face. "Mind if I ask a personal question?"

"No, not at all."

"Is that the real color of your eyes or are those contacts?"

"Real. Nothing artificially enhanced."

"You have beautiful eyes. Exotic and a little mysterious. Like the twilight. You know what the day has held, but what the night will bring is still a mystery."

Cam lost a beat in her pace. Did he have a clue how totally sexy he was? That low deep voice, soft-spoken words and penetrating eyes were enough to have her feeling decidedly damp, and it had nothing to do with the physical exertion.

"If this is a ploy to raise my heart rate, you're doing a damn good job."

"Honey, my heart rate's been elevated since I turned and saw you standing there."

"Flirt," she said with a grin.

"Damn skippy."

They shared a laugh and finished their warm-up with a few heated looks and verbal sparring. When she hopped off the machine, he followed, grabbed a couple of towels from a stack and tossed her one.

"Water?"

"That'd be great," she said and mopped her face and neck.

Lee went to the social/bar area of the gym where members could sit and enjoy a healthy light meal, or get a protein shake or water. He grabbed a couple of bottles of water and headed back into the gym.

Cam was stretching, bent over with the torso of her body flattened out on her legs. The legs of her gym shorts rose with the position to reveal part of her firm, round rear, making one part of his anatomy start on the road to a full salute.

He took his time crossing the gym, enjoying the show. She moved effortlessly from the forward bend to an upright position, her arms over her head. Slowly and with impressive grace she bent backward, not stopping until the palms of her hands were flat on the floor behind her.

"That inspires a lot of wicked thoughts," he announced his presence.

She rocked her body forward and recovered from the backbend with ease. "Wicked, eh?"

"Decidedly wicked."

"I like wicked."

"Really?" He handed her a bottle of water. "How wicked?"

"Depends," she said and turned the bottle up to down half of it, then smiled at him. "What'cha got in mind, handsome?"

Lee wanted to say stripping her naked and bending her over a weight bench, but that would not have prolonged the game.

"How about sensual exercise?"

"Sensual? Is there really such a thing?"

"Say yes and find out."

She gave him a look hot enough to have him wishing he had on looser shorts as she answered, "Yes."

He held out his hand, and after a split second of hesitation she placed her hand in his. He pulled her over to a padded section of the gym where various sizes of exercise balls were housed on a low rack. "Let's start with some back extensions."

"I've never done those."

"Then I'll be your first," he teased. He picked one of the balls and placed it in front of her. "Here's what I want you to do. You're going to lie on the ball. Your legs can be bent or straight. Position the ball under your hips and torso. Let your body drape forward over the curve of the ball."

Cam assumed the position, trying to keep her legs straight, but being rather short, the ball wobbled and rolled. "Here, let me help," Lee said, and positioned himself between her legs, bending forward slightly to place one hand on either side of her on the ball to add stability. "Bend your legs if you need to and squeeze the ball a little between them."

It was an altogether sexual pose. Her lying butt up over the ball, legs spread and him between her legs, bent forward and caging her body with his hands. Cam felt a distinct stirring in her sex, a hot yearning that made her throb and grow wet.

"Are you ready?" he asked in a tone that was as sexually teasing as she'd ever heard.

"Bring it on."

"That's my girl. Now, I want you to put your hands behind your head or clasp them behind your back, whichever is more comfortable. You're going to slowly raise your chest up until your body is in a straight line. I want you to make sure that your body is in alignment. Pull your abs in and lift."

She lifted up, feeling the pull in her abs. "Don't hyperextend your back," he said and moved his hands to either side of her hips. "Go down now. Slowly."

Going down was easy. Up wasn't bad. At least the first thirty. After that, it got harder. And it wasn't just the exercise. With his hands on her hips and the feel of her inner thighs pressing against his legs she was getting far more worked up than she'd thought was possible for someone straining every abdominal muscle in her body.

"Come on, baby, you can do it," he encouraged. "Just a few more."

Cam wasn't sure she had much more in her, but she tried. When she reached fifty and lowered back down, she just hung limply. Until she felt Lee's hands on her hips rocking the ball toward him. She pushed herself up as he lifted her by the hips, and came to a standing position pressed firmly against his hard body. One part of which was exceptionally hard.

His hands moved around her, running lightly over her torso. "Feeling the burn?"

"More than you can imagine."

Lee grinned and let his hands linger a few moments, enjoying the feel of her beneath his hands as he played lightly up and then down her torso. He knew she was aware of his erection. He would've had to have been a saint not to react. Seeing her bent forward with her round ass presented to him was like viewing a dessert you really wanted to dive into but didn't want to rush and miss a moment savoring the pleasure.

"You ready for more?" he asked softly, feeling a rewarding surge of excitement when her body immediately heated and tensed.

"Oh yeah."

"Good. You'll like this one." Actually, he figured he'd like it. A lot. He hoped it would be as stimulating for her because today had brought about a decision. He was going to seduce Cam Stockton.

Chapter Two

ℬ

Lee finished writing the card, sealed it in the small envelope and laid it atop the red tissue paper in the box. The clerk closed the box and smiled at him. "We'll have this delivered no later than one this afternoon, Mr. Holiday."

"Thank you, Deborah. You've been a real doll."

"Any time," she breathed.

Lee smiled and left the package delivery shop. Camille was in for a surprise. One he hoped she'd find intriguing and just a bit daring. If he'd misread her there was a good chance she'd slap him silly when he arrived to pick her up this evening. If his instincts were on the mark then they'd both be in for a stimulating evening.

It surprised him a bit at how taken he was with Camille Stockton. Not that she wasn't lovely. She certainly was. Her shoulder-length hair was silky and thick, the kind of hair he could imagine gliding over his chest and down his abdomen as her lips worked their way lower.

Soft, smoky blue eyes, rimmed by thick lashes, and lush lips set in a face more exotic than beautiful, the slightly angular lines giving her an erotic appeal. And her body was certainly made for the art of love. Full breasts and curves in all the right places. Not hard and cut like many of the women who populated the gym, but womanly and ripe, the kind of body a man wanted to feel beneath him. Or on top of him, soft and giving.

But it was more than her looks that drew him. There was fire simmering beneath the surface, a fire he suspected had not been stoked in far too long. The idea of fanning those flames until she ignited was a temptation too great to pass up.

Unless he was completely wrong about her... He suspected he was not. Whatever the case, he'd know before the night was done.

* * * * *

Camille looked up as her assistant entered. "A package was delivered for you."

"Just put it on the desk, Jennie. And did you get the figures from the lighting company on the cost of the October production from the off-Broadway group?"

"I'll have it ready for you in five minutes."

"Thanks."

Camille finished the email she was writing and jotted down a note for herself then looked at the package on her desk. Her phone rang. Still staring at the package, she answered, trying to keep her mind on business and off what might be in the package.

As one of the leading event planners for the city, she was accustomed to juggling multiple projects at once and multitasking, but the package was like a siren's call. A mystery that was diverting her attention. When the call ended, she reached for the package, reading the label. No return address. That was odd. She wasn't expecting anything.

She opened it and inside was another box, this one from the most expensive lingerie shop in the city. Who would be sending her lingerie? A small white envelope lay atop the tissue in the box. Cam opened it.

Wear this tonight and I guarantee it will change your perspective of fundraisers forever. Lee.

Cam pulled back the tissue. Nestled inside was a lacy black garter belt, a matching thong and stockings. She blinked, reached for the lingerie and then pulled back, staring at it. Why in the world would he send her this? Did he get off thinking about her wearing it?

That idea brought a rush of heat to her belly. She barely even knew Lee Holiday but she knew enough to be sure that given the chance she'd be on him like white on rice. Just a look from him pushed her libido meter to the red line.

She reached for the lingerie, and as she lifted it from the box, she noticed a glint. Beneath the black lace and silky stocking was an odd bracelet. She took it from the box.

Shaped like a torc, it was about a half-inch thick. The ends did not meet and were only slightly curved. The bulbous ends were smooth and the whole thing smooth and shiny.

Only it wouldn't stay on her wrist. She tried bending it but the metal was too thick and strong. She held it in one hand, turning it this way and that as she tried to figure out how she was supposed to wear it.

"Oh my god!"

Cam looked up in alarm at the sound of her assistant's voice. "What?"

"That!"

"This?" Cam wiggled the bracelet.

"Yes, that! What are you doing with something like that?"

"What do you mean?"

The red flush and nervous laugh from her assistant had her even more confused. "Am I missing something here?"

Jennie closed the office door and approached the desk. "Don't you know what that is?"

"A bracelet?"

"Not even close."

"Then what?"

"It's...you..."

"What?"

"You insert it in...you know, your privates."

Cam dropped the thing as if it'd grown barbs. "Say what?"

"Yeah. I have a friend who's all into the BDSM stuff and she told me about it. One of her Doms gave her one. You put one end in your—vagina and the other up your butt."

"No way."

"Yes way."

"No."

"Yes."

"Oh my god."

Jennie nodded. "So, boss, just what the heck have you been up to since your divorce?"

Cam snatched up the *thing* and the lingerie and stuffed it all back into the box, slammed on the lid and shoved it under her desk. "Nothing like what you're thinking."

"Then why did someone send you that?"

"I have no idea."

Jennie's eyebrows rose and fell. "Well, you might want to think about whoever it is that sent you that 'cause I'd be willing to bet that he's a Dom. And unless you're into that sort of thing you might want to reconsider hanging with him."

"I assure you I am not involved with any...Dom or playing sex games or—or whatever. Now, about those lighting figures?"

"Oh yeah. I copied it to the external drive under the production company's folder. It's ready whenever you want to check it."

"Thanks."

"Sure." Jennie turned to leave and Cam called out as she reached the door.

"Jennie? If you don't mind, let's not mention this...package to anyone."

"Sure thing."

Cam watched her leave then dragged the box from beneath the desk, put it on her lap and opened it. Part of her was shocked. She was comfortable with shock. What she wasn't comfortable with was the part of her that reached for the *thing* and felt a strange thrill.

* * * * *

Tempt the Cougar Blog

From Cam: HELP!! I have this…situation. Remember the guy I posted about? The trainer who's going with me to the fundraiser tonight? Well, today he sent me a present. Black lace garter, matching thong and silk stockings.

And this…thing. My assistant says it's a torc. Not the Celtic ones (yes, I Googled it), but one that's a sex toy that you put inside you. One end up your twat and the other up your butt.

What the fuck? His card said if I wear the gifts, it will change my perspective of fundraisers forever. What do I do?

Cam, the befuddled.

Cam clicked on the *Publish Post* button then sat back and stared at the screen. She hadn't been able to get the *thing* off her mind all day. Even now, the open box sat on the desk in her bedroom beside the laptop, the *thing* gleaming in the lamplight.

Come on, come on, someone answer. She shouldn't have waited so long to post. In just over an hour Lee would arrive to pick her up. Would he ask about the gift? Ask if she was wearing his present?

What was she going to do? *Come on, girls. Need some help here.* She pushed back from the desk and stood. She'd take a shower. Maybe by the time she finished one of the girls would have answered.

245

Twenty minutes later, wrapped in a thick body towel, Cam padded back into the bedroom and clicked on the bookmark for the blog. Her lips spread into a smile as she read the posts.

Tempt the Cougar Blog

Comment from Edie: Try the thing out. What've you got to lose? Sounds as if I need to get me one of those! And a garter, thong and stockings will make you feel sooo good, if they're good quality. If the thing doesn't work, you can always strangle him with a silk stocking!

Comment from Elizabeth: Stiletto doesn't fit so easily on the other foot, does it? That's why we all needed your encouragement when it was our turn, and now the choice is yours. So I ask you, are you going to go for living your wildest fantasy, or are you going to regret not doing it for the rest of your life?

Comment from Monica: If it's anything like the Chinese love balls that Sam bought me...Oh sweet mystery of life, at last I found you! And I should point out that if the stockings, garter, thong and torc are good quality, they'll last longer than most relationships. Don't look a gift stud in the mouth.

Comment from Autumn: We agreed to try anything and everything, no holding back. The torc sounds like delicious torture. And the stud sounds exactly like the kind of man we talked about. I say go for it all. And by the way, what kind of fundraiser did you say this is?

Comment from Stevie: Sounds like that thing may change your religion! You go, girl.

Cam considered her friends' advice. They were right. If she didn't take a chance and explore the opportunity, she might regret it. And it wasn't as if he was asking her to let him truss her up and whip her or something. It was just a little sex toy.

Tapping out a quick thank-you to the girls, Cam hurried to dress. Lee might be right. This might change her attitude entirely about fundraisers.

* * * * *

Cam smoothed the black sheath over her hips and turned to look over her shoulder at the reflection of her backside in the mirror. No way would anyone guess that beneath the tasteful frock her body was being subjected to an entirely new set of sensations.

The torc Lee had given her just might end up being her new best friend. One rounded end brushed over her G-spot when she moved and the other pressed against nerves in her anus she didn't realize were such pleasure centers. She'd only had the thing in for five minutes and already had a serious case of damp panties. Damn, she'd spend half the night in the ladies room mopping her crotch!

The doorbell rang and she gave her reflection one last glance before hurrying to the door.

One look at Lee took her breath. She'd thought he looked good in a tank top and gym shorts. In the black tailored suit, white shirt and deep gray tie he looked like something out of a fashion magazine. The cut of the jacket emphasized his broad shoulders and narrow waist, and the gray of the tie brought out the startling blue of his eyes.

Bond, James Bond. Yep, he could easily fit into the role of super-sexy uber spy.

"Hi, come in."

He smiled down at her as he stepped across the threshold. "You look incredible."

Cam returned the compliment with a delighted smile. "So do you." She closed the door and led the way into the great room.

Lee chuckled. "So I clean up okay?"

"More than okay. Believe me. Would you like a drink before we leave?"

"I don't drink much, but thanks."

"Okay. Can I get you anything? Water, tea, a soda?"

"Actually there is something you could do."

"What?"

"Are you wearing my gifts, Cam?"

A rush of heat washed over her skin. His expression had gone from cheerful to something hot and hungry. It'd been a long time since a man had looked at her like that.

"Yes."

"Show me."

"Show you?"

"Yes. Lift your dress and show me."

Something in his voice, the look on his face…it was the single most erotic moment of her life. Things swirled inside her that had not been given life until this moment. Excitement, a sense of unease, and a deep desire that she wasn't sure she understood.

Lee moved closer, leaned down, and barely skimmed the side of her neck with his lips. Then he inhaled. She heard him drawing in a long slow breath. He straightened and exhaled.

"Hmmm. I can smell your desire, Cam."

Well no shit, Sherlock. Her pussy was in overdrive. She could feel the wetness on the thong, on her inner thighs. Thank god she'd chosen a black dress or sitting would have been out of the question. Unless she favored the idea of a big wet spot.

"Let me tell you what I think." His voice was a sexy low croon, his eyes pinning her into immobility. "I think inside that cool exterior lurks a bad girl. A woman who longs to be dominated, pushed to explore her sexual appetites — perhaps even a little debased. I think you yearn for it, dream about it, and want more than anything for a man who will strip the control from you, leaving you free to experience all the pleasure and pain your appetites demand."

Good god, had he been reading erotic romance? His words could have been yanked straight from the pages of one of her favorite books. Straight from that secret place she hid from the world, that place where desires that could not be acted upon dwelled in fantasy.

"And you think you're the man to set me free?" Damn, was that her speaking? That sultry voice that carried a hint of challenge? Now *she* felt like a character from a book!

He turned, walked the few steps to a leather wingback chair and sat. His posture seemed almost imperious, his expression demanding yet inflamed. "I know I am. Now, come stand in front of me, lift your dress and show me how well you wear my gifts."

The way her pussy and ass clenched around the torc sent a riot of sensation rocketing through her. Each step she took brought another surge of electricity, taking her perilously close to climax. When she stood before him, Cam took hold of the fabric of her dress and worked it up over the top of the stockings, over the patch of lace that covered her mons, clear up to her waist.

"Beautiful," Lee said with a lusty smile. "Turn around, Cam."

She complied, casting a look over her shoulder to see him looking hungrily at her ass.

"Spread your legs and bend over."

She almost moaned. Her pussy clenched and her clit throbbed. Moving her feet apart, she bent forward. The position spread her ass cheeks, leaving her completely exposed aside from the thin strip of material from the thong that bisected her ass.

Seconds ticked by. Cam started to feel uncomfortable. Lee wasn't moving or speaking. Should she look back at him? Straighten up? As the questions assailed her, she felt his hand move across one buttock, his finger working beneath the thin strap of the thong and moving downward.

The strap of the thong stretched and he pulled it away from her skin. The tiny sting of the elastic slapping her skin when he released it was little compared to the jolt that rocked her when he pressed on the torc.

Cam's legs threatened to give way. His fingers moved between the swollen lips of her pussy, finding their way to her clit. She bit back a groan when his fingers closed on it, pinching, and then rolling it slowly.

"You look good this way, Cam. Bent over and offering. I'm in anticipation of what I'll do to you when this event is over."

His fingers continued to torment her clit as his voice crooned low and sexy. "Tell me, are you as excited as I am about what's to come?"

Cam wanted to shout, "Fuck the fundraiser." She was so close to coming she could feel her belly vibrate and her pussy clench. "Yes," she managed to gasp.

"Good."

With that he stopped. She almost groaned in frustration. Damn, how was she going to make it through this fundraiser? All she could think was whether he'd make good on his promise when it was over. And what exactly he might have in mind.

Cam had never been involved in anything remotely kinky or out of the ordinary. Well, at least not since the day she met her ex, Dan. He was a straight-up, missionary-style lover. Climb on, bang away, and get his.

But that didn't mean she wasn't eager to try something new.

She felt him lower her dress over her ass and she stood, turning to face him. His eyes wore a look that any woman with half a brain could recognize. Lust. But to Cam it was a look she wanted to freeze and hold onto because it was directed solely at her, and it had been longer than she cared to remember since a man had looked at her like that.

"Are you ready?" he asked.

"You have no idea."

Lee chuckled. "I meant to make our first public appearance."

"I know," she admitted. "And I suppose I am. Just one tiny thing. Do you think you could—you know, act like you think I'm the hottest thing since the push-up bra?"

"Baby, I won't have to act."

Cam smiled up at him. "Damn, you're good for my ego."

"And hopefully a lot more than that."

She blew out her breath and stepped back. "Okay, before I decide to blow off this whole thing, let's do it."

Lee laughed at her words. "Your wish is my command."

Cam smiled and fetched her purse. She had a whole lot of wishes. She just hoped he was as good as his word.

Chapter Three

ഇ

The country club was packed, as Cam had expected. The annual fundraiser for juvenile diabetes always brought the city's elite, the power-players who would happily donate tens of thousands of dollars in exchange for being in the limelight for an evening.

She couldn't help but feel a bit smug with satisfaction. Cam had arranged the event and from the looks of things, it was going to be a success.

"Ms. Stockton?" The head of the Juvenile Diabetes Foundation hurried over to her.

"Ms. Smyth." Cam smiled and took the woman's hand. "You look lovely."

"Oh my dear, you've outdone yourself," Ms. Smyth gushed. "Everything is perfect. Simply perfect."

"I'm so glad you approve," Cam replied then noticed the way Irene Smyth was giving Lee the once-over. "Oh forgive me. Irene, this is Lee Holiday. Lee, Irene Smyth. Irene is the president of the Juvenile Diabetes Foundation."

"A pleasure." Lee took Irene's hand in both of his and smiled down at her.

Cam could see the flush that worked over Irene's face and neck. It was clear she was affected by Lee's looks and charm.

"Camille, wherever did you find this gorgeous man?" Irene's question might have been directed to Cam but her eyes were on Lee.

"Camille and I have been keeping our relationship low-key thus far," Lee responded in a low and intimate tone. "This is the first time we've made a public appearance together."

"I'm so pleased you did," Irene replied.

"I do hope you'll save me a dance?"

The smile that took shape on Irene's face was bright enough to rival the bank of lights that lit the stage of the ballroom. Lee had no way of knowing just how many points he'd made for Cam. Irene was sure to insist that Cam organize the next event and that was a definite feather in Cam's professional hat.

"I will indeed. Camille, again, you've done just a marvelous job."

"Thank you."

"Now you two young people take advantage of the bar and mingle. I see the mayor beckoning."

"Have fun," Camille remarked as Irene cut Lee one last smile.

She stepped in front of Lee, tilting her head back to look up into his eyes. "You're good."

"Didn't I mention that already?"

"I mean at smoozing."

"Oh yeah. Well, she seems like a nice lady."

Cam smiled and on impulse stood on tiptoes to graze a soft kiss on his lips. "I'm glad you're here."

His right arm snaked around her waist to pull her close. "So am I."

The immediate burst of heat from the contact had Cam wishing they were not in the middle of a crowded ballroom.

"Champagne?" A server stopped beside them with a tray.

"Absolutely," Lee replied and took two glasses, giving one to Cam. "To you. Ms. Smyth was right. This is really impressive."

Cam accepted the glass and touched it lightly against his. "Thanks."

She'd not dared to dream that the evening would be like this. Lee was undoubtedly the sexiest man in the room and seemed to have eyes only for her. She'd seen the looks on the faces of the women present and felt a bit like Cinderella at the ball—the lucky gal who was with the handsome prince.

And more importantly, the gal who was leaving with the prince. She'd never been more eager for a man, but tonight she would gladly leave early to spend more time alone with Lee and the delights he promised.

Just as she raised the glass to her lips, a voice from behind her had her reacting much the way one would at the sound of fingernails on a chalkboard.

"Cammie? Is that you? Oh my god! Danny, it's Cammie."

The high she'd felt a moment ago was gone. In its place was annoyance and dread. Lee must have noticed something—her expression or the way she tensed because he wound his left arm around her waist as she turned, pulling her snugly against his side.

Cam had always imagined she would feel ill at ease to have her ex-husband see her with another man, and had often wondered if that discomfort would prompt her to put distance between herself and the man she was with. To her surprise, the opposite was true. She'd never stop being grateful to Lee. His big strong body next to hers and the possessive hold he had on her waist gave her strength to look into the face of her ex-husband and smile.

"Dan. You're looking well."

"Camille." Dan didn't return the smile and his eyes barely skimmed Camille before they were focused like twin lasers on Lee. "I don't believe we've met. Daniel Hillford, state prosecutor."

"Lee Holiday." Lee extended his hand. "Pleased to meet you."

"We've already met," Kandy announced. "Remember me telling you, Danny? At the health club. Why, you could have knocked me over with a feather when I saw Cammie with Lee."

Dan ignored Kandy and turned his attention to Camille. "Nice event. Drew a good crowd."

"Yes, I hope it will be successful."

"I'm glad you were able to arrange an escort, Camille."

Cam didn't know how to respond. Was Dan implying that she'd paid Lee to escort her?

"Cam and I felt it was time to make our relationship public," Lee announced.

Cam nearly swallowed her tongue. *Make their relationship public? What relationship?* She shifted her weight from one foot to the other. The movement, like all movement, caused the torc to shift slightly and a short stab of pleasure had her skin growing even warmer.

"Oh?" Dan looked at her. "I wasn't aware you were...involved."

"Why would you be?" she asked, finding her tongue.

"No reason. Let's just say I'm understandably...surprised. No offense, Mr. Holiday, but the age difference..."

That infuriated Cam. And anger had always had a way of freeing her. She laughed lightly and raised her glass toward Dan in a toast. "Kind of like the pot calling the kettle black, don't you think, *Danny*?"

"It's hardly the same," Dan replied without hesitation.

Cam opened her mouth to reply, wanting to wipe the smug smirk off his face, but Lee beat her to the punch. "You're right. Neither of us is cheating on anyone. If you'll excuse us, I want to dance with my gorgeous date."

"I could kiss you," Cam whispered as he led her toward the dance floor.

"Then why don't you?"

Before she could reply, he'd turned her into his arms and his lips were on hers. Ten minutes ago she'd have protested, not daring to be so bold at such a public event. Right now, she didn't care. She returned the kiss with enthusiasm.

When it ended, she was breathing a little faster. When Lee guided her into a slow dance, her breathing hitched. And when he did a sexy grind to the beat against her, wetness dampened her upper thighs.

"You're killing me," she whispered.

"Aroused?"

"To say the least."

"I can take the edge off. Come with me."

"Huh?" Surprised, but without protest, Cam let him lead her from the dance floor.

They made their way across the ballroom with Cam saying quick hellos to people who greeted her. When Lee stopped in front of the ladies room and raised one eyebrow Cam put on the brakes.

"No way."

"Oh yeah."

"Lee, someone might see you go in."

He looked around then back at her. "No one's watching. See if anyone is inside."

Cam felt like a teenager about to sneak behind the bleachers at the high school to make out. It was an unsettling but exciting feeling. She opened the door and stepped inside. This was not a large public restroom but a private powder room. This country club was one of the few in the city that still boasted of such old-school amenities.

"It's clear."

No sooner were the words out of her mouth than Lee had nudged her inside and was locking the door.

"This is crazy."

"Take off the thong."

Again, she was struck by the tone of his voice. Masterful and seductive. It was like he had two sides, the Lee who was fun and flirtatious and the Lee who was some kind of sexual wizard, casting a strange spell over her that made her want to do whatever he asked of her.

She lifted her dress and wiggled out of the thong. Lee took it and slid it into the left pocket of his jacket. "Raise your dress and sit down on the vanity with your back to the mirror."

Cam cut a look at the door then at him. "This might not be—"

"Do it, Cam."

Again, that voice. And not only the voice but also the look of hunger on his face. A look that was directed at her. "Lee, you don't have to—what I mean is, I don't expect you to...to service me or something."

He took her hand and guided it to the inner thigh of his left leg. Cam felt her eyes widen. He had a massive hard-on.

"I need you, Cam. I need to touch you. Taste you. Sit down on the vanity and spread your legs."

He had her at the word "need". She spread a hand towel on the top of the vanity. She hoped it would hold her weight. It looked like an antique, a piece of furniture from another era.

Cam worked her dress up around her waist and took a seat. A small moan burst from her as she settled. The torc pressed deeper inside her.

Lee knelt in front of her, placing his hands on the inside of her knees and spreading her legs. "Beautiful," he murmured as he lowered his head and kissed the inside of her right leg, just above the knee.

"Scoot your hips closer to the edge and lean back."

She did as he directed, feeling a waft of cool air against her damp pussy as he lifted her left foot, removed her shoe and placed her foot on his knee. Cam was squirming as he repeated the move with her right foot. When he pressed her knees out to the side, widening the spread of her legs, she almost whimpered.

He took his time, working his lips up the inside of one leg, his fingers playing advance scout, moving into the folds of her pussy, spreading her.

Cam's body jerked when his tongue slid over her clit in a long slow lick. When he sucked that hard nub into his mouth she moaned then bit her lip, trying to be silent against the onslaught of sensation rocketing through her.

His fingers kept her spread wide as his tongue moved between the labia, working the length of her pussy and back up to flick at her clit. Cam struggled to keep from making a sound, her breath fast and hard and every muscle taut and quivering with need.

A knock at the door had her jumping, but Lee held her in place. "Say occupied."

"Occupied," she called in a broken and breathless voice.

A split second after the word was out of her mouth Lee latched onto her clit, rolling it in his mouth, then running his tongue over it, increasing the speed. Cam forgot about being quiet, forgot about everything but the orgasm that pulsed closer with each beat of her heart.

She panted, moaned and clung to the edge of the vanity in a white-knuckled grip, her legs and belly vibrating. Then it hit. Like a wave cresting, it crashed over her. She heard herself cry out, "Yes, yes yes!" and then lost track of reality.

Lee continued to stroke and lick her until the orgasm faded then he straightened, pulled her to her feet before him, and claimed her in a kiss that had sizzle building again between her legs.

She tasted herself on his lips and tongue and felt his erection pressing hard against her belly. It was like a dream. Was this really happening to her?

Lee pulled back from the kiss and smiled down at her. "And that was just a preview."

Cam blew out her breath. "The full feature may kill me."

He laughed and smoothed her hair back over her shoulders. "Somehow I don't think so. Now, shall we rejoin the others?"

Cam laughed nervously. "Oh yeah, no problem. Come my brains out in the powder room then walk back into the ballroom as if nothing ever happened. Piece of cake."

Lee chuckled. "You have the look of a woman who's just experienced a climax. Flushed skin, swollen lips and a certain heaviness to the eyelids. It's intoxicating. You're intoxicating."

"Are you real?"

"Excuse me?"

Cam laughed, mostly at herself. "I'm sorry but intoxicating isn't a term I've heard applied to me. And this..." She gestured around them. "And you. It's been a long time since I've felt anything like this. A very long time."

"Then you're overdue," he replied. "And tonight I'm going to remind you just how sexy and exciting you are."

"Promises, promises," she teased, a little uncomfortable about her admission.

"Iron-clad, money-back guarantee," he countered.

Somehow, after what she'd just experienced, she was inclined to agree. Suddenly she couldn't wait for the event to conclude.

Chapter Four

❧

Tempt the Cougar Blog

From Cam: How juvenile is this? I should wait until tomorrow but I can't. We're on our way home from the juvenile diabetes fundraiser and let me tell you more was raised than funds. I did it in a powder room! Well, not really did it. But Lee went down on me and I came like the Great Flood. Good god!

Now we're on our way back to my house with a promise of more to come. Girls, I could get addicted to this—and to him. It's downright electrifying—and scary.

"Must be something special to prompt such a smile," Lee commented as Cam pressed the *Publish Post* button on the tiny screen of her iPhone to send the blog post winging its way to her friends.

"Just stuff from friends."

"Male or female?"

"Definitely female."

"Good, then I don't have to go into a jealous pout."

"Somehow I can't imagine that happening. Thank you again for going with me, Lee."

"I believe it *was* my idea."

"Yeah, well thanks all the same."

He smiled. "How's your perspective on fundraisers?"

Cam laughed. "It's for sure that this one tops the list."

"Driveway or garage?"

"Huh?"

"We're about to turn into your driveway. Where do you want me to park?"

"Wherever you like."

"If I park in the drive, the neighbors will know I spent the night."

Cam looked at him in surprise. "Oh? I didn't know you were going to."

"Now you do."

Lee parked the car in the driveway, cut the engine and got out to walk around the car and open her door. Cam smiled to herself. It sure would be easy to get used to this kind of treatment.

Once they were inside, Lee took her in his arms. Cam sighed in satisfied surrender, reveling in the feel of his body pressed against hers and his hands roaming down her back to cup her ass.

Lee backstepped, still locked in the kiss, into the living area. His lips left hers to trail along her face and down her throat where her pulse pounded. His hands slid slowly across her ass then tightened and yanked her up against him again.

His lips sought hers and she eagerly accepted the kiss, lifting her arms to encircle his neck, pressing against him and deepening the kiss. At length she pulled away, her skin feeling hot and flushed and her breath coming quick. "I want you."

Lee smiled at her, running his hands along her sides and up to trace over the swell of her breasts. "And you shall have me. But we're not going to rush. In fact, there's something I've been looking forward to and now is the perfect time."

"What?"

"I want to look at you. Strip for me, Cam."

With that, he released her and took a seat on the couch. Cam stood frozen in place, staring at him. *Strip?* That didn't sound too appealing. She felt pretty secure with her clothes on but to get naked while he sat there fully clothed… She looked away, unsure what to do or say.

"Cam, look at me."

She turned her head toward him. "You're one of the most beautiful, sexy women I've ever seen and I'm more attracted to you than I've been to any woman. I want to see you. I need you to throw away all your uncertainty and more importantly your past, and strip for me. Show me your passion, Cam."

Throw away my past? Actually, that was probably excellent advice. There'd been a time she'd felt like a desirable woman. Dan had ripped all that away from her, had turned her into the perfect Stepford wife—perfectly dressed and behaved and totally devoid of passion.

What Lee offered was a chance for her to reclaim herself. She'd be a fool not to try. Tossing her head, she smiled and sauntered to the stereo. She didn't have a vast library but she did find a sexy song that wasn't too fast that would work.

An idea occurred to her and she turned. "Wait. I have to get something."

She hurried to the hall closet. Sure enough, the old black fedora she'd bought as part of a costume for Dan one Halloween was still on the top shelf. She put it on and returned to the living room. Once the music started, she took a deep breath and with her back to Lee, started to sway.

Lee watched with growing anticipation and sexual hunger that gnawed with increasing ferocity. He wasn't sure she'd have the courage to do as he asked. Despite her looks and intelligence, Cam was a woman who'd had her innate sexuality stripped from her by an unaware, egotistical man who didn't realize her worth.

Music filled the room and she turned to face him. At first, she simply swayed to the beat, her hips undulating ever so slightly. Putting one hand on the hat, she pivoted. The hat dipped low, shielding her eyes as she performed a sexy bump and grind.

When she dropped into a crouch and looked from beneath the brim of the hat, his breath actually hitched. The look in her eyes was of a seductress, the smoky blue nearly eclipsed by the dark pupils to give her a feral, predatory look.

Cam took hold of her dress and began to stand, working it up her legs. The dress rose to expose her thighs, her neatly trimmed sex and her belly. Then she whirled, presenting him with her back. The dress fell to cover her again and then her hands reached behind her, working down the zipper.

Inch by inch her back was revealed. When the dress was fully unzipped, she performed a sexy little shimmy that had it sliding down her body to puddle at her feet. She stepped out of it, removed her hat and turned.

Clad only in the garter belt, stocking and high heels, with the hat covering her breasts, she was the perfect picture of sexuality.

Cam gave him a sultry smile then executed a seductive roll of her hips that had her sinking almost to the floor, knees bent and splayed out to the sides. Lee had to reach down and adjust himself in his slacks. He was definitely going to have her repeat that move later. Only completely naked and with him beneath her.

Cam rose slowly and sauntered closer. She tossed the hat in his direction. As he caught it, she moved her hands to her breasts. His eyes locked onto the sight of her hands, cupping and caressing her breasts, thumbs circling her nipples as her hips continued to grind and roll. His eyes moved from her breasts to her hips. Her seductive movements drove the hunger impossibly higher.

Cam slowly turned and bent forward, the movement presenting him with a view of her luscious ass. The sight of the torc securely anchored in her wet pussy and ass was enough to have his dick pulsing almost painfully. Need that was already

Ciana Stone

burning within him developed sharp claws, cutting into him with razor sharpness.

She straightened and moved to stand between his legs. Lee looked up and her eyes locked with his as she leaned over, her luscious breasts hanging full and inviting as she deftly worked the buttons on his shirt. The moment she parted the material to bare his chest, she lowered her mouth to his skin. Wet and warm, her tongue traced a trail of fire from his neck to his waist. All the while, her hands worked at his belt and the zipper of his pants.

For a woman who had seemed uncertain about her sexual appeal, Cam was doing a hell of a job. It took all the control he could muster not to grab her and throw her onto her back on the couch and bury himself inside her.

She sank to her knees on the floor in front of him as she freed his erection. Her mouth closed on him, electrifying every nerve in his body. Her tongue circled the head of his shaft, creating a burn that spread down its length, into his testicles and radiated out, prompting him to peel off his shirt, toe off his shoes and work his legs free of his pants.

Silken wetness enveloped him as she deep-throated him, each stroke driving the need higher.

Cam could feel the tension that rippled through Lee's body. It was a pretty sure bet that he was close to climax. His hands tangled in her hair, pulling her up to meet his lips. One touch and the need to devour him overwhelmed her. She climbed onto his lap, gripped his face and plundered his mouth as their bodies strained against one another, need bringing perspiration bursting through their pores to slicken their skin.

Suddenly Cam's world narrowed to the confines of the room, then smaller until nothing existed but Lee. Nothing mattered but the feel of his body pressed against hers, the taste of him as his tongue filled her mouth, and the fire that burned

264

within her at the touch of his hands roaming down her back to cup her ass and press her firmly against his erection.

She ended the kiss and started another slow trek down his body, her lips and tongue working slowly toward their destination. As she knelt in front of him, she felt his hands working onto her hair.

His grip tightened when she took him in her hand, running her tongue around the head of his penis, probing the tiny opening. Pre-cum gave him an exotic, spicy flavor that was intoxicating. She licked at the tiny droplets, using her tongue to smooth the lubricant over the engorged head.

When she ran her tongue down the length of his shaft and back up, a low groan came from him that had the fire of her desire flaming higher. It was exhilarating to know that her touch affected him and she wanted to give him more. Take him higher and further than he'd ever gone.

His body was like a drug, one she'd formed an instant addiction to and had no desire to break. The only measurement of time she was aware of was the reactions of his body as she took him close to the edge, time after time. Every time she felt that slight vibration sing in his body, felt his muscles tighten, she would slow, pulling back to circle the head of his penis with her tongue. And each time she felt that tension in him release, she would start again.

Finally, he stopped her, pushing her away.

Lee had never experienced anything like the sensations Cam evoked in him, and he wanted the same to be true for her. Pulling her to the sofa, he pushed her back, working his way up from her navel to her breasts and suckling them until she gasped, that curious sound that signaled a mixture of pain and pleasure that drove her to grind against him and small moans to come from her lips.

He could honestly admit that he'd never experienced this kind of need. The hunger to brand her, to give her what she couldn't hope to find with another. He captured her lips with his, tasting himself on her tongue.

She groaned into his mouth, her hands moving down his sides to pull him more firmly on her. He could taste her desire and it inflamed him almost to the point of breaking. Of forgetting the pleasure he wanted to show her and spreading her legs to sink into her delicious warmth and sate his hunger.

But the desire to pleasure her was stronger. He lingered on her lips a moment longer then released her from the kiss, his lips traveling down her neck to nip at the tender skin.

She pressed against his mouth, her hands tangling in his hair to pull him more firmly to her breast. He flicked his tongue over the peaked nub, letting his hand drift down her body and over her mound. His fingers slid between the wet folds. She moved against his hand then gasped when his finger eased over her hard clit.

Her soft pants and moans flamed the inferno in his mind and body, spurring him to trap her arms over her head and tease her nipple, his tongue circling and flicking over it before finally sucking it into his mouth.

She pressed up into the sensation, her breath coming faster as his fingers worked over her clit, pinching and stroking. When he felt a ripple run through her body and heard her breathy gasp, he knew she was about to come.

Easing back, he spread her legs and knelt between them. Her heavy-lidded eyes watched as he worked the torc from inside her then spread her sex wide and bent forward to lave her from perineum to clit in one slow stroke.

Her throaty groan preceded her arching against his mouth. He raised his head to see her hands moving to her breasts, pinching her reddened nipples.

She was sensuality personified. Gloriously uninhibited. Strong yet submissive to his every need. He wanted to dominate her, possess her and yet the need to pleasure her outranked his own desire. He needed to give her what no other man could.

His finger stroked between the lips of her labia then spread them to circle the silky wet flesh. When he pushed one finger inside her, she moaned and pressed into the feeling. He inserted another finger, gently probing the vaginal walls, pressing deeper. When her body arched he knew he'd found that one spot that delivered the most intense pleasure.

Cam's hips moved in time to the strokes of his hand, her own hands tracing down her body to her inner thighs to spread them wider. The bond between them enabled him to feel her need almost as strongly as his own. It was an intoxicating blend, almost overwhelming in its intensity. He bent forward to lave slowly over her clit and she moaned, moving faster against his fingers. He felt the vibration that raced through her and stroked faster and deeper inside her, sucking her clit into his mouth and flicking his tongue rapidly over it.

"Now, please. Please, Lee. In me!" Her panted words came a moment before her pussy started to spasm around his fingers and wetness streamed from inside her.

Before her climax could end, he straightened and pushed the head of his cock against her wet opening. She pushed against him, her body yielding to him.

The way her pussy clenched on him and her undulating movements beneath him threatened his control almost to the breaking point. She smiled up at him, that expression of sex and lust that said clearly she knew the effect she had on him. He nearly came before he was fully seated inside her.

Running his hands up her luscious body, he gently squeezed her swollen nipple. A prolonged breath preceded her smile. She lifted his hand from her breast and raised it to her mouth, sucking one finger then two. The sight of her sucking the juice from her pussy off his fingers made his dick throb, threatening his control.

She gave him that sultry smile as she moved his hand back to her breast. "Take me."

Her words were an explosion of sensation in his mind and body, a siren's call that could not be denied. He started to stroke, slow and steady, fighting to maintain control and keep the impending orgasm at bay. Her tight pussy pulsed on him, tightening then releasing. Her hips rose and fell, meeting each thrust and matching his pace.

It was not long before they both were breathing hard, trying to hold back the dam of sensation that threatened to burst. She was the first to succumb. "I...I can't...stop," she gasped and arched her body, stretching her arms back over her head in a gesture of surrender. "Please...oh please."

The sight of her submissively offering herself and the husky plea of her words was more than he could resist. He released the bonds holding his lust intact and let the full force of his need be free from all restraints.

Cam groaned when he grabbed her hips and roughly pulled her to him, impaling her on his full length. Her body quaked as he rode her, soft cries urging him on. When he felt her muscles tighten around him, he lowered down, propped on one elbow so that his free hand could pin her arms above her head securely.

His thrusts became more urgent and forceful and her cries deeper but he would not gentle his movements. Nor did she encourage him to do so. This was mating at its most primitive. Here was the moment he'd waited for. Her complete surrender.

"Now," she moaned. "I want all of you."

He couldn't have refused her demand had he wanted to. He drove deep and fast, their bodies slapping wetly in accompaniment to his harsh breaths and her moans. Her body began to quake in orgasm, ending his control. With a hard thrust, he hilted himself in her and surrendered.

When at last reality returned, he sank down on her, listening to the sound of their breaths, their hearts pounding against one another, and feeling their sweat-slicked skin gradually cooling.

He rolled off her onto his side and she shifted to face him, reaching up to stroke along the side of his face. In that moment something completely new to him happened, something he'd never experienced. Lee fell in love.

Chapter Five

℘

Cam finished going over the details of the next event on her schedule and opened her web browser to access the blog.

Tempt the Cougar Blog

From Cam: Sometimes I really love you, Monica. If you hadn't issued that challenge...well let's just say that today I am one happy woman. And well satisfied, I might add.

Grin.

Yes, he spent the entire weekend with me and I think I could become addicted to the guy. Can you say Rock my World? Repeatedly!

Gotta go. Will write more later!

Hugs, Cam.

She closed the laptop as her assistant Jennie entered. "I'm taking lunch now. Want me to bring you back something?"

"No, thanks anyway. I'll grab something in a bit."

"Okay, see you in an hour."

Cam watched her leave then leaned back in her chair. Lee hadn't left her house until that morning when she left to come to work. The weekend had been one she'd remember for a very long time. She and Lee had done things she'd only read about, and when they weren't having mind-blowing sex they laughed and talked and she discovered that not only did she lust for him, but also she genuinely liked him.

Which was dangerous. She hadn't been lying when she'd posted that she could get addicted to him. She was already

270

feeling far more of an emotional attachment than was safe. Nothing could happen between them, at least not anything in the way of a real relationship. She was too old for him.

Which really sucked.

She reminded herself that she hadn't gotten into this for love or happily ever after. This was all about having a good time. And great sex.

That turned her thoughts to wondering why she'd agreed to come to work without underwear. It was a request he'd made of her while they were dressing this morning. Did he want to imagine her working without underwear? Was that a turn-on for him?

A knock at her door turned her attention away from lascivious thoughts. "Yes?"

The door opened and suddenly the lascivious thoughts returned. There stood Lee with a take-out bag from her favorite Thai restaurant.

"Hungry?" he asked.

"Starved."

"So am I."

He walked in, kicked the door closed behind him, plunked the bag down on her desk then pulled her desk chair back and dropped to his knees. Before Cam could blink her skirt was bunched up around her waist and Lee was feasting on her.

And boy could the man feast. His tongue plunged deep inside then withdrew to circle her clit. For one brief moment Cam regretted her "short-fuse" state then surrendered to an orgasm that had her quaking.

Lee sat back on his heels, smiling at her as she blew out her breath. "My turn," she said. "Stand up."

She grabbed him by the hips as he stood and positioned him between her spread legs. In moments his pants were unfastened and in a puddle around his ankles. She wrapped one hand around the base of his shaft and worked the other behind him to grab his ass and pull him closer.

There was a brief intake of breath that came from him as her tongue circled the swollen head then laved down the length of him. She felt his hands tangle in her hair as she took him in her mouth. Damn, he was fine. She gave herself over to the taste and feel of him, lost to everything else until he groaned and pulled back.

"No fair," she protested. She wanted to give as good as she'd gotten and he'd stopped her too soon.

"Plenty fair," he said as he leaned over and locked his lips with hers in a kiss that had her toes curling.

Cam groaned in protest when he pulled away, then smiled as he worked free of his shoes and the pants bunched around his ankles.

Lee picked her up and carried her across the office to the sofa. He placed her on the sofa and pushed her back as he stretched out on top of her, his body hot and hard against her.

Another kiss had her body humming with need and she tried to pull him more firmly between her legs. He resisted, supporting himself on one elbow, his lips traveling down her neck in soft kisses and sharp little bites. And all the while his hand worked slowly down her body.

When he reached her sex, his hand cupped her. She pressed against his hand, eager for his touch. His fingers moved in her wet folds, spreading her lips to stroke and probe.

She didn't even try to stop the moan of longing that came from deep inside her. At the sound, he gave her a wolfish smile and staked a claim on her lips. His fingers moved inside her, deep and slow strokes that had her panting against his mouth and rocking against the movement of his fingers.

"Oh yes," she groaned. "More."

"There's plenty more, baby." His whispered response preceded him sucking her bottom lip into his mouth and biting softly on it before moving to nip at her chin and work his way down her neck.

"I'm going to leave you so satisfied you'll barely be able to walk."

"Promises, promises," she breathed throatily.

His hand tangled in her hair, pulling her head back. She looked up into his eyes eagerly then gasped as his fingers penetrated her wet core.

"Yes," she moaned as his fingers stroked her closer to orgasm.

His smile was predatory as he unbuttoned her blouse and pulled on her bra to reveal one breast. He lowered his head, his mouth closing on her breast. The light bite he gave to her nipple had her moaning. Not in pain but hunger. She worked her hands down his body, circling his shaft. "I want you."

"And you'll have me," he said against her skin then raised his head to smile at her. "But not just yet.

He sat back, took hold of her legs and forced them into a bent position, spreading them wide. Her hands worked into fists, clutching at the sofa cushion as he licked her wet folds. He spread her legs more, sucking her labia into his mouth and then slowly moving his tongue up her length to suck on her clit.

She moaned when his tongue worked down and plunged inside her. A gasp followed when his tongue stroked over her clit, sending a spark of electric sensation tearing through her.

Her hands moved to her inner thighs, pressing them out and down, fingers digging into her own skin as the intensity increased. "That's it, baby," he crooned against her, and released her legs to use his fingers to spread her wide, exposing her clit.

Her fingers dug deeper into her flesh when his tongue flicked over her clit, teasing and circling it. She was panting by the time he captured it in his mouth, his tongue tracing over the hard nub.

She trembled, spreading her legs wider, wanting more yet fighting to stem the wave that threatened to wash her out into that sea of release.

Lee pressed two fingers inside her, his strokes slow and deep as he continued the sublime assault on her clit. It was too much. She couldn't hold back.

"Ah, oh...Lee," she moaned a moment before the wave crested.

Her body trembled. She felt him move, pulling her to him and pressing his hard shaft against the entrance of her sex. The wave pounded down on her. A mindless void of sensation took her as he penetrated her, stretching her.

The wave intensified, leaving her mindless to everything but the sensations. He pushed slowly, deeper and deeper, until the length of him was embedded inside her.

Her body strained to accommodate him. She felt stretched to her limits, clenching on the hardness that filled her and all the while imprisoned by an orgasm that had her panting and moaning, her hands gripping his shoulders like claws, digging in and holding fast.

He took his time, stroking slow and drawing the pleasure out so that every time it seemed the intensity would abate, his pace would increase. Hard and deep he rode her, bringing her back to a fever pitch of sensation so intense all she could do was surrender to its power.

When his movements began to slow, she sucked in a breath and panted at him. "No, don't stop. More. Now. Please."

"I want to watch you play with yourself. Play with your clit." He sat back on his heels, pulling her forward so that she was bowed, her hips elevated by his thighs.

She had no problem complying. Securing her position by digging her heels into the sofa on either side of him, she rocked her pelvis forward. Her hands moved between her legs,

274

fingers spreading her sex to expose her clit. She saw his eyes tracking her movements.

She ran one finger then two over that hard bud of flesh, feeling the resulting spark that made her sex clench on him. He gripped her hips, measuring his pace with her. Slow at first, then increasing in speed and depth as her body started to tense with the onset of climax.

She felt the vibration begin, and at that moment he drove deep inside her. She screamed his name in pleasure and tightened her legs around his waist to pull him down on her.

The slap of flesh against flesh was an accompaniment to the beat of their fast breaths and her soft groans.

"Ah damn. Baby, slow..." he groaned as she started to contract on him. "You're going to—"

"Come with me," she panted, milking him with strong contractions. She felt him let go, felt him pulse in time with her contractions and she crested, letting herself freefall into sensation.

When at last the wave had passed, he lowered himself down, rolling over with his arms locked around her so that she lay against his side. With her head on his chest, she closed her eyes, listing to the rapid pound of his heart and feeling her own breath trying to stabilize.

For a long time he held her then drew back and looked into her eyes.

"What?" she asked.

"Just surprised. I thought you'd be more inhibited considering we're in your office."

"The only ones in the office," she corrected and looked at the antique clock on the credenza behind her desk. "For another—oh shit, less than ten minutes."

"Then I guess we don't have time for round two."

She raised one eyebrow, feeling her sex clench in excited anticipation. "I wish."

"So do I. But there's always tonight. Why don't I come over when I finish with my last appointment?"

"What time is that?"

"I can be there by nine."

Cam smiled. "Sounds good."

"Great. I'll bring champagne."

"Oh? Are we having a party?"

"Celebrating."

"Celebrating?"

He gave her a sly smile. "I got the job."

"You got the...oh my god, you got the job as sports medicine specialist for the pro football team? Lee! Why didn't you tell me earlier?"

"I had other things on my mind."

Cam rolled her eyes at the teasing smile on his face. "This is fantastic! You've got to be over-the-moon excited."

"Yes and no."

"What?"

"Yeah, I'm glad I got the job. It's what I've been working for a long time. But..."

"But what?"

"It means I have to leave in two days and will be gone for a couple of weeks."

Cam wasn't sure why that would be a problem. "And?"

"And I won't get to see you for two weeks."

Something changed in his eyes, in his expression. She could hear it in his tone of voice. This wasn't a man just having a good time. As impossible as it seemed, somehow he was emotionally invested in what they were doing. Cam couldn't explain how she knew that, but she felt it in her gut.

And it scared the crap out of her. This wasn't supposed to happen. They were supposed to have mind-blowing sex and...and what? Suddenly it dawned on her that she didn't want to think of Lee not being in her life. Crazy as it was, she'd allowed herself to fall for him. And that wasn't smart. Not at all.

He was watching her, waiting for a response and she didn't know what to say. No way was she going to admit that she'd fallen for him. "Well, there is this little thing called a cell phone. And I've heard about this thing called sexting. Maybe we could give it a try."

"Sexting?"

"Yeah, you know, like phone sex but with text."

"You want to have text sex?"

She chuckled and moved off the couch to adjust her clothing. "Maybe. And hey, I'll be here when you get back. If you're interested."

Lee stood and pulled her into his arms. "I'll be interested."

"Good," she murmured a moment before his lips closed on hers.

"Holy shit!"

Cam jerked at the sound of her assistant's voice. She pulled away from the kiss but not from Lee's arms. "Jennie," she addressed her assistant who stood with rounded eyes and mouth hanging open at the door. "I didn't hear you knock."

"Oh! Oh I'm sorry. I—I—sorry." She turned and fled.

Lee chuckled and lowered his head to rest against Cam's. "Guess you've got some explaining to do. I better let you get back to work. See you at nine?"

"I'll be waiting. And congratulations on the job, Lee."

"Thanks. See you tonight."

He gave her a quick kiss, dressed and left. Cam hurried to the washroom adjacent to her office and looked at her reflection. What she saw wasn't a woman who looked like she'd just had incredible sex that had left her a bit disheveled

277

and flushed. Instead, she saw a woman who'd done the one thing she'd vowed to never do again. She'd loosened the reins on her emotions and fallen for Lee.

Chapter Six

ᔥ

Tempt the Cougar Blog

From Cam: Sorry to have been out of the loop for the last couple of weeks. To be honest I've been doing a lot of thinking. And having a lot of phone sex. I know! Who would've thought that I'd be spending my evenings having phone sex with a young hottie?

So much has changed since I met Lee. And that's what I've been doing so much thinking about. The sex is great. He's great and I love being with him, in and out of bed. But...well the truth is, he wants more than just sex. He's dropping hints about the future, how to arrange things so we don't have to be apart so much.

It scares the hell out of me!

I like him. A lot. Maybe even more than like. I don't know. Well, maybe I do, but I can't admit it, not even to you guys. I mean, he's ten years younger than me! And he's just getting his foot in the door on a career that will have him on the road most of the time. It can't work. It just can't. My life, my job is here.

I don't know what to do. He'll be home today and is coming over tonight. He wants to talk.

What do I do?

Cam the confused.

Cam pressed the *Publish Post* button then leaned back in her chair and stared at the screen. She didn't expect her friends to solve the dilemma for her. She knew she had to do that herself. But she needed to know what they thought.

Was she insane to even consider getting into a long-term relationship with Lee? Part of her wanted to throw caution to the wind and take the chance. Another part was just too scared. There were too many obstacles to overcome.

First was his age. She knew it wasn't an issue with him, but it was for her. Despite the happiness her friends had found with younger men, Cam couldn't stop thinking about the "when's" — when he was forty she'd be fifty. When he's fifty, she'd be sixty. She might be holding up fine at forty-two but eventually the difference was going to show a lot. She didn't know if she could handle it.

And what if he decided one day he couldn't? How could she set herself up for that kind of hurt?

Then there was the matter of his new job. He'd be on the road with the team most of the time. That was also a major factor. How could you have a successful relationship when you're apart so much of the time?

She closed her eyes and tried to breathe slow and deep. She needed to find her balance, to be able to be calm and reasonable when she saw him.

But thoughts of seeing him prompted anything but calm. Excitement, anticipation and a huge case of girl wood, but not calm. Cam blew out her breath and straightened in her seat. She'd just have to wing it and hope for the best.

Unless one of the girls came up with some excellent advice. Mentally crossing her fingers for that, she turned her attention to getting through the rest of the day.

* * * * *

Lee threw the last load of his laundry into the dryer then stretched out on the couch. He had a few hours before time to go over to Cam's and still had some things to work out in his mind.

Like where their relationship was headed.

During the two weeks he was on the road they'd burned up the phone lines, talking and texting. Sure, they'd had some amazing phone sex and had even tried the sexting, complete with photos, but it was the conversations that had been the important moments.

He'd learned a lot about Cam and most of what he'd learned he liked. The only thing that bothered him was her reluctance to let their relationship move forward. It was as if her one failed marriage had tossed her into an emotional prison that was unbreakable. You went in and never came out.

Well, that wasn't entirely true. He knew she cared for him. Maybe she was even in love with him. But she wasn't ready to admit it, much less act on it. Was it the age thing that was holding her back? If it didn't matter to him, why should it matter to her? Couldn't she trust that he was sincere when he said it didn't matter?

Or did it matter what he said? Maybe this had nothing to do with him and everything to do with battling her own demons. The question was how did he go about breaching the impenetrable prison she'd sequestered herself in and make her see that what they had was too important to turn her back on?

And how the hell was he going to figure out the answers in less than three hours?

* * * * *

Tempt the Cougar Blog

Comment from Monica: Don't overthink it. The core is your relationship. All the rest is just stuff you deal with. If you have genuine feelings for him then that's all that matters. Life is waiting for you, Cam. Don't let it pass you by because you were afraid to step out of the shadows and kick it in the ass.

Comment from Rachel: Only you can decide if Lee is worth the extra effort, but from what you've told us, I think you'd be a fool to throw away the chance at something wonderful just because it might be too hard. Where there's a will, there's a way, Cam. Go for it!

Cam finished reading the comments that had come in from her friends. Intellectually she knew they were right. She was not only overthinking the situation but also acting rather cowardly. The question was why? Was it just a matter of her vanity and the fear that one day he'd view her as old, or was it the fear of rejection?

Despite the brave front she put on for everyone, when Dan cheated on her and then left her, it had been devastating. Not simply because he preferred another woman over her but because she'd been so stupid she'd never suspected.

What if the same happened with Lee? What if he decided he was tired of her and cheated on her or walked out on her for a younger model? What if she was blindsided by another train that she never saw coming? Could she survive another hit like that?

The ring of the doorbell cut her questions short. Dashing out of the small study, she ran for the door.

Lee swept her into his arms, claiming her with a kiss the moment the door opened. He backstepped her inside, kicked the door closed behind him and continued the assault.

When he released her, Cam felt a little rubber-legged. But then he did have the power to turn her into a quivering glob of female goo.

"God, I missed you." He smiled down at her, running his hand along the side of her face and into her hair.

"Me too," she admitted. "I wasn't sure what you wanted to do about dinner but I could order something. Unless that's dinner." She gestured to the small duffle bag he'd dumped inside the door."

"Baby, food is the last thing on my mind. And no, that's not dinner."

"Then what is it?"

"A surprise."

"What kind of surprise?"

"Remember that little bondage game we played on the phone?"

Cam felt a rush that dampened her panties. "Oh yeah."

"Well, this time it's not pretend."

"Really? Well in that case, I'm all yours."

"You sure?"

"Absolutely."

"Then let's take this to the bedroom."

"Whatever you say." Cam gave him a sexy smile and proceeded to the bedroom, leaving him to follow.

She took a seat on the bed. "Okay, what now?"

Lee placed the duffle bag on the chair next to the nightstand and rumbled through it. His hands emerged with a set of restraints and he walked over to the bed.

"Lift your hair off your neck."

Cam lifted her hair and held it on top of her head as Lee fastened a soft, padded leather collar around her neck. He stepped back and she let her hair fall back to her shoulders.

Lee's dick jumped at the sight. He'd longed for this since the moment he met her, and knowing she was willing had him half ready to forget what he'd planned and simply spread her luscious legs and bury himself inside her.

But that wasn't the plan. First he'd give her a fantasy, show her pleasure she'd never experienced. Then he'd deal with the matter of the relationship.

"Stand up," he ordered, half expecting her to balk at his command.

But she didn't. She stood, waiting as he crossed the room to the docking station on her dresser. He scrolled through the music on her iPod. "What's your favorite music to strip to?"

She smiled and cocked her head to one side. "Hmmm. How about 'Wild Women' by Natalie Cole?"

"Oldie but a goodie," he said with a smile and selected the track. The speakers projected the music as soon as he hit the play button.

"Strip," he said and lay back on the bed.

Cam began to sway and pump her hips to the beat. Within moments her grind had the hem of the short robe she wore riding up to reveal the lacy thong she wore beneath it.

She turned her back to him, lowering one shoulder of the robe then the other, all the while shaking her ass at him. When she whirled to face him again, the robe was barely covering the tips of her breasts.

With a sexy, come-get-it smile, she lifted her arms over her head then lowered them, her hands caressing their way down her body, lowering the robe so that her breasts sprang free. She cupped them with her hands, her hands splayed out over the firm globes, her body undulating so that the robe shimmied down to her hips where it lodged.

Lee's dick throbbed in his pants. He'd never seen a dancer who could match her moves or her looks. With a sexy pout on her face, she moved her hands down to lower the robe one tantalizing inch at a time. When she stepped free of it and was clad only in her barely there thong and sexy stiletto heels, she moved closer to the bed to grab the bedpost.

She pressed her mound against the post, then bent her knees and worked her way down the post. She wiggled her way back up, arched back and swung around, letting go to spin on her toes to the center of the room, her enticing ass to Lee.

He watched her work her panties down and step out of them, then she spread her legs and bent forward, reaching between her legs to stroke her hands from her ankles up to the vee of her legs, her fingers trailing along the sides of her sex.

The sight of her bent over and exposed was enough to make him reconsider his plan again and get right to the part where he was stroking away inside her. But he wanted more. He wanted to do things to her that he'd been dreaming of. Hear her pant, moan, beg and scream.

"Come here." He was surprised at the roughness of his own voice, the need that was evident.

She straightened and walked to the bed as he rose with the restraints in hand. "I think it's time for these."

Cam felt a shiver of unease. Sure, they'd talked about it, pretended over the phone, but to actually let him bind her meant a loss of sexual control.

"What's the matter?" He moved closer. "Scared?"

Cam tossed her head in what she hoped translated as confidence. "Of what? Are you planning on hurting me?"

"Only if you want me to," he replied, sending a spike of excitement straight to her pussy.

She smiled and held out her arms to him. He secured the padded restraints to both wrists then knelt down to fasten similar restraints to each ankle. "On the bed," he said as he stood.

While she lay back on the bed, he fetched the rest of the restraints from the bag. Cam felt perspiration break out on her skin as he pulled her arms up above her head and secured them to the headboard.

He fastened nylon straps to the ankle restraints and pulled her legs up and back toward her head, forcing her to bend her knees as he secured the ends of the straps to the bedposts at the head of the bed, raising her ass up and leaving her splayed out and completely vulnerable.

It was a feeling that made her anxious and excited at the same time. Lee got off the bed and just stood there for the longest time, looking at her. She started to feel uncomfortable and nervous. Suddenly he turned and crossed the room to the dressing mirror.

He picked it up and carried it back across the room, positioning it at the foot of the bed. He looked at the reflection then moved to the head of the bed to look at it again.

Cam looked and saw herself, legs bent up nearly to her chest and pulled back so that her pussy and ass were raised and spread wide. Panic bubbled in her stomach. Maybe this wasn't such a good idea.

"Wait, let me fix this." Lee lifted her head to put a pillow beneath it. "I want you to be able to see everything I do to you."

Her pussy clenched at the gravelly tone of his voice and the hunger on his face. She said nothing but watched as he got off the bed to get the bag and dump its contents on the bed.

He climbed on the bed, looking at the assortment. "How about these?" He held up nipple clamps. "They can be very stimulating.

"But," he continued as he leaned forward, "do they work as well as this?" He lowered his head and ran his tongue around the areola of one nipple, circling then flicking the nipple, over and again until Cam started to wiggle and squirm.

He moved to the other breast, giving it the same treatment while he used his thumb and index finger to pull and pinch at the nipple his mouth had nice and wet with saliva. Cam felt the burn, welcomed it, but after a few minutes the pleasure began to be tinted with pain. "No, stop. Please."

"Can't take it?" Lee raised his head but kept one nipple prisoner, pinching and rolling it with his fingers.

"Uhhh." She bit her lip, wanting him to stop, yet feeling a measure of pleasure from the small pain.

"I didn't think so," Lee said with a smile and reached for the clamps. Cam gasped as he fastened one to each sensitive nipple. It created a ribbon of sensation that ran through her, culminating at her pussy and making it clench.

"Baby, you're so hot." Lee ran his hand to her pussy and plunged two fingers inside her. "But not as hot as you're going to get."

"Ahhh," she moaned as he stroked her, his fingers sinking deeper each time.

"Uh-uh, not yet." He removed his fingers as she started to cream. "No coming yet. Not 'til I say so. Remember, you're mine. I call the shots."

He picked up a tube of lubricant and coated a beaded anal probe then smeared lubricant from her clit to her ass, spreading her lips wide and loading her with the slick substance.

"Look how your pussy opens for me." He seemed transfixed on the sight. "So soft. So wet." He inserted two fingers inside her. "So hungry."

Cam switched her gaze from his face to the reflection in the mirror. Lee's fingers moved in and out of her pussy, each stroke making her cream so that it ran out of her pussy and trailed to her ass. Watching as the sensations raced through her made it even more exciting and she wiggled against his probing fingers, wanting more.

He looked up at the mirror and grinned. "Not yet. I have a little something for you."

She knew what was coming but still was not quite prepared. The anal probe was six inches long and had a series of beads, each larger than the other. Lee squirted a generous dollop of lubricant on her anus and smeared it around, probing his finger inside her tight hole.

"God, you're tight," he commented, sinking his finger up her ass to the first knuckle.

She moaned at the invasion. She'd been on the giving end of this kind of play several times but the receiving end was another matter and one she'd avoided for the most part.

"Have you ever been ass-fucked, baby?" he asked, moving his finger in deeper.

She shook her head back and forth, not trusting her voice.

"You gonna let me be the one who breaks you in?"

"It would seem so," she gasped, her traitorous body already tuning in to the sensations, making her pussy run wet.

"Loosen your ass, baby."

"I'm trying!" she moaned.

Lee withdrew his finger and ran the end bead of the probe around her anus, finally pushing it in. Cam gasped and strained at her bonds, but her pussy opened wider, making it obvious that she was excited.

One bead at a time, he slowly inserted the probe. Cam's moans increased with each bead. He was less than halfway when his free hand moved to her clit, spreading her pussy wide to expose it.

Cam nearly screamed as he ran his finger back and forth over her clit then down to sink into her pussy, all the while pushing the probe in deeper. "That's it, baby. Take it," he crooned. "One more, one more."

With his hand alternating between tormenting her clit and finger-fucking her pussy, and the probe stretching her ass, going deeper and deeper, Cam finally surrendered control. "Ahhh, yes!" she screamed as he stroked his fingers fast inside her, taking her to the edge of climax.

"Noooo!" she protested when he stopped, but left the probe in her ass, making her feel stretched and full.

Lee shifted so that he could lean down and run his tongue down one side of her pussy and back up the other, then again, nibbling on her lips, sucking them, and then moving up to her clit.

He began pulling the probe out, very slow, one bead at a time, all the while licking her pussy, sucking on her, lapping at her cum. When the probe slipped free, she relaxed then moaned as he sunk a finger up her ass, his knuckle rough against the sensitive muscle.

"Never gonna be able to fuck you up the ass if we don't get you loosened up." He raised his head long enough to watch in the mirror as he withdrew his finger and gave her another squirt of lubricant. Cam cried out when he used two fingers, her tight anus protesting against the invasion and yet welcoming it.

Lee stroked her pussy from clit to opening, spreading the lips, stroking and pinching them, then somewhat roughly pinching her clit and rolling it between his thumb and finger, all the while ass fucking her with his fingers, pressing deeper inside her to the first knuckle.

His fingers spread, earning a scream from Cam that was of either pain or supreme pleasure. She wasn't sure. It all seemed to be mixed up, combined. All she knew was that her nipples ached from the clamps, her ass burned and her clit felt as hard as a rock.

"Oh god," she moaned as he began focusing on her clit, rubbing up and down, circling and stroking. "Please, pleaseplease."

"Please, what?"

"Please, I want it."

"Want what?"

"To come!" she screamed.

"Then beg for it. Beg me to fuck your tight little ass and lick your sweet clit."

"Yes, please."

"Please what?" He toyed with her, all the while stroking and probing, feeling her nearly vibrate with hunger.

"Please fuck me. Fuck me! Just let me come!"

"No." He suddenly stopped everything and sat back on his heels.

Cam screamed and thrashed around. "Okay, enough. Let me loose!"

"Oh no, we're not even close to that," he replied calmly and leaned down to nip her on the chin. "Like I said, this time I'm in control and I'm going to enjoy your luscious body all night. And when I do let you come you're going to have a half-hour orgasm, and after that, no matter what you do with the rest of your life, you'll never forget this night or the man who made you come like you'll probably never come again."

And with that, he started again. The evening turned to night and night gave way to the first streaks of dawn when Lee's own hunger finally gave way. He licked Cam's swollen clit to orgasm and as her body started to quake, he climbed between her legs and slid inside her.

She screamed so loud it should have had a neighbor calling the police, but Lee barely noticed. All that existed for him was the clenching wet pussy milking his dick, taking him by the second closer to ultimate bliss.

Cam had never come so hard or so long. The climax was just subsiding when she felt Lee's orgasm crest. It pushed her headlong into another body-shuddering orgasm that nearly had her eyes rolling back in her head.

Lee groaned and fell forward, bracing himself on his hands with his eyes closed. When he finally opened his eyes again he smiled down at her. "Baby, I don't know what the hell happens after tonight, but I want you to know that you're the most incredible woman I've ever met and as long as I live I'll remember this night."

"Ditto," she said with a smile. "And I'd love to put my arms around you right now, but I think my arms have lost all feeling."

Lee unfastened the restraints. Cam's arms tingled as circulation was restored and she pulled Lee to her. He wrapped around her and they both lay silently on the bed. Inside of a few minutes his breathing slowed.

She waited a few minutes more until she was sure he was asleep. More than anything she wanted to just stay there, curled up in his arms. But that couldn't be. If she stayed she'd never be able to walk away again. She had to leave. Had to get up, shower and go to work, pretend this was nothing more than an incredibly wild night of sex.

It was not what she wanted. Not at all. She wanted to simply sink back into his arms, close her eyes and sleep. But she couldn't. When he woke, he'd want to talk and she couldn't face that. Not after the night they'd just had.

What the hell was she supposed to do? She couldn't let the emotions pressing in on her take control. She couldn't be in love with him. He was too young, and she...well, she wasn't sure what she was except a very confused woman who'd stumbled into a relationship she didn't know how to handle.

She should just walk away. Pretend it was just great sex and nothing else. Never let him know that she was losing her heart to him. Maybe he wouldn't want her heart anyway. Maybe for him this was just a passing thing, a relationship he thought now that would last, but one that would lose its appeal down the road when a younger, more attractive woman caught his eye.

But what if he did care? Really care? She knew what it felt like to be hurt. If she walked away, would he be hurt? Did she want that?

God, what a mess! She wished she had the courage to just do what her heart told her. To allow herself to love this man and say to hell with the consequences, the "what if's" and uncertainties.

For a long time she lay beside him, listening to him breathe and feeling the warmth of his skin against hers. What would life be like to have this every night? To wake to his smile and anticipate the night to come in his arms?

No. That was a fantasy. A dream. It couldn't work in real life. She had to remember that. She hadn't gotten into this for love. It was supposed to only be about sex, about reminding herself that she wasn't a loser just because her husband had dumped her for a younger model.

She wasn't supposed to love Lee and she darn sure wasn't supposed to leave herself open and vulnerable to being hurt again. And that, she realized, was her biggest fear. That one day he'd walk out on her.

Cam couldn't face that. Not again. Better that it end now while she had the courage to walk away and try to forget.

Before she could change her mind, she slipped out of the bed, grabbed what she needed from her closet, and tiptoed down the hall to the guest room to shower.

Once she was dressed, she scribbled a note and left it for him on the nightstand. Then, with her heart breaking, she went to work.

Chapter Seven

℘

Cam tossed her purse and briefcase on the chair and picked up the phone to check her voice mail. Lee still hadn't called.

She'd screwed up. Royally. She never should have left the morning after their bondage thing. She should have stayed. But chicken-shit that she was, she ran. And hadn't heard a word from him since.

The girls had offered advice ranging from letting it go and moving on to tracking him down and telling him she'd made a mistake. Several of the newer women who'd joined their group had suggested that she just call and act casual, test the waters and see how he'd react.

That might be a good plan. She could call. Again. But what good would it do? He hadn't taken calls from her the past three weeks — what made today any different?

Cam wanted to cry, to kick something — probably herself. How could she have been so stupid? How could she have turned her back on something that could have been so good?

What the hell was she going to do?

Edie's voice sounded in her head. *Well, what are your choices? Do nothing and it's over for sure or take a chance there's something still there and go for it.*

Cam grabbed the phone before she could chicken out again. The phone rang three times before Lee answered.

"Cam?"

"Is this a bad time?"

"No. I just got off a plane and was headed home."

"You've been out of town?"

"Yeah."

"Oh, well...well, I—uh, I wondered if you might have some free time?"

"For?"

Cam nearly lost her courage, almost hung up. But she sucked it up and replied, "I'm sorry. I was wrong and...and I wanted to talk."

There was a long pause before he replied. "I'll stop on my way home."

"Thanks."

"See you soon."

She hung up the phone and just stood there, her mind in a whirl. He was coming over. Now the question was, was she brave enough to admit the truth to him? Hell, was she brave enough to admit it to herself?

An hour later, she was sitting on the couch, freshly showered, and dressed in a soft casual gauze dress, no shoes, and her hair still damp. She hadn't bothered with makeup. If she was going to be completely honest then she'd be honest in her appearance as well. Nothing enhanced or masked.

The doorbell rang and her stomach clenched. When she opened the door and saw Lee standing there the world seemed to go completely silent and time screeched to a halt. She nearly staggered as the realization hit her. She was in love with this man.

"Are you going to ask me in?"

"Oh, I'm sorry. Yes."

There was an awkward silence between them as she closed the door behind him and he turned to face her. For a long time they simply looked at one another. Finally, he broke the silence.

"Why did you leave?"

"Fear," she replied.

"I don't get it."

Cam gestured toward the great room and Lee followed her, took a seat on the sofa beside her. "You want to explain?"

"I don't know if I can. I mean, I don't know if it will make sense."

"Try."

A comment from her friend Elizabeth came to mind. *I had many of the same feelings! I ran through the list of pros and cons, and the one that hit home the hardest, that sticks with me still, was asking myself if I could face every day knowing I hadn't even tried.*

Yes, taking the leap to be in a relationship with Kevin took a lot of faith. No matter how it turns out in the long run, the reward has already been worth it.

Elizabeth had nailed it. It was a leap of faith. She blew out her breath. "I'm scared. Scared of how you make me feel, of how I feel about you."

"Cam, I'd never hurt—"

"Don't," she held up one hand. "Please, let me get this out while I have the courage."

"Okay."

"When I found Dan in bed with that woman it knocked me for a loop. I never even suspected that he wasn't happy with me—that he was screwing around. Then when he left me...well, I guess it did a number on me. I felt...less than. Embarrassed, humiliated and rejected.

"When you and I met I wasn't looking for happily-ever-after. Just a man to make me feel good about myself again, to make me feel like I was still desirable. Not less-than."

"And I don't do that for you?"

"Oh god, no, it's not that. You do. You've made me feel like...like someone special. Sexy and desirable and interesting."

"Then what's the problem, Cam?"

"I'm the problem. I couldn't stop at just feeling good and enjoying it. My emotions pushed in and I started to fall..."

"In love with me?"

Cam nodded, not able to meet his eyes. "It scared me. I couldn't leave myself open to the kind of potential hurt love brings. What if one day you look at me and see an old woman? A woman who's not desirable? What if one day you're away on the road and some young beautiful woman comes on to you and suddenly you wonder why you're wasting your time with an old lady like me? What if—"

"What if I don't?" he interrupted. "Cam, I love you. I want to spend my life with you and no matter how old you are, you'll always be the most exciting, sexy woman in the world to me. Sensuality—sexuality, it's not just about what's out here," he touched her face then moved his hand over her heart. "But what's in here. I'm in love with you, Cam. All of you, not just your body."

"I want to believe that," she whispered. "So much. But I don't know if I believe in happily-ever-after anymore."

Lee chuckled and pulled her into his arms to hold her close. "But what's happily-ever-after other than a series of happy-for-right-nows? Life shouldn't be lived for tomorrow, or next week or ten years from now. It's the now that matters. All the experiences and closeness of the right-nows are what build the happily-ever-after."

Cam looked up at him, surprised by his words. "That's beautiful, but how can I trust it?"

"A day at a time, baby. That's all we have. And if you give me a chance, I'll prove it to you a day at a time."

Cam looked into his eyes, saw the sincerity and love shining bright. She'd be such a fool to turn her back on what he offered. And she didn't want to be a fool.

"I do love you," she admitted.

"Is that a yes?"

She nodded and he smiled at her. "Then maybe we should celebrate this moment—our first in the never-ending series of happy-for-nows."

She returned the smile. "What'd you have in mind, handsome?"

"Did you lock the door?"

"Huh?"

Lee laughed and lowered his lips to hers. Cam surrendered as the masculine smells and tastes intoxicated her senses. The sensation of maleness enveloped her, passionate, strong, willful and wild.

When Lee pulled back, she protested with a groan. He smiled, grazed her lips once more, and rose to lock the door, shutting the world out and their passion in.

Cam stood to meet him on his return. He lifted her hair away from her neck, running his tongue along its side and around to the hollow of her throat.

His smell filled her, speeding her pulse. His touch inflamed her, heating her skin. He lowered the straps of the thin dress she wore and it slithered down her body to pool around her feet. His hands moved around her, over her belly and then up toward her breasts, his lips moving on the skin of her shoulder leaving trails of fire in their wake.

Her nipples tightened beneath his touch, the palms of his hands warm against her skin. Her own palms grew moist in anticipation. Lee's eyes racked over her scantily clad form back to her face.

"No woman has ever affected me the way you do."

When his head ducked down to take her breast into his mouth, she arched toward him, pressing into the sensation. Lee raised his head long enough to give her a sexy smile then began a journey down her body with his tongue. A trail of elation ghosted his mouth, making her skin tingle.

When he knelt and licked her navel, his hands slid up the back of her smooth legs to massage and squeeze her ass.

Cam's breath hitched when he slid the thong down her legs and his mouth covered her mound, his tongue raking past the tight curls to search out her clit. Moisture dampened her inner thighs.

Lee's tongue moved lower, laving her swollen lips, sucking and biting. "You're so sweet, so damn sweet. Let me take you to bed, baby, and love you all night. Every night."

"Anything you want," she replied, quoting his words back to her.

"Promises, promises," he retorted teasingly.

"Yes, it is," she replied. Lee was right. Happily-ever-after was the product of all the happy-for-nows. And right now, she was very happy.

Epilogue

ဆာ

Tempt the Cougar Blog

From Cam: Sometimes I really love you, Monica. And the challenge you issued. Were it not for that, and the friendship and support I have with all of you, I wouldn't have had the courage to get out there and see what life had to offer.

When we all met, we were pretty dismal, weren't we? We'd let life defeat us. What a difference a year makes, eh? Look at us now!

To all of you ladies who've recently joined our intrepid little group, let me say thanks. You're such a fun addition, and while right now you may feel that the future looks bleak, take a look at what happened to Monica, Stevie, Autumn, Edie, Elizabeth, Rachel, and me.

We came together as women afraid to pursue our dreams. And today we're women living those dreams.

It can happen for you too. You just gotta believe.

(And post all about it for the rest of us, of course!)

Can't wait to see you all at the next RomantiCon!

Hugs, Cam.

Also by Desiree Holt

ဢ

eBooks:

Cougar Challenge: Hot to Trot

Cupid's Shaft

Dancing With Danger

Diamond Lady

Double Entry

Driven by Hunger

Eagle's Run

Ellora's Cavemen: Flavors of Ecstasy I (*anthology*)

Emerald Green

Escape the Night

Hot Moon Rising

Hot, Wicked and Wild

I Dare You

Journey to the Pearl

Just Say Yes

Kidnapping the Groom *with Allie Standifer*

Letting Go

Line of Sight

Lust Unleashed

Mistletoe Magic: Elven Magic *with Regina Carlysle & Cindy Spencer Pape*

Mistletoe Magic: Touch of Magic

Night Heat

Once Burned
Once Upon a Wedding
Riding Out the Storm
Rodeo Heat
Scalded *with Allie Standifer*
Scorched *with Allie Standifer*
Seductive Illusion *with Allie Standifer*
Switched
Teaching Molly
Trouble in Cowboy Boots
Where Danger Hides

Print Books:
Age and Experience (*anthology*)
Candy Caresses (*anthology*)
Demanding Diamonds (*anthology*)
Ellora's Cavemen: Flavors of Ecstasy I (*anthology*)
Erotic Emerald (*anthology*)
Mistleoe Magic (*anthology*)
Naughty Nuptials (*anthology*)
Rodeo Heat
Where Danger Hides

About the Author

ຂໆ

I always wonder what readers really want to know when I write one of these things. Getting to this point in my career has been an interesting journey. I've managed rock and roll bands and organized concerts. Been the only female on the sports staff of a university newspaper. Immersed myself in Nashville peddling a country singer. Lived in five different states. Married two very interesting but totally different men.

I think I must have lived in Texas in another life, because the minute I set foot on Texas soil I knew I was home. Living in Texas Hill Country gives me inspiration for more stories than I'll probably ever be able to tell, what with all the sexy cowboys who surround me and the gorgeous scenery that provides a great setting.

Each day is a new adventure for me, as my characters come to life on the pages of my current work in progress. I'm absolutely compulsive about it when I'm writing and thank all the gods and goddesses that I have such a terrific husband who encourages my writing and puts up with my obsession. As a multi-published author, I love to hear from my readers. Their input keeps my mind fresh and always hunting for new ideas.

Desiree Holt welcomes comments from readers. You can find her website and email address on her author bio page at www.ellorascave.com.

Tell Us What You Think

Also by Mari Carr

About the Author

ဢ

Writing a book was number one on Mari Carr's bucket list and on her thirty-fourth birthday, she set out to see that goal achieved. Now her computer is jammed full of stories—novels, novellas, short stories and dead-ends—and many of her books have been published. Mari found time for writing by squeezing it into the hours between 3 a.m. and daybreak, when her family is asleep and the house is quiet.

To learn more about Mari, please visit her website or join her Yahoo! group to get in on the fun with other readers as well as Mari Carr! http://groups.yahoo.com/group/Heat_Wave_Readers/join

Mari Carr welcomes comments from readers. You can find her website and email address on her author bio page at www.ellorascave.com.

Tell Us What You Think

We appreciate hearing reader opinions about our books. You can email us at Comments@EllorasCave.com.

Also by Mari Freeman

ʓᴑ

eBooks:

Beware of the Cowboy

Birthright

Cougar Challenge: Sin on Skin

Love Doctor

Print Books:

Birthright

Plan for Pleasure

About the Author

ॐ

Mari Freeman lives, disguised as a normal suburbanite, in central North Carolina. When not penning romantic erotica, she enjoys horses, hiking, traveling, good food and friends. An outdoors girl at heart, you can often find her at the lake with laptop fired up, fishing line in the water and her imagination running wild.

In her previous lives, she's held an interesting array of occupations. She's been a project manager, a software-testing manager, sold used cars, pumped gas at a truck stop and worked in a morgue.

Mari's favorite stories include Alpha females in love with even more Alpha males. She finds the clash of passionate, strong-willed personalities fascinating. She writes contemporary, paranormal and a little science fiction/fantasy.

Mari Freeman welcomes comments from readers. You can find her website and email address on her author bio page at www.ellorascave.com.

Tell Us What You Think

We appreciate hearing reader opinions about our books. You can email us at Comments@EllorasCave.com.

Also by Ciana Stone

&

eBooks:

Acid Rayne *with Nathalie Gray*

Cougar Challenge: Cam's Holiday

Hearts of Fire 1: Memory's Eye

Hot in the Saddle 1: Chase 'n' Ana

Hot in the Saddle 2: Molding Clay

Hot in the Saddle 3: Scout 'n' Cole

Hot in the Saddle 4: Conn 'n' Caleb

Riding Ranger

Sexplorations: Finding Her Rhythm

Sexplorations: The Thing about Cowboys

Sexplorations: Working Up a Sweat

The Hussies: A Taste for Jazz

The Hussies: All in Time

The Hussies: Sin in Jeans

Wyatt's Chance

Print Books:

Hot in the Saddle: Unbridled

Hot in the Saddle: Unrestrained

Wyatt's Chance

About the Author

ℰℭ

Ciana Stone has been reading since the age of three, and wrote her first story at age five. Since then she enjoyed writing as a solitary form of entertainment, before coming out of the closet to share her stories with others. She holds several post graduate degrees and has often been referred to as a professional student. Her latest fields of interest are quantum mechanics and Taoism. When she is not writing (or studying) she enjoys painting (canvas, not walls), sculpting, running, hiking and yoga. She lives with her longtime lover in several locations in the United States.

Ciana Stone welcomes comments from readers. You can find her website and email address on her author bio page at www.ellorascave.com.

Tell Us What You Think

We appreciate hearing reader opinions about our books. You can email us at Comments@EllorasCave.com.

Why an electronic book?

We live in the Information Age—an exciting time in the history of human civilization, in which technology rules supreme and continues to progress in leaps and bounds every minute of every day. For a multitude of reasons, more and more avid literary fans are opting to purchase e-books instead of paper books. The question from those not yet initiated into the world of electronic reading is simply: *Why?*

1. *Price.* An electronic title at Ellora's Cave Publishing and Cerridwen Press runs anywhere from 40% to 75% less than the cover price of the exact same title in paperback format. Why? Basic mathematics and cost. It is less expensive to publish an e-book (no paper and printing, no warehousing and shipping) than it is to publish a paperback, so the savings are passed along to the consumer.

2. *Space.* Running out of room in your house for your books? That is one worry you will never have with electronic books. For a low one-time cost, you can purchase a handheld device specifically designed for e-reading. Many e-readers have large, convenient screens for viewing. Better yet, hundreds of titles can be stored within your new library—on a single microchip. There are a variety of e-readers from different manufacturers. You can also read e-books on your PC or laptop computer. (Please note that Ellora's Cave does not endorse any specific brands.

You can check our websites at www.ellorascave.com or www.cerridwenpress.com for information we make available to new consumers.)

3. *Mobility.* Because your new e-library consists of only a microchip within a small, easily transportable e-reader, your entire cache of books can be taken with you wherever you go.

4. *Personal Viewing Preferences.* Are the words you are currently reading too small? Too large? Too… ANNOYING? Paperback books cannot be modified according to personal preferences, but e-books can.

5. *Instant Gratification.* Is it the middle of the night and all the bookstores near you are closed? Are you tired of waiting days, sometimes weeks, for bookstores to ship the novels you bought? Ellora's Cave Publishing sells instantaneous downloads twenty-four hours a day, seven days a week, every day of the year. Our webstore is never closed. Our e-book delivery system is 100% automated, meaning your order is filled as soon as you pay for it.

Those are a few of the top reasons why electronic books are replacing paperbacks for many avid readers.

As always, Ellora's Cave and Cerridwen Press welcome your questions and comments. We invite you to email us at Comments@ellorascave.com or write to us directly at Ellora's Cave Publishing Inc., 1056 Home Avenue, Akron, OH 44310-3502.

ELLORA'S CAVE
Romanticon

Annual convention
for women who
refuse to behave